Deliverance

Umesh Moudgil

Published by New Generation Publishing in 2012

Copyright © Umesh Moudgil 2012

First Edition

www.newgeneration-publishing.com

 New Generation **Publishing**

"Live life to the fullest and never let
anyone put you down."

"Respect and like who you are. Listen to
your heart, but act with logic and
be generous to the people around you."

Preface

When I was a boy, I used to dream that one day I would achieve great things in my life; I would own a *Porsche 928 Series 4* - my dream car. Watching *Risky Business*, I just fell in love with it, and since then dreamt of owning a sleek black 928 one day. However, as I grew older, my dreams changed. I started thinking about someone else sharing my life, falling in love, and having a perfect family. Throughout my younger life, I was always too shy of girls and was never the ladies' man. I would run away a mile from them and words would come out wrong while talking to them.

The only problem with this perfect thought is that we are not perfect people; we have faults that we find hard to fix and the world has a cruel way to remind you of them. When you think you have turned the corner and you are on the top of things, again you get knocked down. They say, when you get knocked down, you get up again and fight to say to yourself that "I am good and everything I do is correct." You shed tears, but alas, time waits for none and the journey of life goes on.

I always found it hard to portray my feelings, and when I did, who understood? I am not sure if the people who knew me did. Saying "sorry" is the hardest word. In my mind, I have said this so many times to the people I love, to myself for being who I am, and to God.

Life is a journey of understanding. There will come times, when you do not understand what is happening around you and then you start asking questions to yourself. The response you get back will depend on how you are asking the questions and how your mind reads into the answers. There will be many trials and many roads for you lead and walk until you find the right direction. Most people believe in their faith, and this guides them. Some others use their education to lead the way and climb up the corporate ladder. There are also some other people like me who wonder aimlessly in life with plenty of imaginations, always restless and searching for an answer. There will once come a point in your life that will change things for you, personally, and suddenly you feel the need to change your life. Another important question here is, "Do people, who are close to you, really know who you are, the person that you want to be, realise your inner thoughts, and your feelings"? Sometimes, it feels like being back at school where people pick on you without knowing who you are and really do not care, but you end up feeling hurt and scared, hiding those feelings inside you.

Deliverance narrates an account, which is very personal to me and the character is based upon my thoughts and feelings. This is a story that came from my heart, leading to a world of discovery and some answers, which I found hard to comprehend. The reason why I found it hard to comprehend was because I did not want to hear the truth. The truth that you are in charge of your destiny and every move you make adds colours to your life. *Duty*, *Karma*, and *belief* are important, but they do not answer all the questions. If we leave the energies of our life behind, what does that mean? The stories of ghosts we hear, are they real and do this mean that these poor souls have not crossed over? *The paranormal* is an interesting topic. Though I am not qualified enough to answer these questions, but I can say that we all have a sixth sense, however, we do not use it.

This book investigates, in a fictional sense, *the theory of life after death, and where we go thereafter*. Science has not disproved that the paranormal phenomena of life after death does not exist. Even, all religious teachings talk about our soul being immortal and our body as just a vessel containing our soul. Science has also not disproved that physical dimensions do not exist, so we could possibly pass into these dimensions or parallel universes once we transcend from our material bodies. The question about life outside our universe has been a mystery for eons. Scientists even fight amongst themselves regarding the concept of evolution and the big bang theory, and how all these began on the Earth. Were Adam and Eve created by a higher being or did they evolve from single cell organisms? The main question is – where did our soul come from? This is what makes us different from each other.

A *near-death experience* (NDE) refers to a broad range of personal experiences associated with impending death, encompassing multiple possible sensations including detachment from the body; feelings of levitation; extreme fear; total serenity, security, or warmth; the experience of absolute dissolution; and the presence of a light (*see Wikipedia Definition*).

These phenomena are usually reported after an individual has been pronounced clinically dead or very close to death, hence the term NDE, but I suspect that people also have this experience when they are within the final moments of their lives. I believe their whole life story goes through them, and then on the final moment, they walk away and leave their mortal remains behind.

The concept of outer body experiences (*OBEs as they are termed*) is disputed by scientists as the mind playing tricks, however, there are people who have experienced this outer body experience. People experience different things; some say they see rays of light and some others experience themselves standing outside their bodies and watching what is happening around them. Some event in our life at times triggers an experience that we cannot explain and most people are even embarrassed to talk about these openly thinking that others would laugh and ridicule. The trigger for an OBE could be anything from our past, a NDE when we are involved with, or it could even be a memory.

I saw a movie a while back called, "Somewhere in time"; where a young playwright was approached by an older woman who gave him an antique watch uttering the words, "Come back to me." His journey of discovery started from there and his obsession to discover flowed through the story. I am not saying that this is true, but I do feel in my heart that lives are linked and we are drawn to certain things. In my case, it is the search for love and a better understanding, which I need. I often sit alone and wonder how I have been made; I judge my character, my beliefs, and what my direction is. Like the young Christopher Reeves in "Somewhere in Time", I also become obsessive in my attitude and always returned to the same question - *was I here before and what is my purpose?* In the movie, Christopher Reeves cannot accept life without his lost love and he gets to meet her only in the afterlife. His character could not accept life without his love. Some time ago, I had spent time looking at ways of unlocking my past by talking to a past life specialist (by regression hypnosis), but I could not break down a blockage that would take me to my previous life. I have read many accounts on the internet that describe, in detail, what people have experienced, and they do make you question many things.

An example of one of these accounts was that of a forty year old man going to a seminar, run by a past life transgression specialist. Within the seminar, the specialist asked her audience to go a place where they felt safe and then let themselves relax. In the relaxed state, she asked them to think back of a time where they felt there was happiness and then go back further into the womb. Once they had achieved this state, she asked them to go further to their previous life. After thirty minutes, all audiences came around and she then asked them about their experiences. This man, in his forties, described that he found himself standing in Ancient Rome. He was dressed as a Roman solider and he could remember in detail what he was doing. Apparently, this man was haunted by images of war, rape and death, and he felt uncomfortable around scenes of death and violence.

What does all this mean? Neither, I can answer this question, nor deny about its truth or falsity. Does this mean that there is actually life after death, and that our souls just move on and our bodies are pure vessels that we shed like our skin? Thus, when we see the immortal light, we cross over into a new dimension, place, or life.

People have reported OBEs for eons and most people, after they have experienced this, have changed for the rest of their lives. Their perspective on life changes just after a few seconds or a few minutes, technically, after they were dead. If we really cross over, where do we go, and if we do not, does that mean that our very life's energy stays and we walk in limbo for eternity? Would this answer as to why people say that there are ghosts – life energies that have stayed and not moved on.

Life and death are part of the life's fabric itself, and as human beings, we are driven by emotions of the heart and the logic of the mind. Science would definitely make you believe that all that I have described above can be explained as our sub-consciences, making up these stories as truth. In other words, our imaginations gone wild or mad. There are suggestions that if we have control on our minds, we can transcend to higher planes and can truly be masters of our self. In Holy Scriptures, like the *Bhagavad Gita*, it is written, "lives are led by Karma (actions and deeds)." Many religions also commonly preach that our actions and deeds in this life will affect our well-being when we enter God's realms. In the first chapter of Bhagavad Gita, Lord Krishna takes his devotee into his confidence and says, "lift yourself up my friend, do your service and believe in me. This is your duty and not a sinful action. Lift your bow and prepare to do your service." Initially, his devotee was hit by his remorse feelings, but the Lord takes him into his confidence and relates his teachings.

*The central teaching of the Gita is the attainment of the final beatitude of life, perfection, or freedom. This can be attained by doing the duties of life or *Swadharma*. The lord says to his devotee, the mighty Arjuna, "therefore, without attachment, constantly perform the action, which is duty, for, by performing action without attachment, man verily reaches the Supreme" (this text is from the Bhagavad-Gita's Gita text and the commentary is by Sri Swami Sivanada).

The holy Bible quotes, "to enter the kingdom of heaven, we must be born new. One thing is for sure in life - one day we die. What is not clear is where we go and that is where our belief comes into. Our religion's teachings will tell us what happens to us, but do we really have the answers? Scientists would make us believe that there is an explanation for everything and the teachings of old age religions are purely fable and fiction." Does this answer the question of why we believe in ghosts and demons and are there really angels out there looking over us?

10

The Bible, in conclusion, says, "Your spirit and soul leave the body. Your body returns to dust, and your spirit and soul returns to God. God then accepts or rejects you depending on if you accepted Him or rejected Him in this life."

Eccl. 12:7 (of Bible) states that "then shall the dust return to the earth as it was and the spirit shall return unto God who gave it. Does this mean there is no life after death? First of all, we need to understand just what we are. What is man?" Genesis 2:7 (of Bible) states, "The LORD has formed man from the dust of the ground and breathed the breath of life into his nostrils after which man became a living soul." According to God's word, we were formed out of dust. God then put the soul and spirit into the mound of dust he had made. Genesis 3:19 (of Bible) states, "For dust thou art and unto dust shalt thou return."

We do not have any answers to these until the last moment of our lives and then we do see something. Some people, who have experienced OBEs, state that they see a bright light and their bodies are caught up in it. Some others describe of seeing faces of their loved ones waiting for them in the next life. We do not know what is the truth and what is the fiction in this, but what we do know that is something is waiting for us or we want to believe that there is something waiting for us, perhaps to judge us or perhaps to comfort and love us.

Islamic beliefs preach that the present life is a trial in preparation for the next realm of existence. The Qu'ran very emphatically states that "the Day of Judgement must come and God will decide the fate of each soul according to his/her record of deeds." So, we still comeback to our deeds, and if we are measured on our deeds, does that mean we have to live like saints to attain the entry into heaven or do we have to collect enough points?

When a person of Islamic belief dies, he/she is bathed and wrapped in a clean, white cloth (usually by a family member) and buried after a special prayer, preferably the same day. It is considered to be a final service that they can do for their relatives and an opportunity to remember that their own existence here on earth is brief.

I truly believe that we are driven by some inner soul that makes us who we are. The soul is the very essence of a person and it is immortal.* Plato described the words of his teacher* Socrates, "As bodies die, the soul is continually reborn in subsequent bodies." Our actions and battles exist within ourselves and we always look for answers of our sheer existence. The question here is - do we over think issues or things? In reference to God and in my views, there is only one high and mighty, and he exists in many forms and guises. He exists in every fabric of our lives and he has given us the biggest gift of all – *our life*. If I was a non-believer, I would say that we have made the fable of God actually being real – we have created this being who we believe is perfect and he/she is the almighty.

What we must do is to look after this gift that he has given us, in the best way possible. We fight our own battles, desires, wants, and needs. To attain freedom, we must first release our bodily desires and reach out for our sixth sense. The masters who achieve this do this through dedication, meditation, and a complete surrender to the higher and mightier. This is what Lord Krishna asked to his friend and devotee, Arjuna; he said, "believe in me and do your duty, and I shall deliver you."

A lot of characters in this book are also based on people whom I know, but the characters do not portray them fully and no personal feelings is meant towards them. I suppose, you can look at this book as being my story in the main character's eyes and his feelings portray what I feel and my aspirations. My biggest desire and need is always to be loved and sometimes this makes me feel very restless. Some people may call this as my insecure and fragile nature, but I look at it as a continual hunt for something, which I crave for and that something is the understanding of our very existence and love. The word *love* can mean many things and I still find it *hard to define*. Our emotions are in a mess when we are in love, our hearts fly high, and we are immersed in a warm, but safe feeling. Love also brings despair, disappointment, anger and tears. I believe that love and hate are the same emotion and we ambush them for our own needs. Fear is the biggest emotion that exists within us, and sometimes our fears let in other things, like despair - a feeling of not being wanted, and, thus, we fail to succeed. This is when we let dark thoughts come in and fester, and then we let the *Dark One* inside. The question here is "what and who is the Dark One"? Is he *Satan* or is he the devil within us when we despair or when we are scared? I believe, we all have both, good and bad inside us, and until we accept our frailties, desires, and needs, we truly cannot master our feelings and control ourselves.

This book is dedicated to my family and to the people I hold dear to me. I hope that one day they can forgive my shortcomings, if not in this life time perhaps in the next. In many ways, this is a very personal story of redemption, forgiveness, and self-judgment. Someone told me years ago that I should not judge myself harshly or beat myself up. I think the reason why I did this is because I wanted to punish myself; because I felt that I was wrong - *the insecurity rears its ugly head again*. Some people would describe this as a childish behaviour, but I would classify this as insecurity, and lack of self-confidence and belief.

As human beings, we are always looking for something. We are masters of our own actions. Is there a high place of existence and can we let ourselves go to be able to see the very fabric of life itself? Guru Kirpal Singh quotes in his writings, "Man know thyself. Saints say that nature has designed man to leave his physical body at will, transcend to higher spiritual planes, and then return to the body."

These words have a profound meaning that we all need to explore our self and this is done through mediation, yoga, and having the ability to let go. If man is to live for eons, we need to be at one with nature and really expose our minds and hearts to the other dimensions that exist. This may sound like sci-fiction, but I truly believe that we have the ability to see and do more, and we have do the will power within ourselves to achieve this. The human brain is the biggest gift we could have been ever given. If we could harness more of its power, we truly could transcend. At the moment, we are only using a small percentage of it to just amble through life.

God has sent us many messengers who we call prophets or Gods, like Jesus Christ, Krishna, Mohammad, etc. We need to truly listen to their words and not use them or their preaching to attack each other on basis of religion, colour, caste, or creed. When Lord Krishna showed his infinite *roop* (being) to Arjuna on the battlefield, this truly opened his eyes.

Man know thyself is truly what we need to strive too. My thought pattern on this is that "until we do not understand ourselves, we cannot truly let go of our materialistic lives." I am the worst at this and cannot lecture, but can only hope that one day I can enter this journey.

The journey of my character, *Raj* in "Deliverance" is not only about of forgiveness, but also of accepting who he (Raj) actually is. We spend too much time beating ourselves up because we feel that we have sinned or done something wrong. We are only following our paths and we need to make mistakes to learn from them. The day will also come when something monumental will occur in our life to change what we do, forever.

For me, this book tells a personal journey of someone who is trying to find himself. Along the way, he has to get past his demons and accept his destiny. In my life, I have always been seen as someone who starts something and never ends it - this is how my own people see me. To the readers, this book may feel dark at places because, as a writer and story teller, that's what I have felt and that's what a lot of people, who are insecure about who they are and what they can achieve, feel.

The best advice, I was ever given, was from a customer years ago and I would like to thank him for it now. "Peter you were right. I needed to step out of the shadows and put myself first because I know I can achieve and be the best. You are right my friend and I appreciate this advice of yours. I have never looked back, but always offered this to other people."

Life is a journey and for my main character in this novel, he goes through many changes and discovers that our very souls are woven so finely that it is hard to decipher what they really are, unless you have control on them. We keep wondering throughout our lives, some with a purpose and others are happy to go lucky. I wanted a purpose in my life, but got screwed up many times. Now, I am trying to understand and win the battle. As human beings, we wish we could turn back the clock and relive certain moments in time, but this does not happen in real.

Here, in this novel, Raj has the chance for

redemption and deliverance from the past, but it is a long journey of understanding, hurt, and discovery. It will require all his strength, and belief in himself and his God. There will be times when he will question his own sanity and his judgement also he will need to master his emotions. For a man like Raj, this will be hard, because in his previous life, he could not do so.

My message to all the readers is, "Reach down to your own souls and ask the question - What is it all about and why am I here?"

The answers that you will get back will shock you to the core and you will be asking yourself the same questions that Raj asked himself at the point of his death.

The conflict between good and evil, as Wikipedia describes it is, "The conflict between good and evil is one of the precepts of the Zoroastrian faith, first enshrined by Zarathustra over 3000 years ago." It is also one of the most common conventional themes in literature and is sometimes considered to be an universal part of the human condition. There are several variations on this conflict; one being the battle between individuals and ideologies, with *Good* on one side and *Evil* on the other side. Another variation is the inner struggle in characters (and by extension, humans in reality) between good and evil.

Conrad's version of the inner evil conflict, known as the *Heart of Darkness*, is a human's struggle with his own morals, and his battle with his hidden evil. Although first chiefly used in the novel, this improved device was commonly used as opposed to the old devices used in literature before the turn of the century. It is a conflict that exists outside of literature as well, making it an universal truth of the human condition, and finding all humans as having an "inner evil" or Heart of Darkness in his novella of the same name."

The key message of the book is to understand who you are. Do not pity yourself, do not talk your abilities down, and look at life as a gift. With that in mind, strive forward and live your life to the full, not as a saint but as a human being with feelings, strong commitments, and direction. Always remember, you are like a child playing in a vast expanse where everything is very fluid and change can happen at any time. Be at one with your surroundings and do not live outside of who you are as a person. Smile, laugh, cry, and love are our natural feelings; we can be in control, but learn how to control and lift outside the norm.

For me, I have my aspirations, my desires, and my needs, but I really cannot explain any of these. I was picked on at school and hid my feelings away. Perhaps that affected me and I wanted to be different and not hide behind large rocks. Perhaps that's why certain parts of me became who I am today and perhaps that's why I run away from problems rather than tackling them head-on. We all make choices in our lives and discover them further as we get older and I made mine.

They say in life that you have to like "YOU." Only then, you can find true happiness and you have to be at one with your convictions. This book is *my redemption, my deliverance,* and I have written it from my heart. It took me five years to pen down my thoughts and create my character, who I have come to like over his journey of acceptance, but most importantly, over the *deliverance from his past.*

Acknowledgements

This story is purely a work of fiction that I have developed and nurtured over time. I have made references to a few external sources, which I would like to hereby acknowledge. These include:

- Wikipedia quotes from Conrad;
- Wikipedia quotes from Plato;
- Quotes on *Life after Death*;
- Quotes on *Near Death Experience*;
- Sir Isaac Newton's Quote;
- Bhagavad Gita - Quotes from Lord Krishna's Beliefs;
- The Bible's quotes on the soul;
- Frank Sinatra and extract from his song;
- Ms. Geeta Kumar for her help in proof reading and editing; and
- *Never Alone* by Rodney Belcher.

This book is also dedicated to my family - you are the best gift that God ever gave me and this is for you. Also to all my friends whom I met over the years - you have enriched my life and have offered me your support and love.

Hey Dad! Now you can be proud of me. This is for you and for my kids as well – *believe in who you are and stay open with your hearts to everyone whom you meet.*

The Old Man

The weather in London, in the middle of July, is a very wet one, and tonight was no exception. The clouds had gathered early that day over the capital and people were running for shelter as the first wave of rain droplets hit the ground. It's since the last few years that people blame global warming for changes in the weather patterns. The summers in UK were getting wetter and colder. Sheltering under a large oak tree in Hyde Park, Raj sat slumped against the old bark of the tree that had been in the park for hundreds of years.

The rain droplets felt like giant boulders tumbling down a mountain side, hitting his weathered cheeks with vigour and ferocity. He had forgotten how many winters and summers he had spent in the park. Raj had never imagined that he would end up like this – sleeping rough and living his last days like a hermit. Perhaps this was his own making, and yes, he can blame himself for this. The mental scars of his past cut deep within his chest, and for a man like Raj, it felt like a vice gripping his heart and slowly closing it tight. The rain was getting heavier, but his eyes were transfixed; lost somewhere in time and space. Sleeping rough in London can be very harsh, and the streets can be cold and demanding. However, nothing seemed to matter Raj, neither the cold nor the rain. His eyes were transfixed in a death gaze, and in his mind, he, near the end of the sands of time, was near.

Today, however, he seemed immune to everything. Even the rain did not make a difference, and his mind was elsewhere in a different time zone and dimension. His life had gone through so many changes; most of them were his own making and now he was all alone in a dark stormy night. As he sat there, two policemen walked by on their evening patrol of the park. They turned their heads and smiled at Raj; they knew him well, and normally left him alone and this night was no different. They simply waved their arms and continued walking away towards the lake, in the middle of the Park.

Life is a gift, and so the saying goes, but today it feels like a burden. It got heavier and heavier day by day. Raj asked to himself, "How could I live with the responsibility?" He was too scared and ran so far away, and now he was sitting alone pondering when death will claim him. He thought that even God had forsaken him because he had run away and had committed the biggest sin. The feeling that he had given up all those years ago had not left him and all that was left was self-pity and remorse. The stupid thing about all of this is that he could have predicted this twenty years ago.

Raj smiled. The park reminded him of memories of when he was young and courting his wife to be. Raj, being Asian in origin, was born in India and had come to England in 1970 when he was only five years old. He had three sisters, all older than him, and so he was the spoilt younger brother who got away with murder of his parents. His father had arrived in England shortly before his birth, in 1965, with the aspiration that he would take further his career in teaching. His father had been in teaching in India for almost ten years and had been a History Major. When the opportunity of going to England on a teaching voucher came to him, he jumped on the chance to make a better life for his family.

Raj's mother was also an English teacher in India and was the only daughter of her parents. Like all Indian women, life had not been easy for her and she had suffered the loss of her younger brother at a very young age. Raj had never met his maternal grandparents, but his mother always used to say him that he was like them.

The rain had not stopped, and instead, lightening rattled and screeched over the skies. Raj still sat there with his eyes fixed in a lifeless gaze, haunted by his own demons and thoughts. His mind again drifted away to the past, and today, he seemed to be living his life again in his mind.

Raj had arrived in UK, when he was only five years old, with his mother from India. For a five year old child, it was an exciting time to be sitting on a plane, flying to a new home. Knowing that his dad would be waiting for him on the other side excited him even more. Life was never going to be the same again for this five year old boy, and looking back on this, now he wished that he had never arrived here and would have stayed in India. No, he cried, I didn't mean that. I lacked direction throughout my whole life. Astrologers said that it was because I was born in between changes of birth signs. If only I had listened to my head and not my heart, knuckled down and studied hard, but how true could I be then? I had everything, great parents, a lovely loving wife and great children, so why am I here, sitting on my own in this wretched body?

In years gone by, he had written a poem about life of what he thought it was like. It went something like this:

Life is like a chess game
You could be a knight and fight beside your queen;
You could be a pawn and die for your king;
Life is like a chess game.
Every move on the board marks a new step in your life;
Some good,
Some bad,
Life is like a chess game.

It was strange remembering that poem again after all these years, but tonight was like yesterday to Raj and along with the rain droplets, he cried a little. He was good at that; showing his emotion and crying. He wished now that he was different and didn't hang his emotions on his sleeves,, and had been more level-headed. However, he in is younger days, thought it was good to have a feminine side because it made him human.

Tonight, was indeed a strange night at other places as well and Raj was not alone thinking about the past.

In a city called *Reading*, in the heart of rural Berkshire, a young beautiful woman sat in a meeting in the main board room of a major blue chip company. She listened to the owner of the company as he presented the second quarter results. Her mind was not really in the meeting room, but drifted elsewhere. Tears seemed to flood into her beautiful large black eyes. Her mind, also like Raj's, had drifted to old times and was not here in the meeting. Dad, she whispered to herself.

Meanwhile, not so many miles away, a young man was driving home from his office after a hard day. He was in his thirties and his hairs were showing their first signs of greying, just like his father's, some years before. The day had been a stressful one and his bosses were demanding results from him, which he was trying to deliver. It had been a hard quarter in the IT business and he was responsible for a large regional sales territory, and so held great responsibility in delivering figures for his team and company. He smiled as he turned the corner from his house and was glad to be back home. The town, he lived in, had not changed much over the years. He admitted that his town had got more congested and he often wished that he would had moved out years ago, but something always held him back. Brought up in an Asian family, where boys were always streets ahead of the girls, had some pressures and in many ways that made him stay there.

He stopped the car a few hundred meters after turning the corner, next to a very smart large house, which was set upon within a small group of prestigious houses. This whole area had changed over the years and, where in the old days there was a housing estate, here now it was a small set of large houses set on their own. His parents would have been proud of him if they were here, he thought as he stepped out of the car. The weather was changing again; the rain had not stopped the entire day and the evening was growing darker earlier today. He pressed the button on his car keys and locked the car doors. He then walked to the front door of the house and then pressed a hidden entry button on the door. The door opened quietly and he walked in.

As he entered the house, he was greeted first by his young son, who was nearly ten years old now. "Where's your mum?" he inquired.

"She's in the kitchen dad, and did you bring my XBox game?"

Joy smiled and pulled out the console game from his coat packet and whispered, "Don't tell mum."

For a minute, he remembered his dad coming home after work and doing exactly the same. He would always buy him something and say, "Don't tell your mum." His dad had always given him everything, supported him for years on his sporting activities, like his cricket. His bond with his sisters grew and they held him together. He sighed heavily. Even though his family were now complete and he loved Hannah so much, he wished his parents were with him to see his children growing up. He missed them both today and even if he was smiling, he was hiding the hurt that still was in his heart.

Elsewhere, in a different continent, there was a

25

conference being held by a very large well known worldwide organization's PC manufacturer. They were holding their annual sales conference in Austin, Texas. There were 2,500 delegates at this conference and this was quite a historical day because the owner and founder of the company was stepping down and passing the reigns over to his son.

The conference was being held in a plush conference centre in downtown Austin and Micro T had grown their reputation as one of the leading computer companies of our times. The conference hall was extremely well set-up and there was ample room to hold a conference of this size. The main stage stood ten feet away from where the company delegates were seated. On the stage, were seated the senior management, including the owner and his son. At the very end, standing in front of a presenter's table, was a very beautiful, elegant woman.

She was going to open the conference and welcome everyone. She was also going to go through today's proceedings and make formal introductions to all the VIP's present there. This was a real honour for her and she was really proud of her achievements with Micro T. She had been with the company now for ten years, and worked and lived in New York. Originally, she was born in England where she had grown up. Her family had always been strong and there was a great bond between all, however, her parents shared a strange love-hate relationship. They always seemed to argue and make up in the end after sometime, but one day all that changed. She knew her parents loved each other and, no matter whatever happens, they would always love each other. However, when her mum died her dad lost it. He could not handle it and walked out. Her dad could not cope up with his life without the person who kept him on the straight and narrow. He used to joke that she was his sergeant major, but she knew he didn't mean that. There were some days when she was young that her dad used to sit upstairs in her loft bedroom and moan, but again she knew that he didn't mean it. Her dad's problem was that he didn't listen and he would cry like a baby if things do not go his way. However, she still loved him.

It had taken her over ten years to recover from this, but she did it because she was strong and she always had been. She never married unlike her siblings and instead concentrated all her thoughts in her work. Her mother had died after she moved away from home and her father had left home shortly afterwards. He had never really recovered the loss of his wife; in his eyes he had always blamed himself for her death.

Now, she stood in front 2,500 delegates, opening the major conference. Her emotions were in check, her tears held back, and her head pushed back in pride. She wished that her parents were here today to see this and she knew they would have been proud – as they always were. She knew her mum would have loved this moment, standing somewhere in background, watching her. She was sure that her mum was here with her today, standing next to her, with her arm around her and supporting her. Dad would be walking around looking to where to eat and she smiled thinking about that.

The old man cried a little more as he slumped back against the oak tree, thinking of his past. He wished it would all end now; life was now becoming a burden to him, which he could no longer carry. The rain had not stopped instead got stronger, but still Raj did not make a move; he sat there in almost a trance, completely absorbed in his own thoughts. Memories drifted him back to the time before his marriage, which was fixed by his parents to Asha. He smiled when he thought how his brother-in-law had asked him his views on Asha. From there everything was history, he began to see her on-and-off in London, where she worked, and formed a relationship. They had spent many visits walking in Hyde Park, talking and sneaking the odd hug. It was funny to remember those times – they were the happiest days of his life – "I miss you Ash" he murmured.

Raj was still restless, though, like all young men, he would still look at other women and he had always revolted into what he was told by his parents to do. In his time, he went for higher education and messed that up because he really did not study and flunked his graduation. I am sorry Dad. You gave me everything I wanted and I think that is where everything went wrong. Did I show enough respect? Looking back now, the answer must be no. You deserved so much more from me. Asian parents give their lives to their children's upbringing; I am not trying to say that other cultures do not. Everyone was right. Perhaps my parents had spoiled me, but whose parents do not? To our parents, we are always kids and they will always be there for us.

Thinking about things now, there was a lot he wished he could change, but life was now drifting away. His heart pined for his children who had walked out after Asha's death. They did not deserve that and he knew that. It was his mistake. He was not strong enough, but he could lecture others that they needed to be. He remembered, being told by a past life regression specialist that he should not beat himself up but that was all too easy to say. Raj was a expert at this and that's why he panicked when things went wrong, and was not level-headed enough to resolve the problems.

Was he ready for marriage at 23? I am not quite sure if he really understood the virtues of marriage until it was too late. Why had he not changed earlier? Why hadn't he stopped his urges to spend too money and gamble it away on stupid selfish things? Thinking about things now, how many people can actually say that they have understood their other halves fully, and their needs, wants, and desires? Ash wasn't perfect, but she had her head screwed on because she wanted security and that was obviously important in every marriage. Raj was a law into his own hands, he didn't really understand what his responsibilities were and had left everything for Asha to do.

Not all was doom and gloom. Raj had always been first to help his family; he had a good heart and his intentions were never to hurt, but he was just misguided. What really let him down was his temper; I think it came from his father's side. He had a quick temper and it would flare up without thinking, and then he would afterwards sulk. This would be then followed by crying and remorse on why he did that, but that was the nature of the beast. In his heart, he wanted none of this, would cry himself to sleep or sit in the dark and never go to sleep. Self-blame was the name of the game and it justified everything, but it didn't fix a thing. What he really needed was to tell the truth and accept that.

As the rain continued to fall, Raj rose his head. Something caught his eyes; someone was walking towards him. Initially he could not make out who it was because of the rain and his weak eyes, but as the person got nearer, his eyes started get wider and his face lost all colour. It was Ash and she was standing in front of him now.

She looked so different; almost like the young woman whom he had met so many moons ago. As he stared harder at her now, he could make out her features and facial expressions. She looked beautiful; a warm glow radiated from eyes and her smile just blew him away. She now stood a few paces away from him, staring at him intensely.

Was he dreaming? Was she really there? He reached out his arm to touch her but she was too far away. He then tried to get to his feet, but his weak body did not support him to move. "Damn this wretched body", he said to himself. "Asha", he whispered, "I am so sorry."

In seconds, her happy appearance changed into a more devilish angry face and her eyes were blazing with hatred. She knelt down beside him, still looking at him intently, but now in disgust. "I warned you this would happen Raj and when you die no-one would be there," she sneered.

"Look around you Raj, there is no one here now and you will die alone," she shrieked and with that she was gone. The impact of seeing her in that form had a massive effect; he could feel the vice holding his heart tighten harder and with each turn, he was ready to explode.

Raj's world started to crumble around him. The vice now had closed completely and the pain from his broken, bleeding heart was sending lightning bolts through all his veins. Tears streamed down his eyes, but they were of blood from cracked vessels in his eyes. Blood started to trickle from his mouth and droplets from his eyes ran down his cheeks. He slumped back against the old oak tree, his head crashed down hard on the bark, creating a horrible looking wound. His end was near, not the one he hoped for, but the one he talked himself that he deserved. The grim reaper was now ready to claim him and in a single instant, he thought he saw him walking towards him before his eyes started to close.

As Raj drifted away into the emptiness, he felt himself been sucked out of his body and started to float upwards. He thought he could see his old body still slumped against the old oak void now of life. Asha was right; he did die all alone, without even a goodbye bid from anyone. As he drifted further into the emptiness, other visions flashed by him of his father and then his mother, and then a fleeting glance of Asha with her parents, looking happy. He could swear that she turned, looked, and then turned away towards her parents who were calling her. He didn't understand what these visions were, but he hoped that they meant she was happy and his parents were well. It was strange. He had always imagined when he was young that the master of death, the grim reaper would come, get him and claim him. Perhaps this was happening now to him and the lord of death was indeed claiming him.

After what seemed like an eternity, Raj found himself standing in a small blacked out room. It was pitch black; he could not see anything. In minutes, the silence was broken by a booming voice that called out to him, "State your name."

Raj was confused. He could not reply. Again, the voice called out the same question. This time, Raj answered, "My name is Raj Sharma."

"Do you know why you are here Raj and not with your family like Asha? You said I would judge you one day. Well here I am."

At this point, Raj fell to his knees and started to sob, "Father, I knew this day would come."

"Why do you cry my son?" The voice answered back.

"I have done many things wrong Father and I am responsible for nearly spoiling my children's' future and for sending my wife to an early death."

The voice laughed, "No Raj, those things you did not do, and they were the paths that have been written. You were just following those. Yes, I admit that you could have followed a different path that I had set, I

31

had often reached out for you, but you ignored me. This much is true my son. I know there was no malice and I know where your soul originally came from, so you were only following your own *karma*. Your destiny was different to Asha's, but your souls have been intertwined for centuries and that will not change. You will always be a part of her and she of you, and yes you will meet her again, in a different time and space.

Raj, I gave you all the time you needed to change. I tried to reach out too you so many times, but each time you pushed me away. Your heart is good my son, but your deeds have much to be desired in some cases. You loved your children, but you could not offer the same love for Asha. Now stop crying and stand up", the voice demanded, "and follow me."

Raj wiped his tears away and slowly rose to his feet, and when he did, the room where he was standing, suddenly lit up into a brilliant white blinding light that initially hurt his eyes. As his eyes grew accustomed to the light, he started walking towards a door that was opening near the far corner of the room. As Raj passed through the door, he entered into a massive expanse that seemed to stretch out for miles. As he stood there, he noticed that there were people floating by him in great numbers. They came in all shapes and sizes, some old, some young, but all with one look on their face and that of pure emptiness, but, also of freedom. It was like they had shed themselves of any worries and thoughts, and now they drifted towards the next part of their journey. As he watched the constant stream of people floating past him, he saw someone he knew - it was Asha.

He called out to her in the vain hope that she would look, and she did. Unlike others, she stopped in the mid flow and started to flow towards him. She looked radiantly beautiful, her hair glowed like silk, and her face just blew him away.

He started off again by saying he was sorry, but she shook her head and placed a finger on his lips. He feverishly reached for her hand and she accepted it gracefully.

"I love you", he said, "I always have, but I could never really tell you. It is my fault that I could never give you the life you deserved."

She again shook her head and smiled at him. "I have to go Raj", she whispered, "it's my time and they have found a place for me."

"Don't leave me", he cried.

She again smiled, "I will see you again Raj", and with that she turned and drifted towards the sunset. For a split second, she stopped, turned, and shouted, "I loved you too", and with that she was gone.

"She's happy Raj, don't worry she will be fine, her soul has always been pure and you have been too blind to see this. Instead you saw lust and money to resolve your problems."

"No God, that's not true", he answered back, "You know that I have never cared for money, I just spent it. Yes, I did crave for lust, but that was not my fault; it was how you made me and I could not stop myself. I asked you many times to stop. I cried every day when I slept on my own when I was cold, but nothing changed. I did not want to be like that and you know this. I know there was more in our lives than sex and money – it was love. That's all I wanted. All I ever wanted boss was to love, not fear and not cry, and when I reached out for help there was silence", he cried. Falling to his knee, he whispered, "I never wanted this, … was a fool….."

After a few seconds of silence, he asked the Lord where Asha was going. It wasn't for him to know. "She must follow her own soul quest as you will, but I will promise that you will meet again", the voice replied.

"Where do I go lord?" he asked quietly.

"Now that's an interesting question", replied the voice. "Raj I want to show you something, so bear with me, ok and then let's talk about what you are going to do for me." Raj was confused, but he did not say anything. He stopped. His thoughts drifted to Asha for a minute - how he met her, and what happened leading to her death and him leaving home. "We all make mistakes", he told to himself, "my biggest mistake was that I didn't believe in myself and when the world knocked me, I thought I deserved it and felt sorry for myself. His grief was still strong in his heart. He had messed up and again he thought of her.......

Asha

Lives of Asian women are mapped out from their birth itself, to some degree. Their parents will already be thinking about how to save money for their daughter's marriage and how they are going to find a suitable groom for their daughter after their daughter passes a certain age. Raj was no different. In fact, he thought about it a lot, but money to him was fluid and it never stuck in a saving's account, rather went off his current account like water from a flowing stream. This always made Asha upset because she wanted security for the family and a good life for their kids. When she got married, she had to adjust living with a new family, her in-laws, because everyone lived in a joint family, which can be hard for anyone, but for Asha, she took it in her stride.

She had been brought up in UK, but still her parents had taught her well. Responsibility was written all over her. As a young girl growing up in England, she had the best of both cultures, so both the west and east were enriched within her. Her parents, like Raj's parents, had come to UK to make a better life for themselves and their children. When she was very young, at the age of eight, her family suffered the loss of her only brother. He was killed in car accident and this really affected her and her parents. Her thoughts about life changed a little and she had to be strong for her parents. They never really recovered from the death of their son and to make things worse, her mother could not conceive another child. Her doctors told her that it was too risky and could lead to death. Ash became the only son/daughter overnight, but she accepted this, buried her loss deep within her heart and carried on with life.

Even for marriage, when her parents talked to her

about Raj, she agreed because she and her family knew that it was in her best interests and her family knew Raj's family well. She had always known who she was going to marry because the families knew each other so well. So, for Ash, making a decision was easy as she knew that her parents would not make any hasty decisions. They say that marriages are made in heaven and people come together for a reason. Raj and Asha also might have been together for eons; they may not have met in the last life, but their souls were never far away from each other. Sometimes, she thought in the marriage that Raj was not always there. Initially things were great, they got on really well and were a young couple getting to know each other. However, they were different people. He was an extrovert in his ways; sometimes he would be up in the world and other days, she felt that she did not know him at all. That was her fault, she thought, because they never really talked like friends, even though they were married. Marriage is a bond of two souls, two friends, two hearts, but something was always missing in their relationship.

As life went on, she saw many ups and downs. She wanted him to settle down, get his head into gear, think about investing in a new house, save money, etc., but that never seemed to happen. Instead, money came, money went, and nothing was saved. They had a great family. Kids were level-headed and loving, but they were also hard, because they saw what happened around them. Their attitudes towards things were different and Raj was to be blamed for that because he thought he could joke around and let Ash do the role of coaching and steering.

At times, Ash would sit and wonder, "How am I going to survive this?"

Her bond grew stronger with her daughters; they kept her alive with their drive and push. They also pushed Raj hard. Sometimes this caused friction, but he knew they were right in many ways. Raj was close to his parents; they were his backbone and everyone knew this. His weakness was that he could not say no to anything. His parents supported everything he did and thought Ash was driving him different ways, but really it was his fault in acceptance and talking responsibility. Ash felt trapped, she wanted to shout some days and other days they were so much in love.

Then one fateful day things ended; Ash died. She gave up and Raj walked away from the family unit. His second backbone had left him as she couldn't face life with him anymore. Raj felt there was no one left in his life. His selfish pride and guilt drove him out of his family and his home.

As her soul drifted away out of her hurt body, she could see her kids gathering around her bedside. They were distraught. She could also see Raj near the doorway. His eyes were bloodshot, he had not shaved, and he looked as if he was drunk. She saw him fall on the floor when she had passed away. Sobbing uncontrollably, the kids rushed towards him, but he ushered them away.

"Dad!" they shouted. She saw him get up, look towards the bed and the kids, and then run out.

As she drifted away, she felt a warmth in a brilliant light that evolved her, and as she looked up, she could see some faces that she knew. Her mum and dad, they were smiling. They greeted her and hugged her. Was this real?

"This is my child", came a response in the back of her mind, "You have left your material body behind and now you are in my world. Rest dear, it will be time to move soon", and with that the light got brighter and brighter, and she could see no more.

The Boy

The journey of discovery had started for Raj. He stood there for one minute watching this vast area where people floated into the sunset to their new lives and disappeared, and another minute, he found himself standing in the middle of a park, somewhere in the middle of the night. "Where the hell am I?" he asked himself.

About 20 yards away, straight ahead of them, a young scruffy looking lad was loitering around the park bench. He was soon joined by two well built, well dressed men. Raj couldn't make out the conversation between them, but he guessed from the tone that the men were not happy. Quite suddenly, one of the men thrashed out a right hook to the boy's temple and knocked him down. Now, the other joined in with kicks to his mid-riff.

The young lad was helpless, he tried to raise his hands and arms up to protect his face, but he ended up with good old beatings. Once the men were satisfied that he had enough, they stopped and hauled the young lad onto the park bench where they proceeded to rape him and carry on their brutal assault.

At this point, Raj turned ahead, he wanted to shout out in anguish, but alas, what could he do, he had no body and could not help. Despair filled him and he shouted out to the Lord to stop this insanity. As Raj turned around, the men had finished their deed and left the boy lying lifeless on the bench and started to walk away from him.

"Why have you bought me here Lord, why are you showing me this?" he pleaded.

"I am showing you this because I want you to work for me."

"What do you mean work for you?" asked Raj in surprise.

"Well it goes something like this. Currently, I cannot send you through the right doors because the deeds in your last life did not score enough points. I cannot even send you down to my brother because your intentions were never evil, but just misguided. So, what I am offering you is the chance to redeem your soul, and to do this you will need to work for me as a fixer."

"A fixer? What the hell is that?" he replied in astonishment.

"Get that thought out of your head Raj, that joke is a dirty one."

Raj chuckled as he realised what he was thinking about. In his past life, Raj had been told a joke about two con men who had had gone to heaven and met God at the purely gates. God had given them a chance to redeem themselves by saving enough lost souls, and the guy, who would be able to convert enough, would enter through the gates, and the other down to hell. After a week, both of them returned to the big gates.

God asked the first man, "How many people have you saved the last week?"

He replied confidently, "a thousand people." Now the other man was smiling and laughing; well he was an Irish man after all.

God asks the same question to him and he replies, "ten thousand people Lord."

"How the devil did you do that?" God asked. Again the man laughed and replied,

"Well Lord, I took my ring off and then my bangle, and told them showing my ring that this is the size of your arse before you go into jail and then showing my bangle, I told them that this is the size of your arse when you come-out," he laughed.

"Let's talk about this, but not here, back in my

office," God said incredibly and with that Raj's surroundings changed again. Now, he found himself now sitting on a chair in a plush office. He could not help smiling to himself. If this was the afterlife, he thought, it would make a great Hollywood film. He remembered the Nicolas Cage's film, where he played the part of a fallen Angel in LA, fell in love with Meg Ryan, and then jumped off a tall construction site so that he could be a real human and be a part of her life, only to find she dies in a freak accident with a lorry. He now also expected Danny De Vito to walk out as God, with a big massive cigar in his mouth and an oversized white suit. What a cliché that would be, and quite amusing he thought.

Some part of that was true; a man did appear in front of Raj, but he certainly was not Danny DeVito. Mind you the resemblance was mighty close.

"Well Raj, a *Fixer* is like Nicolas Cage in that film you are thinking about, but this time it is real. I'm going to send you back on Earth to help that young boy in the park, back to his feet. I want you to help him and those around him."

"Why this boy?" Raj asked.

"Why not this boy?" God replied. "He is my child and he needs my help!" He shouted.

"But why me lord?"

"Because you have the heart to and I know you will not fail me."

"Am I going back as a man?" he asked.

"Raj, if you do this well, then you will have a choice whether you want to go through the doors or stay back on earth doing this job.

"Is this my destiny?" he asked.

"That is for you to decide Raj and you must face your own demons now my son."

There was a minute's silence and then God said,

"Let me show you something."

In a glance, the room vanished and instead Raj found himself floating in space. He was floating in what looked like a Milky Way. He was in awe. All around him, the stars shone so bright, almost as if they were souls floating around until it was there time to return.

"You would be right about that Raj," said the lord, reading his mind. "They are indeed souls waiting to be reborn again and the universe is infinity mass for you to comprehend. The grains of your DNA make up the strands of life itself and this is infinitely vast. Any one of these souls could be born in any dimension, any lifetime, and any place in the universe. There DNA joins them to the strands of life itself and that decides where. So, there is life after death, the journey just starts all over again."

"Each one of these souls follows his or her own path, and in some way he is following his own destiny and he alone will know when he has completed his task. Then he can rest in my haven in the glorious Milky Way", the Lord replied. "Whether you believe in me or not, it is irrelevant, but I am giving you a chance to redeem yourself, this is your duty/destiny, whatever you say."

"How I am going to help that kid? I couldn't help my own well enough."

"Raj how can you say that? One thing you were, was a good father, and they worshipped you, they still do today."

"How can they boss?" came the reply. "When I walked out on them, when I could not handle my own selfish guilt, when Asha died? I don't want to hurt anyone anymore boss, just in case I hurt them as well."

"Come with me Raj", ordered the Lord and with that their surroundings changed, and he soon found himself standing outside a large house. Parked outside the house was a brand new BMW 9 series, which looked like it was just out of the showroom. Raj smiled and this brought back memories of how he first owned his first BMW working for Intel, years ago. It was the same colour, perhaps not as expensive as this one. As he looked through the windows, the car was full of gadgets and a gorgeous red Dycota leather trim.

From the car, he looked around his surroundings and at his own clothes, he was wearing a black suit and a long tweed overcoat. As he looked up at the sky, it was overcast and rain was in the air.

"Where are we?" he asked.

He replied, "Your home Raj. This is Joy's house. After you walked out, Joy rented out the old property as it brought back too many memories. He and Hanna bought this house. By the way, he also got a new job with a large law firm as a senior partner and it pays him a good six figure number. Now, how can you tell me you weren't a good father?"

"No, Asha did this boss, she pushed him when he was young, I just spoiled him with things. I thought this way I could buy his love."

"Hey, this is me you're talking to, and I know so shut up and eat some humble pie, please."

"Are you going to stand there or going to walk in?"

Raj looked shocked, "how can I just walk into his life again?" he retorted.

"He won't be able to see you, no one can, so move yourself."

At that, Raj turned his attention to the house, it looked magnificent. My son is a senior partner in a law firm. I thought he was going to be a cricketer at one stage – all those matches I took him to through his young career and then it all ended when Ash got unwell and passed away. He bowed his head for a minute, wiped away a tear, and looked up again. He started to think about Joy, and this made his heart swell up and head pushed back with pride. He started to edge towards the big house and then he stopped; looking directly ahead of him, standing in front of the house, was Asha. "How could this be? She was on her way to her new life", he tried to utter some words, but nothing came out of his mouth.

She had not seen him yet, she was dressed casually, in jeans and sweater and was staring at the house intensely.

"Asha", he called. She looked around and saw him walking towards her. She did not move, but now looked at her approaching husband. In her eyes, he looked younger, the same as he did when he came to see her in London for the first time.

"I knew you would come", she said. "They said I had a few hours before I started my journey, so I asked if I could comeback. Raj what did we do wrong?" Asha asked. "Don't be sorry, you raised a lovely family and look at your son, he's done really well", comforted Raj. "He is happy Raj, and the wounds healed that we gave him, with all our fighting."

"You raised a level-headed young lad Ash, and this is the fruits of your labour, so don't worry."

She smiled and said "you know I have loved you, even when you were a dick to me, even when we did not talk."

He let his guard down now and tears whelmed in his eyes, "I know and I always will love you, and I hope that one day you will forgive me. I never understood what love was and always confused it with other things. I lost myself Ash and I lost you many times."

At that, she flung her arms around his neck and they embraced for the first time after so many years. The warmth of her arms held him there for what seemed like an eternity and he closed his eyes savouring the moment.

When he opened his eyes, she was gone and once again he was alone. Had it truly happened or was it in his mind?

As he started to the walk towards the front door of the house, Asha reappeared in front of him. She looked around and stretched out a hand towards him, which he grabbed eagerly. They did not exchange any words as they looked forward towards the door.

"Just walk in Raj and remember you're not from this world anymore." This should be interesting, he thought as he proceeded to walk right through the door and into the front passage of the house.

As they both stood in the passage, they marvelled at the size of the house; it was like a mansion, as seen in movies. Raj had always wanted a home like this one day, and his son had achieved his goals. The silence was broken, when the phone started ringing and a woman came running in to answer it.

"Hello", she answered quietly. After a few seconds, her facial expressions changed to a gentle smile on recognition of the other caller, "Hi Ojal, where are you? We are waiting?" she asked. Again there was a pause as the other caller responded and then the woman, on the other side of the phone, replied, "Okay, we will see you in the next five minutes."

Asha and Raj could barely hide their excitement; they were going to see their youngest daughter as well as their son today. It seemed as if someone had really planned this. There was a slight chuckle in the back of Raj's head. The woman who answered the phone must be his son's wife, Hannah. She had now put the receiver down and walked away, followed by Raj and Asha.

As they followed her around the corner, they could

hear her shouting Joy's name. They walked into a magnificent kitchen–cum-dining area. Hanna proceeded cutting a salad, just as Joy walked in causally. "What's up Han?" he asked "Was that Ojal on the phone?" Hannah nodded and replied that she would be here in five minutes.

"Get the table ready Joy."

"Where is Ashok?" he asked.

"Probably on his X-Box," was the reply from Hannah.

Raj and Ash exchanged glances; this whole thing was so unreal. Here was their son almost living a mirror image of their lives, the only difference was that Joy had done well for himself compared to his Dad. A moment later the doorbell rang and Joy hurried off to answer it. Raj followed Joy as he did.

Raj laid his eyes on Ojal, his youngest daughter. She was tall, leggy, beautiful, and all dressed in a professional business suit. Following directly behind her was a well-dressed man; his facial features were striking, he looked slightly older than Ojal and he extended his hand to greet Joy warmly.

"Hey Joy how are you?" he asked.

"I'm well thank you", replied Joy. Together they walked and passed Raj, oblivious to his presence, into the dining area where they were greeted by the girls.

At that moment, the voice inside Raj's head spoke again, "I told you they were happy. They must lead their own lives now and it is time for you to move to your next phase."

"Wait Father," Raj replied, "can I say goodbye to Ash?"

"She's gone already Raj," and as Raj looked around, she actually had. He walked into the kitchen area and gazed at his children. They are happy, he thought and then whispered "I love you guys."

45

At that very moment, Joy looked up, "Dad is that you?" Hanna reached out her hand to hold her husband's, but Joy got up and walked over to where Raj was standing, looking at his son. Hanna tried to reach her husband, but Joy had already moved away.

"Not again Joy, your mum and dad have gone."

"No", he whispered back to her, "he's here."

"Joy please", she pleaded. "Please, I cannot go through you hurting yourself again."

Ojal walked over to Hanna and put her arms around her, "Joy stop this!" she shouted, "they are gone, dad left us."

Joy turned to his sister, "How you can be so hard? Someone makes one mistake and you don't forgive him for that."

"I didn't mean that Joy", as Ojal reached out for him, "You know this. I cannot hurt anymore thinking about mum and dad, life has to go on. Joy", she whimpered as she laid her head on the back of his shoulders and arms around him. The whole ambience of the room had changed. There was tension in the air and everyone was caught by surprise on Joy's reaction, but also how deep his feelings were being hurt. Hannah like Ojal, wanted to hold her husband, he was so good, he had worshipped his dad and his mum, had been their strength. She wished Sonya was here; She was Joy's older sister, as she would have handled him.

"Dad, I know you're here, I can sense you." Tears whelmed in Raj's eyes, his chest felt as if it was going to burst.

"I love you guys and I am sorry for the heart break I caused. You see I could not handle things, I panicked, I was a fool. Joy I am so sorry, I did not realise that I had hurt so much and you know I would not do this to any of you. All I ever wanted was the best for everyone

He was crying openly. He tried to lift his arms to

reach Joy, but his astral form did not allow him to do so. He was filled with self-pity and self-remorse again and felt things spiralling back, where they were twenty five years ago. He felt a throbbing pain in his chest, his eyes started to roll, and his conscience started to loose. He was going into a full blown panic attack again and every bit of his body was crying out to stop.

As Raj drifted into the darkness, he realised how much he had let so many people down. Life for him had been a joke; he never took responsibility seriously. It was always about him. Asha was right, and now he felt really sick. He closed his eyes for a minute, but all he could see was Asha's and Joy's eyes piercing his heart with a toothpick. He started to question himself on how the Lord could think that he could help anyone. His own demons were re-surfacing again, and once again despair was given an opening to crawl in. His world again was falling around him and he was being swallowed up in his own pity.

When he opened his eyes, he realised that he had stopped moving and now was standing in a large hall, but it was void of any people or any living thing. He was alone and he felt cold; a touch frightened, what was going to happen now. It was funny, he always said he hated being part of a family and now standing alone, he felt cold, scared and again fighting his demons.

"What's wrong Raj?" asked the voice inside his head again. "Was the experience of seeing your family been too much or was it that you felt guilty that you weren't there too see them grow up to be fine characters and people?"

"What do you want of me?" he shouted. "You know how I feel, you know everything about me, and still you choose to taunt me."

"I am not taunting you my son, but showing you what your actions…."

"Yes, I deserve this for all the shit that I have done, but I am not the only one, I didn't commit murder."

"Yes you did Raj, you did worse than that, you betrayed peoples' trust, your own people's trust. You were selfish, you were driven by materialistic things, the need to have everything you could not afford. Instead of being contended, you were always...." Again, he did not finish the sentence. "Raj before you can move on, you must come to terms with your actions, and accept who you are and come clean. I bought you here for a reason my son, and again it is not inflict pain or hurt but to open your heart and mind."

Raj fell to his knees, "What do you want me to say?" he whimpered. Tears now flowed down his cheeks uncontrollably, "I know..." he kept on repeating until he could speak no more, until he passed out on the cold floor of the hall.

"I don't want you say anything Raj, I want you fight and believe in me. In your life, you were always a soul that would go one way and another, a Jackal and Hyde character – *not in the bad sense*. I want you to think about what certain actions to do. Every action has a reaction. Is that what you learnt in Physics, Raj? I want that young boy back whom I had put on this earth to be kind and generous to others, not a whimpering mess. All my children are important to me Raj. Lift your head my son, if you believe in me. Over the next couple of months you will feel pain and be hurt, but you must be strong. Like Lord Krishna quoted, 'lay your belief in me and I shall deliver you' – you always talked to him and asked for forgiveness, but really the only person who can forgive is you yourself."

LA

The City of Los Angeles (commonly known as LA), California (the "City"), is the second most populous city in US, with an estimated population of 7 million persons. LA is the principal city of a metropolitan region, stretching from the City of Ventura to the north, the City of San Clemente to the south, and the City of San Bernardino to the east.

Founded in 1781, LA was, for its first century, a provincial outpost under a succession of Spanish, Mexican, and American rule. It experienced a population boom, following its linkage by rail with San Francisco, in 1876. LA was selected as the Southern California rail terminus because its natural harbour, unlike San Diego's, seemed to offer a little challenge to San Francisco, the home of the railroad barons. But, what the region lacked in commerce and industry was that, it made up in temperate climate and unspoiled real estate. Therefore, soon tens and then hundreds of thousands of people, living in the north-eastern and mid-western US, migrated to new homes in the region. The City's population climbed to 50,000 persons in 1890 and then swelled to 1.5 million persons by 1940. Agricultural and oil production, followed by the creation of a deep water port, the opening of the Panama Canal, and the completion of the City-financed Owens Valley Aqueduct to provide additional water, all contributed to an expanding economic base. During this same period, motor cars became the principal mode of American transportation and the City developed as the first major city of the automotive age. Following World War II, the City became the focus of a new wave of migration, with its population reaching 2.4 million by 1960.

The City's 470 square miles contain 11.5% of the

49

area and 38.7% of the population of *the County of Los Angeles* (the "County"). There are over 3.9 million people living in LA and over 36 million people in the state of California.

Jose had lived all his life in the city of angels. His parents had passed away when he was child and he had been brought up by his dad's friend, who had promised his pa' that they would look after him. Jose, on the other hand, had his own ideas. At a very young age, he had got involved in a gang and there were many such in LA. By the early 80's, there was a record of over 30, 000 different gangs operating in LA and by 1982, gang members started to deal in drugs, and the homicide rates increased by the mid-80s and gang warfare, over particular patches, were rife. It was estimated that there were over 1,20,000 gang members in LA, which is still growing now, but the gang culture now has become more violent and brutal. Guns and drugs were part of their lives, and once you were in, you could never leave again, unless it was in a box.

Jose was part of this culture. With his Latino heritage, he joined his local boys' home and started dealing in crack, petty robberies, and even did a stint as a rent boy. At the age of 12, he had experienced more in his life than any other human being would have experienced in a lifetime.

To Jose, being part of his homies, one of the 100 Hispanic gangs in Compton, was the only family he had experienced and it was hard for him to move away. 'Homies for life' was his gangs phrase; they would cover each other and even take a bullet if they had to, as well. In Compton, there were over 500 different gangs, all operating in a tight area. Gangland warfare was a part of life in some areas and even the police would not travel down to some streets on their own, without back up.

Jose was now eighteen and had been a part of the Compton homies for five years now. Gang life was a part of his very fabric, so even the thought of moving away was a no go. This morning, however, he was on a mission. The homies were heavily involved with a Columbian drug lord and a new shipment of crack had pushed the homies' way. They had at least three kilos, worth some cool million dollars, and their job now was to distribute these throughout all the pushes, pimps, schools, etc. They didn't care who got hurt, as long as they made money. The homies' leader, a beefed up creep, called Ramon, called the troops in for a meeting. Jose now, fairly high up in the gang, was by his side.

Ramon was a sly character. He had come to succession as a leader a few years ago, when he had basically murdered the last one with a sneak knife attack. He had blamed a rival gang for the murder and he had even slashed his own hands to lay credit to his story. The only problem was that Jose had witnessed the murder, hence, why Jose thought he was safe was because he held Ramon's secret.

Ramon divided the troops into three groups; Jose would lead one of them and start distributing the crack to the club bouncers and door guys. He was also given a gun for his protection, but what he did not realise was that the gun was of a cop, who was killed a few nights ago again by Ramon, when he was high on ice.

This was Ramon's way of getting rid of another obstacle in his path and he made sure that the guys with Jose were his men. Ramon had a lot riding of this shit selling, otherwise the Columbians would come looking and these guys knew how to conflict pain.

That night, Jose set out would be a fateful night of his life and would change him for good, with the gun, pushed under his belt, the crew jumped into a waiting low rider and set off. Joining Jose tonight were Louis,

Freddie, and Frankie. They had all joined the brothers when Ramon had taken over, so Jose did not know that well and, to be honest, he didn't like them either. Still he had a job do, so they headed out to the first club on the south side of their turf. The guy, driving the low rider, Frankie, was your typical looking gang banger; his red bandana signified that he was from one of the Compton's homes. His head was shaved and he had a nasty looking scar running from his cheek bone to his throat area. He always seemed as the loose cannon in the group because of his temper, and he would not hesitate to slit anyone's throat, if was provoked. Shifting the car's gears, they glided effortlessly around the corner and then to their first appointment.

As they turned the corner towards the club that was barely 50 yards away, they were forced to stop their car. The brakes were jammed hard as three other cars headed directly towards them with their headlights blaring. There was no time to think as Frankie banked the car towards left, but his reactions were slow as the first car slammed into the side of the car, instantly killing one of them, Louis, in the back seat. The bone crunching sound would stick to Jose's mind for a long time, and to see the shock on the dead boy's face and hit him hard.

With the car slammed to one side, Frankie was the first to jump out; this was not a part of the plan to get the kid into trouble tonight, he thought. He reached for the knife that was hidden under his belt, but again his actions were too slow. In an instant, there was a sound of a rapid gun fire and Jose could see bullets ravaging Frankie's body, sending a mist of red blood everywhere. With Frankie down, Jose crept out of the other passenger's door; his first reaction was to run, but he couldn't as there was over one hundred grand worth of shit in the car and he would be killed if he lost that.

He then reached for the gun, a semi-automatic 9 mm one, and pulled back to cock the gun and release a bullet in the chamber, ready to fire. He had never fired at a moving person before, but only at tin cans at the gangs hider way. This, however, was real and he was terrified, but he didn't want to die, so had to.

When he looked around for their last team member, he could see his broken body slumped in the front seat of the car. Jose saw the drugs tucked up in front of him in a grey bag, so he grabbed for them, but just at that time, a hail of bullets washed by his head. He fumbled around for a few minutes for the bag, and once he had it, he pulled back and started to creep away into the blackness of the night. For a minute, he thought he had escaped, but was confronted by a big black brother, holding a 38 mm, straight at him. The man urged Jose to pass over the bag to him, and as he started to do so, he pulled the trigger of the 9 mm, hidden under the bag. The bullet hit his assailant straight in the throat, causing the man to fire his gun as he struggled to reach for his neck with both of his hands. Unluckily for Jose, the bullet that he had fired off, struck a glancing blow on the side of Jose's head and he fell backwards onto the path. The bullet had grazed his skull and his head felt like it was on fire, but he still struggled to get to his feet. His vision was in a daze; he grabbed the drugs and started running away from the hellish scene, with gun fire blazing behind him.

Crawling away from the hellish scene was so unreal. Even though Jose had been a gang banger for a few years and most gang members usually carried knives and guns as bravado, still all were shit scared to use them.

Jose could hear police sirens behind him, lots of them, and so he started running. He could still feel the trickle of blood from his head's wound, but he didn't care, he just wanted to get out. He also realised that he still had the gun in his hand, and that he needed to get rid of it quickly. Ramon had set him up, and he was convinced of it, but who were the men that attacked them. As he now started to run down the 42nd street, he jumped into a small dark alley way where he found a dumpster to leave the gun.

After that, Jose continued to run and walk, and he totally lost direction on where he was, until he arrived at the park. He thought he was safe here, but he was wrong again. Before he knew what hit him, two burley men hit him from all sides. He had no energy left to fight with them and they just bounded fist after fist into his face. He was ready to pass out. He dropped to the floor, bleeding from all over his face, totally helpless. Once on the floor, one of the brutes kicked him viciously in the lower stomach area, completely knocking the window out of him. The other guy now proceeded to pick him and then dump him over the back of a park bench. What happened after then would remain with him for a very long time and never leave haunting his mind. Both men then proceeded, one by one, to sexually molest him, and violate him without mercy and thought.

Both men were satisfied over their night's work. They picked up the bag of drugs and left Jose to die, slumped over the park bench. Joy had lost all thought patterns by now and his eyes were glazed with shock. He was even oblivious to the pain in his lower back area, where the men had molested him sexually.

The dreams and nightmares seemed to role in like massive waves inside Raj's head smashing against every sensor inside his brain. He could see many different faces and hear many different voices talking to him, shouting at him, and searching for him. He himself was running, trying to flee away from his own life. He was in self-denial mode, or even self-pity mode. He knew that there were things that he would like to forget, but not others, who were so key to his life. Facing your own demons was always hard, but in the past, he had always shied away from them.

He tried to open his eyes, but they were closed shut, almost as if they had been glued together. Right now, he was in a place of hurt and there were no exit doors to let him out. Man had always questioned what came after death; Was there real life after death and does our life force really pass through some invisible doors into a new plain of existence? Now he remembered a conversation, he had in the car, driving home with his kids and Asha from South Hall one day. His eldest daughter had asked a question about God, and if there was a parallel life where people lived and went through, which we could not see, also if there was really a God? Raj had made a quick remark, but Asha had rebuked it by saying, "tell her to decide herself about God."

"All I meant…" Raj argued back, "is that God is in our hearts and we should believe it and who knows where we go after death. Who knows if we see a white light that guides us to the stairwell leading to heaven and peace?"

"We make our own destiny", was his last reply on the matter and the conversation soon fizzled out and the mundane of everyday life carried on. The questions, however, stilled haunted his mind and he knew he could not answer the questions asked. In his own mind, he believed, but he also dreaded what was out there; was there another dimension? Now he knew the answer.

His mind drifted further back in the past, when his father-in-law had passed away. The grief was hard to take. He could still remember everything like it was yesterday and his heart still ached. He could remember leaving his kids that fateful b*oxing day* and then getting the news when they reached home. The days that followed were hard, but the body was in automatic mode and he tried to be strong. His own parents were out of the country; what more could they have done, but provide support on the telephone? He felt cold inside and it was hard trying to comfort Asha, as from inside he knew that she blamed him for a lot of things. Worst of all, was the blame of not allowing her to go back home often enough to spend time with her parents. He wanted to plead aloud, but no words would escape from his lips, "I am sorry Asha, I tried my best!" he pleaded inwardly. The death of a parent was hard, but he knew he would have to face the death of many other loved ones in his life; like his own parents also the death of his wife. That really broke the camel's back and he never gave himself for that. She had always been there for him, picking up the pieces when no one else could or even knew about. Every step of the way, he had made mistakes and never seemed to learn the basics, and at the end, him walking out one day to sulk in his own pity killed her. He was guilty as charged for that, and he always said that he would never leave her side and follow her to her next life to atone for his mistakes done in this life. Again, he was being selfish, feeling sorry for himself and unable to think about anything else.

The ones who really suffered in this life were his kids who had to witness the constant bickering and arguments about nothing. He had a quick temper and would fly into his stupid rages that really did not make much sense.

In his own mind and heart, he loved her a lot, but sometimes this was not enough. He wished always that he could have provided her with what she wanted and that was security for her and their kids, rather than wasting things away on a bottle.

Lying on the cold floor, he started to sob again. His eyes were still shut, but now he did not want to open them. He wanted this bad dream to go away so that he can sleep, but he knew this was impossible. He had to face his demons one day, perhaps it was now, if he was to move on. He didn't want to be one of those life forces that could not move on and just remain in limbo.

Before he could dwell in his own pity, he could feel someone standing next to him. He looked up and there was indeed a tall man standing next to him. He was very distinctive looking; his jet black hair was gelled back and he was wearing a very smart looking black silk suit. The most distinctive feature was his piercing blue eyes that were staring at him with contentment.

"Well, look at what we have here, my brother's new project. I don't believe it, he called me from my golf game to talk to you and here you are lying on the floor sobbing like a little girl." Raj looked at the man and could not help himself from saying, "Are you the local pimp dressed in your fancy silk suit? Whatever you're offering I don't want it."

For a split second, it looked like the man was going to explode on fire and beat the shit out of Raj, but he recovered his composure and smiled. "Get off the floor and let's talk", he retorted. "I have a dinner engagement and I don't want to miss this", he sneered. Raj noticed that the man's eyes went from being black to a violent red in colour as he gazed upon Raj for a fleeting minute.

Raj got up slowly and sat up. He faced the man in front of him who now was also seated himself on a chair in front of him.

"My brother told me that he wants you to be his new fixer and I told him that I wanted you to work in my

57

realm, firing up the ovens." He laughed and continued, "That sounds really cliché and a bit corny, but it is true. Let me introduce myself. My name is Luther, some people call me the devil and women call me horn", he laughed again. He then looked at Raj and said, "Look kid, I know this sounds really cliché, like something out of a cheap B class TV movie, but it's real. Your soul was on the borderline, but my brother took pity on you, and the committee made a decision to keep you and give you a chance. I wanted to burn you, but as usual I lost."

"Are you trying to frighten me Mr. Horn sir?" Raj asked very sarcastically. "I may be shit and may be crying like a big girl's blouse, but I know I am better than some dickhead, dressed like a pimp. I know God is playing with my mind and, if you are the devil, you don't frighten me."

"You know all about whores. Don't you Raj?" came the reply and he spat the words out, "I was the one you let in when you were weak with fear, so don't lecture me on how I look to you. I was the one who offered you all those materialistic things like money, cars, and lust for women. You were my soul to be had, but, no, my brother would not have this. You make me sick. You call yourself a man? You're nothing, but a whimpering little boy. You and me will always have this dance. Remember this well and when you are crying, I will be there quietly waiting for you to slip back into your black moods and then I will devour you, boy. Do not judge me or what I can do by the way I am dressed. That is in your mind and in the way you perceive me to look. You are nothing, but an insect underneath my feet that my brother protects. Beware of me boy because that is what you are – not a man."

There was a limit to this insult. Raj got up and questioned the demon, "Who do you actually think you are? I may feel pity for myself and I may have a different way of dealing with my problems, but who do you think you are to dig the knife any deeper than it already is?"

The devil was not used to people standing up to him and speaking to him this way, so his rage was growing stronger. There was fire streaming from around him and his features started to change into something that Raj started to whimper away from. "Little man, you will reach for me and when you do, I will be there to devour your soul and have you work in my realm forever. There will be no one there to protect you, and every day I will take pleasure in stripping your soul of every bit of humanity that may exist. Everything you love will be taken way and you will remember nothing", saying this he started to laugh and then looked at Raj." His eyes pierced Raj's heart, "I am here in you, don't forget this", and with that, he was gone. All Raj could hear was laughter.

It was getting colder and the wind was starting to blow stronger. Raj felt a little breeze run through the corner like a swift serpent. He felt the cold and the wind hitting against him. He tried to open his mouth and the next thing he noticed was that the demon disappeared. Raj looked around, but couldn't see anyone. He fell to his knees once again. His body was shivering, not just from the cold, but from fright. Was this a test or had he truly just met the devil. He thought to him that maybe it was another dream. "No", said a voice out of nowhere. "You are not leading a dream so don't go under that illusion young man." Raj felt as if he had heard this voice before, he felt that he recognised it.

"Hi God, where have you been? Observing the fun with your brother?" There was a chuckle from the voice.

"I must admit that was funny the way you spoke to him. His golf game is going to be hell for the next couple of months. All the words he spoke, my son, were to make you feel weak and to scare you. My brother loves to torment souls that he can do away with. Weak souls like you, and you must get him out.

This is the first step to redemption or deliverance Raj, but there will be more like him, you know this. It is time you stated to walk straight, rather than where you were going. It's time to face the music and come to the dance."

"What do you want God? I am going to be a lousy fixer, drugged in my own thoughts, rather than helping some kid in LA."

"Don't go there again Raj. I know my brother wants to comeback to have a chat." He chuckled again.

"God, where are we exactly, because it's awfully cold here, freezing my nuts off?"

"That makes two of us", said God with a huge laugh and the scene changed into one that he had seen before.

Raj stood once again in the park in LA. The dawn was breaking above the south side of the park and the city was getting up to another day. As he looked around, the park cleaners had already started their work; picking up the litter and clearing out the park bins with the rubbish we leave. He then looked at himself. He was dressed casually in a pair of loose faded out jeans and a black leather jacket.

"Am I real God, down here? Will people be able to see me? Do I have special powers like you like the way we see in all the Hollywood flicks?"

"This is real Raj and this is much about saving that poor kid, we saw in the park, beaten up by those thugs. You are human again, but you have powers to change things, but they will only come out once you start to trust yourself. Believe in your ability and your soul, and

60

everything will shine; remember my brother needs no excuse now to come after you."

"In terms of who you are, look in your jacket pocket and pull out the wallet." Raj did so and he soon had in his hands a lovely soft brown leather wallet, which he soon opened. Inside the wallet, he noticed quite a few credit cards and at the very sight, he winged. Credit cards had been a bane to him in his other life and had caused some of the major rifts in his personal life. This was one of those called demons that he had to face. He reached out for one and pulled it out of the wallet. The card was an American Platinum card, very expensive he thought, and the name imprinted on the card was Johnny Raja."

"Before you ask me who Johnny Raja is, Raj, let me tell you." Over the next half hour, God narrated the story of Johnny Raja.

Johnny Raja was orphaned at a young age when his parents were killed in car crash in Bel Air. Johnny had been ten then. He had been in school when the accident happened on the freeway, when his parents were returning from a business trip. His parents had come across from India before he was born and were successful business people who had made it rich in the land of freedom, i.e., the United States of America. Their business venture was trading in gold and fine jewellery that ran in their family for decades, back in India. They now had used their knowledge to open up a string of Asian jewellery stores in LA, San Francesco, Los Vegas, and Portland. Their business was now bringing in more than 10 million dollars a year for them. They were good people as well; they always helped the poor and regularly donated more than a million dollars to local charities in LA and India. He is now in his mid-thirties – one of the richest Asian businessmen in the UK.

They lived in an expensive part of Hollywood in a house worth nearly two million dollars. It had been the dream of his parents and grandparents to reach this pinnacle in their lives. They only had one child and that was Johnny, whose birth name was Jitendra, but his parents called him Johnny. Their wealth was their son and all their dreams were for him, this is why they worked so hard, but one stormy day their dreams came to a tragic end on the freeway in a freak accident.

Johnny had been orphaned at ten, but he also was the heir to a healthy business, which needed someone to run it. Once Johnny's grandparents learnt of his parents demise, they flew in to take care of things and fortunately, for Johnny they were good people who raised him with the same grace as his own parents. The business flourished and grew under the leadership of his grandfather who was a tough, but fair businessman. Johnny grew up fast and worked in the business, and learnt all about the jewellery trade. At eighteen, he got qualified for Princeton University, one of the most recognised places to study in the world. There he excelled and attained an Honours' degree in Commerce and Business Studies. He had been a model student and a good friend to many in the factuality.

After Princeton, he can back to LA to take control of the business from his grandfather, who now needed rest. The old man had done his best to look after his son's company and now he was tired. He was such a proud man that Johnny really wanted to make him proud. The business had grown so much now over the last 15 years that it was now rated to be one of the highest grossing privately own jewellery houses in US. The business was now worth a staggering 100 million dollars and had well over 200 stores around the western side of US, also now in Mumbai.

Home for Johnny was still LA and the house was

still the ones where his parents' had dreamed about some many years ago. It had a massive drive in and looked like a palace; his parents would be looking down now so happy. His grandparents were the best, they had always been there for him, they had lost a son 15 years ago, but they had brought in back in Johnny's eyes. For nearly three years, Johnny ran the family business, he attended the best dinners money could buy and mingled with the richest and most well-known people in the world, but he always felt as if something was missing.

His grandparents wanted him to marry, and yes, he had known some beautiful young women too, but he had not met that one who would steal his heart. He was also very religious like his grandparents and would sit for hours on his own in the family's temple area, which they had built in their home in LA. He would ask questions like most of us, about what life was about, and try to talk to his parents. There, however, was never any answers, apart from one stormy night.

That night he stood in the man-hour and asked the same questions and this time a voice came to him and asked him for a favour. This favour would ask him to change his life for 30 days and it asked for someone else to come, and own his identity and life to save another life. In return, he would be given a chance to spend some time with his parents whom he never knew, but needed to know.

"This is what you have been asking for the last 15 years my son and now I am granting you this wish. Look over there, there they are." As Johnny looked, his parents were standing a few paces away. They looked radiant and happy. Johnny ran towards them and fell into their arms, and then the white evolved them.

"So you see Raj, you are Johnny Raja for the next 30 days, you will have his memories, his thoughts, his life and everything that comes with it. Within these 30 days, you know what you have to do. You have crossed over and there is no turning back now my child. You have to face your demons because they are still there in your mind, but there also is a light at the end of tunnel, but you have to reach for it and want it.

Find the boy, save him and you will save yourself, and that is all the advice I can give you. Use these days wisely as you will share someone else's body and his life, so don't abuse that, but treat it as another chance. Find yourself Raj and then you will find freedom and the shackles tied around your feet will be freed."

Johnny Raja

For a few minutes, Raj stood there absorbing the words that God had spoken. They had hit some sore areas, but he knew they were correct. He again looked at himself; he was someone else, he could not make the same mistakes he made before. What terrified him more was that Johnny had money. Raj had always abused money, it slipped out of him like water. He took out Johnny's wallet again and looked at its contents. The first thing he examined or reached for was Johnny's driving licence. The first thing he noticed was the striking face of the young man in his photograph on the licence. He was blessed with good looks, but his eyes were sad, they somehow did not match the face.

Johnny's age, according to the licence, was 27, but from his photograph he looked older. Having lost his parents so young had affected him in a big way. Raj could feel the young man's emotions, his eyes whelmed with tears, which he tried desperately to hold back. He put the licence back in the wallet and looked at all the credit cards that Johnny had. Taking one at the time, the young man held very high rated cards from American Express, MasterCard, Morgan and Stanley, etc. Each card probably had a credit limit of 20,000$ or more.

He decided to put the wallet away in his jacket pocket and then he reached for his other jacket pocket and withdrew a bunch of keys. Among these keys, were that of a car that Raj had only dreamed about and that was a Ferrari 699; this car was worth over one hundred and seventy thousand pounds. Suddenly from nowhere he could hear a phone ring; it was coming from inside of his jacket pocket. He quickly pulled the phone out and looked at its LCD screen. The title read *Grandpa*, he smiled and clicked the hook button.

Hey Gramps how are you he answered. "Johnny where are you? We are worried, you never came home last night." "Sorry Gramps, I was caught up at friend's house and lost all notion of time, I am on my way home now." "Ok hurry up, we have visitors coming around." "Ok Gramps, I'll be there in 20 minutes." With that, he hung up the phone and started walking towards the exit of the park. It was strange, but Raj could remember where he was. He was indeed sharing Johnny's thoughts. As he walked out of the park, he could see the car parked across the road. He smiled at the sight at the fiery red blood 699 parked there. It was beautiful and for the next 30 days, it was his. For a minute, he thought he could hear someone chuckle behind him, but there was one there.

He crossed the road and walked towards the car, and then pressed the remote control in his hands for the car alarms and its doors. With a noticeable beep, the alarm disarmed. Before he got in, he admired the classic Ferrari lines.

Stunning all-aluminium two-seater coupé is summed up rather succinctly by its name and delivers everything that this promises. The Ferrari 699 GT Giordano, in fact, sets a new benchmark of excellence in the sports car world.

With its 1000 bhp Enzo-derived 5,999 cc V12, the 699 sprints from 0 to 62 mph in an astonishing 3.0 seconds and boasts a top speed in excess of 270 mph. These impressive performance figures are backed up by cutting-edge technological solutions, from the new generation F1 gear box, which guarantees shifts in just 100 milliseconds, to the sophisticated F1-Trac traction and stability control for even greater cornering grip, and the magneto rheological (MR) fluid suspension for unbeatable body control.

Raj had always loved cars and had always driven

news cars in his life. He could remember owning a Triumph Stage then a Jaguar sports to his Land Rover sports. His immediate family hated him because they always thought he was lucky, but in Raj's eyes this was because of his job and nothing else. Was he materialistic? No, he loved everyone, dearly but he was lost to himself sometimes.

He opened the doors of the Ferrari and slipped into the sumptuous leather sport driver seat. Italian engineering gone made with the 699. Joy and Sonya would have loved this. The first thing he noticed in the car was that the seats had been personalized to suit the driver and they even had the driver's initial embossed into the leather seats. The high tech delayed layout of the cockpit of the 699 took his breath away. He recalled when he drove a 360 around Silverstone, that was special, but the 699 was a dream.

He pulled the seat belt over and locked it in, and then pressed the start button of the engine. The 699 roared to life and he proceeded to put the car into motion. He couldn't help smiling to himself as he could feel the big massive engine of the Ferrari growl and want to pull more torque and power straight-away from a standing start. The car was stunning in every detail. He had imagined one day buying one of these for his son, but kismat was not on his side – how could he afford a $200,000 car. Ash would have rather spent that on their kids' future, marriage, and education. This is where Raj was selfish, he never really thought about those things, and today sitting in the driver seat, all these memories flooded back in.

As he pulled away on to the road, he could see signs for the freeway leading to Beverley hills and his home. His mobile started ringing and his hands free kit kicked in. "Hello", he answered. "Johnny where are you?" "I will be there soon", he answered his grandma,

"I am in car, coming home", he replied. "You knew the girl was coming around today to see you, don't let me down."

Raj's world suddenly just came to a halt. "A girl coming to see. Oh shit! How the hell to handle this one God?" he shouted in the car, you will find a way Raj, you have too. As he turned off the freeway into Beverly Hills, his home was only a short drive away. How was going to handle this and find the kid that needs him? God was having a real laugh putting him in this situation. He turned the 699 slowly into Shoreham drive where Johnny's house was at the end of the exclusive living area. The houses down this road were worth in the access of nearly 5 million dollars. As he got to the end of the drive, he turned into the driveway in front of a massive wooden gate. He remembered that on his keys he had a remote control that opened the massive gates. As he pressed it gently, the gates began to open.

Once there was enough gap for the 699 to slip through, he released the clutch, slowed down the accelerator, and the car responded in like and lurched forward into the huge winding drive way. The house grounds were magnificent and he approached the house. He felt as if he died again and went to heaven. He and Asha had always dreamed of buying a house like this, huge driveway where they could park the cars, and enough space so they could live comfortably with their kids. If only she could see this now, she would be so happy.

As he turned the car in, he came to a halt and turned the engine off, and got out of the 699. She was a beast and she was beautiful. As he closed the door, someone came running out of the front door of the house shouting his name. "Master Johnny, come quickly, everyone is waiting for you, you are late, this is not like you." The person who had addressed me was an old black man in his late fifties, white speckled hair and very kind looking eyes. Johnny smiled, "Jeffery calm down, you will have a heart attack at this rate." The old man didn't listen, instead he grabbed Raj by his arm and dragged him half running and half walking to the house.

Once in, he didn't give him any time to look around, but simply guided him up the stairs and into the last bedroom down the long corridor.

"She is downstairs waiting for you Johnny and you are running late. Please get changed, I have put your suit on the bed."

"Who's downstairs waiting for me, Jeffery?"

"The girl from Dallas whom your grandparents want you to marry my young Master."

Raj could swear that he could hear someone chuckle again in the background at his expense.

"OK, Jeffery don't worry, I will be there in a minute. You go and tell them that I am coming." At that Jeffery left him to it.

"Oh boy, what do I do now? I cannot ruin this guy's chances with this girl, so how do I react? The grandparents are God to Johnny, so I have to respect this and I cannot let him down." He quickly dashed to the bathroom that was located on the right of the huge bedroom, which was lavishly decorated. This guy certainly lived in style and Raj too remembered the hotel suite in St Lucia in 2007 and the Cricket World Cup.

He entered the bathroom and quickly headed for the sink. For the first time, he really looked at his face in the mirror. It was not that of Raj, but the very good looking face of Johnny Raja. A kid who had it all, but whose eyes betrayed a kind of sadness that Raj had seen years ago in his own eyes. He ran the tap, and

69

quickly washed his face and wet his hair. He again remembered how as a young man he used get ready in the morning to go to work, having a quick shave and then washing his hair. Next came the hair mousse and then the hair dryer to get his style. The same applied now, but he hoped he could use Johnny's memory on how his hair went.

Once he had showered and shaved, he hurriedly put on the clothes that Jeffery left him on the bed and then rushed downstairs to meet his suitors. Reaching the end of the corridor and the beginning of the stairs, he stopped, took one look up and a long breath, and then headed downstairs. At the bottom of the stairs, Jeffery waited and gave him a beaming smile as he approached.

"That's better, now you look respectable," he commented with pride at Johnny. "They're waiting for you in the main study, she looks great by the way," he winked. Raj smiled as he strode towards the study.

As he approached the doors to the main living room, he could hear and recognise voices coming from the room; one of these was from Johnny's grandfather who was a very proud man. He always boasted about his grandson's achievements and how well he had coped with his parents' death all those years ago.

He stopped by the door, gathered his thoughts, caught his breath, and then strode through the doors. As he did so, he stopped in the mid stride because he had to catch his breath. Sitting on the cream leather sofa, ahead of him were people he knew very well.

"Johnny my son, come in, you are late."

Gathering his composure, he looked at his Grandfather, "Sorry Gramps I got held up at a friend's place. You know the score, you get talking and time flies."

"OK," his grandfather repeated, "come sit by me so

70

that I can introduce you to these lovely people who have come from a long way to meet you."

"I know Gramps, I know," was all he could say, which got a strange look from everyone in the room. He walked over towards where his grandparents were and seated himself down. Then his grandfather introduced their visitors, "Johnny, this is Ojal Sharma, her brother Joy and their sister Sonya."

"Ojal is a beautiful name my dear," Johnny commented, "Your parents choose wisely. Do you know what it means?" he asked.

Ojal shook her head, Mr. Raja smiled, "It means vision."

It was hard holding the tears back as he intensely looked at his three children through a stranger's eyes. They looked ever so grown up, but yet so beautiful. Ojal sat upright, neatly presented in Indian outfit. Her short shoulder length silky hair was her calling card and she had small little dimples. On the other hand, Joy sat there looking around the lavish living room, his eyes intently studying every wall and thing. His eyes then crossed over to his eldest, Sonya. She looked stunning, but also her eyes looked a teeny sad to him. She was the eldest and she had seen a lot. She was strong and always used to put her point across, but today, her eyes showed deep sadness as she looked at through Johnny's eyes. "What have I done?" he said to himself, he wanted to pull away but he knew he could not.

"Well Johnny, like I said, these nice young people have come a long way to meet you. You remember I said my friend Rajesh talking to me about a possible match for you. Well he was talking about this young lady," as he pointed towards Sonya. Those single words sent shock waves running through his body, he then looked up and lightly swore under his breath, "You set me up."

"No Raj, it was in your daughter's kismat that she is here. Johnny is a good lad and Sonya needs stability and love. What did you leave her? A broken heart because you walked out, because her parents passed away, and she had managed the fort?"

"You are right."

"I said you would have to face your demons and your past and here is your past but there future."

"Johnny did you hear a word I said?" repeated his grandfather in some annoyance.

"Yes grandpa, I heard all of it. Sorry guys, I did not realise this was happening today, so I apologize. Have you guys come from far?"

It was Ojal who replied very quietly, but also sternly, "Yes." Both she and Joy had travelled from UK, but Sonya was based in Austin.

"Austin?" Johnny asked.

"Yes, Sonya works for Micro T. They are a computer hardware manufacturer based in Austin and she got a great opportunity some years ago to relocate to US. She now lectures and presents training programmes all around the world. She is a corporate Legal Expert for the company and heads up a new division in Austin."

At this point, Johnny's grandfather interrupted and led the conversation, and said that these folks were here to discuss the possibility of marriage proposals for Johnny and Sonya. "Rajesh Uncle had introduced me to Ojal and Joy last year when I was over in UK. Don't you remember?"

"I do Gramps, just forgot for a minute," he smiled.

"Look I am sure you guys would like some tea, let me organize this," Johnny said. This time his grandmother interrupted and said, "You sit down and I will go and organize." With that she was off, leaving the men to it.

"So Sonya dear," grandfather asked, "how do you enjoy US, you must be getting homesick?"

Sonya looked up. "Its good, I have always wanted to live in US", she replied.

"Really?" came back the reply from Johnny's Gramps.

"Yes when I was young," she continued "I used to tell my parents that I wanted to study in US and then get a job there. My late father wanted me to attend Harvard and do a Law degree. He said I could really earn some good money in corporate law and that is what I did."

"Did he leave you when you were young?" asked Gramps quietly in a very caring voice. This time Ojal replied, "Yes he did and our mom passed away a few years later."

"I am sorry" was the reply.

"Hey guys you have to excuse me for a minute," Johnny said, "I got to go to the loo." With that he left the room towards the bathroom.

Once in he locked the door behind and collapsed on the floor.

"Boss I cannot do this," he said, "this is not playing fair. I cannot do this for him, it's my daughter in there boss."

"I know Raj," came the reply softly. "That's why I am talking you out for a little while and bringing Johnny back in. He knows the score already, his grandfather has already shown him pictures and mentally he has already agreed."

With that Raj felt himself step out of Johnny's body and standing next to the young man, who looked back at him. "Don't worry, I will look after her," he smiled and moved, passed Raj and exited the bathroom.

Raj followed the young man out and entered the lavish living room. He watched Johnny take his sit next to his grandfather who looked anxious towards his grandson. Behind Raj, the door opened and Johnny's grandmother walked in with one of the maids with trays of tea and buffet snacks. Raj walked around so he was closer to the kids. He watched them intentionally, but then suddenly he stood up very straight. Even though he was technically dead, he felt the small hairs on his neck standing up. He turned around and there standing a couple of feet away from him was Asha.

"Don't say a thing Raj, she doesn't know you are here. She asked the handlers if she could see her kids before she moves on."

"Move on, what do you mean Boss? I thought her life was linked to mine?"

"Hush Raj and just watch."

Raj looked hurt, but he had to turn back to the kids. Now Johnny spoke, "So guys, you have travelled all the way from London, I am honoured. Also heard a lot about you guys from my grandparents."

He then looked at Joy and asked him a couple of things about where he worked and his family. He knew Raj was there watching. Joy answered Johnny's questions and asked a few of his own, in terms of his own situation. He then commented of how impressed they were on how well he had done. Johnny smiled "It's not me," he remarked, "my grand-parents have been my rock and they had helped him drive the business and his education. Yes, I admit", he carried on, "it was loneliest times, but I had them behind me and I know my parents would want to carry on."

"Do you remember them?" Sonya asked. Johnny looked up towards her, his face lit up and he smiled broadly, "Oh yes, I see them every day, and they help me through the good days and the dark days."

Sonya for a minute looked up directly into his eyes and could see the love he had for them and thought this

74

could be it. She returned his smile with one of her own and then looked down again. Johnny's grandfather was watching all this and seeing the glances that both the children made at each other, he smiled.

At this point, Johnny's grandmother interjected that the tea and the snacks were getting cold and she urged everyone to start to eat.

As Raj looked on, he too had noticed the interaction between the kids, and in his mind, he heard the voice saying, "Yes this is what I had planned for her."

He then turned his attention to Asha. She was still standing there, but now she was looking directly at him. She had tears of happiness in her eyes, tinged with sadness. He wanted to go over and hold her close, but his legs would not move; all he could was whisper in his mouth, "I am sorry and I love you." She then turned her attention to the kids once again and slowly moved towards them.

As she reached Sonya, she gently bent down and kissed her eldest daughter's cheek. She also did the same to Ojal and then to Joy. They all looked up and looked around, and it was Sonya who stood up and said "Mum," looking towards Asha. Asha had already backed up and edged away, "Mum, I love you too," Sonya said, "I know you are here."

Still Raj could not move his legs, "Raj wait, this is not your moment."

"But Boss she needs me."

"Hush Raj," came back the stern reply.

"I have to go Sonya. Look after them for me," said Asha, "but don't worry Dad will be around now to watch over. I love you guys." She then turned to Raj, she smiled at him and with that, she started to fade away until Raj could see her anymore.

At this point, Johnny stood up and walked over towards Sonya, "You okay?" he whispered. She turned around to see him standing close to her. She was drawn to him. She felt safe with him and just nodded her head.

At this point, Raj understood that his kids would be okay. He still could not move, but there were tears running down his cheeks like water tumbling down a mountain cliff.

"Raj, we have to leave Johnny here for a while, I need you somewhere else for a little while," came God's voice and with that Raj also faded away from the living room to a more undesirable location.

The Hospital

Mercy hospital was shroud in a rainstorm that hit LA in the last few hours, but the work of the doctors and staff still went on. Most hospitals in the poorer part of LA always found it hard to get sufficient funding, and Mercy was one of them. Doctors and nurses here worked long 16 hour shifts, with little appreciation, and today was no different.

Dr. Rogues was on his shift in emergency ward and when Jose came in, he was in a bad state. The boy had been beaten up severely and was sexually assaulted. They took Jose, who was unconscious, straight to the emergency room and started their magic. After two hours in the consulting room, they moved Jose to the critical ward where he was sedated quiet heavily. He was attached to glucose drips and heart monitoring machines, so they could keep an eye on him overnight.

"Well Doc, what's the verdict? Is he going to survive?" asked the CSI officer, Wells. His officers had found the boy in the park and then called in the paramedics. "The kid is lucky to be alive officer, he has taken a real beating. He has four broken ribs, sever bruising all over his body, and lacerations where he was sexually assaulted. Whoever did this to him wanted to leave a message and they did. The officer listened quietly, mused over the doctor's words, and then started to move closer to the boy's bed. He stood beside the bed for a few minutes and then turned his head towards the doctor. He could see by that the guy was affected and by what he had seen today, he decided not push with any more questions. "Alright Doc, we will catch up with the kid tom," and with that he walked away.

The experience for Jose in all this was a little bit different; he had what we call an outer body experience

(OBE), but had never thought that he would experience this himself. After the beating, which he took in the park, he drifted away in oblivion from all the pain and as he drifted, he seemed to literally step away from his damaged limp body. As he stood looking at his beaten up body in the park, his eyes were frozen with shock and terror. What was happening, was he dead? He could not avert his eyes from his motionless body on the park bench. Have I crossed over, am I dead? He thought. Finally, he pulled his eyes away because he could hear distant sirens coming towards him. The men who had done this had already left the scene and just left him to die.

"You have not crossed over yet Jose," said a voice in his head.

"It's not your time but you have to be strong."

"I can't be!" he screamed in his head, "I have had enough of running, fighting, and cheating. My papa did not come to America for this son," he cried.

"I know my child and that is why it is not your time, you shall have help, trust me."

Jose looked around there was no one there. Who had just spoken to him? Before he could think more, the police had arrived with the paramedics. He left himself being sucked back into his body as the paramedics started to revive him.

"NO!" he shouted, "I don't want to go back, please," he pleaded, but the paramedics had already done their magic and he was now drifted back into the living where he found himself being lifted onto a stretcher. The pain from his wounds were unbearable. His eyes were pleading to the paramedics for some pain killer, which they listened and injected him with some morphine. The pain eased and he slowly started to black out. His eyes closed into a deep sleep where he saw his parents smiling at him.

"Papa, I am sorry," he whispered.

"Hush Jose, sleep now, we are here."

"Papa…" With that he slipped away.

The ER ward at Mercy Hospital continued to work throughout the night as nurses and doctors welded their magic to save lives and bring patients back from the brink of death. Life and death go hand in hand. We are born and one day we will eventually die. I admire the work that doctors do; they work for long hours, and caress the sick and dying with their gifted hands.

The following morning, before the night shift changed, Dr. Rogues checked up on his patient. He was still heavily sedated and the nurse reported that he had a quiet night. They had changed the medication slightly and he had come through the night well. The doctor sighed heavily, "Who could do this to a human being and why?"

Mercy was in one of the poorest parts of LA and by now, the doctor had seen his fair share of violently attacked patients who come into the wards. However, he could still not understand of what drove people to do this. As he was about to leave, he noticed that the CSI officer had also returned to check on the boy.

"Any change Doc?"

"He made it through the night, Officer," was the short reply. With that, Dr. Rogues walked off as he finished his shift for the evening.

Roger

In another part of LA, Roger Davies, a young law student, walked home from his part time job at the local Pizzeria. His job was paying for his evening studies so that one day he could become a high flying corporate lawyer, Roger had a sad past. His family was killed at a young age in a car accident and he was the only survivor. This happened nearly 20 years ago, and he had been raised since then by his aunt and uncle. Roger was convinced that he would pay his own way. He had heard some stories about what his parents were like by his uncle, and he wanted to respect their ideas and thoughts on how to live.

Roger was an outgoing young man; he worked hard and enjoyed the company of his close friends. However, something still held him back from sharing his most inner thoughts with anyone. Roger was also an aspiring martial artist. He had taken part in quite a few district events and had reached the national level for his country. His art was *full contact karate* and he had been practicing for nearly 15 years, since his uncle had introduced him to the sport by taking him to see "Bruce Lee's Game of Death." Ever since then, he was hooked and he wanted to learn martial arts. He, therefore, joined a local Karate Club run by an ex-marine (Master Roberts) whom his Uncle knew. Five years ago, Roger had moved out of his uncle's house into his own place, which he was proud of. He was making his own way and his life seemed to be going the right track. Once he had finished studying, he would be able to have a better life and help his aunt and uncle.

Life has a habit of not wanting to play ball with the best laid plans. Tonight, as Roger walked the short distance to his home, he was jumped upon by a gang of four hooded men. One had a knife with him and stabbed Roger in the stomach, whilst the others kicked and robbed him before they ran off. As Roger lay on the ground groaning in pain, he heard voices coming towards him. He looked up to call out, but there was no one there. From where were the voices coming from? Roger wondered. He was blacking out now. He tried to shake it off, but he could not, and that's when he passed from one world and entered another for a little while.

"This is great boss, you always make me see someone who gets beaten up, killed, hurt or…"

"Raj shut up", came a short sharp response.

"This is Roger Davies. He is 27 years old and its not his time to leave this earth, so that's why you going to take his place and see this world through his eyes for a little while. He's a good kid Raj, he has seen his parents die young, and I am going to give him the opportunity to spend some time with them until you finish your task.

When you take over his body, remember the responsibility that I have given you and remember who you are and who he is. You will feel all his pain, all his fears, all his strength, and you will have all his memories and like Johnny know all his friends, like they were yours. Be wise my son, you have it inside you.

"Hey boss, this is not Quantum Leap you know, like that in TV series, where he jumped into people's life and made changes for the good, and once done, jumped out, and you're not Ziggy telling me what the probability is that something is going to happen."

God laughed, "And why not?" was the reply. "I quite liked the program when I got time to watch it. It gave me the best ideas, those Hollywood screenwriters are terrific."

"Boss you really are mad," Raj retorted.

"Raj, this is serious, no more jokes, using Roger's

body is ideal for what we agreed you would do."

"I earlier thought we were going to use Johnny's, but I suppose he is sorted to a certain degree, thinking about the kid." replied Raj.

"Raj, Roger does not deserve to be here and it was not my idea that he would, but it has happened. Now you will take his place for a little while and complete the task that I asked you, i.e., to save Jose, and in the end, yourself. If you can help Roger, well that will be a bonus along the way. This is reality Raj and not a TV sitcom. Don't you think I know this retorted Raj? Let's do this."

With that, Raj could feel himself being lifted and then sucked into Roger's limp body on the cold alley floor. For seconds, nothing happened and then Roger's body started to move, at first very slowly, first on an arm and then another, and then his head came up, and then finally the body pushed upwards to a vertical position. Raj had passed through okay and now he was inside Roger's body. He lifted his arms up to see his hands, he squeezed his hands into a fist, they were behaving themselves. He then moved his hands down to where Roger had been stabbed. There were no signs on his body of any stab wounds. Yes, there was a patch of red stain on his white t-shirt, but thank God, no stab wounds.

"Raj I have to go," came the boss's voice inside his head, "Help the boy and if you need me just call. For now go home, have shower, and get accustomed to Roger's life. He's a good kid."

"I know boss, don't worry and anyway you know what's going to happen, you wrote the script already." With that Raj spotted on the floor Roger's wallet and proceeded to pick it up and examine the contents. Nothing was missing, the money was still there, and his credit cards were also there, so why was he attacked?

What was the purpose of this charade tonight? Someone had other reasons for this, but who?

Now if I have Roger's mind, I will know where his home is, so he started walking towards the main road out of the alley. Once he reached it, he turned left and walked the short 20 yards to the entrance of his apartment blocks where he lived. What was the number he thought, "Ah that's right, its 23 and it's on the 2nd floor", he smiled and proceeded to go up the stairs towards his apartment.

Once he got to the door, he realised, he didn't know where his keys were, his hands rifled through all his pockets, but they were not there. "Wait a minute. I keep a spare key under the front door mat, so he bend down, lifted the mat, and there was the key. He placed the key in the lock and turned the gold handle to open the door to home. Roger's place was great. Raj could not have imagined a student having these sort of digs, but hats off to Roger, he had worked hard and put a lot of pennies into doing his home up.

As Raj closed the door, he put the key down on a table near the entrance and walked into the main living area, which was really spacious. Raj reached for the lights and switched them. The room came to life. He could see the time and effort that Roger had spent to have a decent place to call as home. Raj instinctively walked through the lounge area and into the kitchen area. Once there, he headed for the fridge, pulled a bottle of beer out, and started to open the bottle. As he did so, he could hear Roger's telephone started to ring. Having a quick swipe of the beer, he looked around for the phone, which was lying on the couch. He walked over and picked it up.

For a split second he stopped before he answered it and thought, what was he going to say, would he know who was calling? Sure, he would, he thought, I have

Roger's thoughts and memory. He pressed the receive button and said "Hello."

"Roger is that you mate? Where have you been, you know we were supposed to go out tonight?"

"Hey slow down partner," was Raj's reply, "I have just got in Kenny, give me 20 minutes to have a shower and to get changed. I will meet you downstairs in front of the apartment." With that, he put the phone down and headed for the bath.

He was living Roger's life. He had his memories as they were his and it was now time to get to work. The only thing that truly haunted him was that who could have ordered the hit and run on Roger and why did they make it look like a robbery?

Twenty minutes passed. Roger was all refreshed and changed into new glad rags. Raj was waiting outside the apartment for Kenny. Kenny was Roger's long time school buddy with whom he had grown up. His uncle and aunt did not approve this friendship much because Kenny was black. Roger's relatives were, in that respect, racist, but that ran through some of their family. Roger on the other hand, was the opposite, he had always hung around at school and then at college with the black crowd, Spanish kids. He had never seen a colour difference.

Kenny, like Roger, was also a martial artist from the same club. They both had made district level together and now had reached the first national levels. They both held 2nd Dan black karate belts and were both recognised as up and coming stars in their club. Like Roger, Kenny had also come from a sad past; his dad had been shot and killed in a gang related incident four years ago. He was not a gang banger, but just an innocent bystander, caught up in a fire fight, which he got shot straight in the heart and died on the spot. His mother, ever since then, had to raise three kids on her own and it was hard. Money was tight, but she never gave up. Her church gave her the strength and her kids the will power to continue. Kenny was the eldest of the kids. He had not married because he could never find a steady girlfriend. He was always scared to commit and could never tell a girl how much he cared for her.

Kenny turned up outside Roger's apartment in his busted up 1970 black trans-am to pick Roger. Roger cringed; he always hated getting into his car because Kenny was a real pig; he had food everywhere in the car, never cleaned it, and therefore, it smelled.

"Don't tell me you forgot to clean the car again."

"Hey buddy", came the reply from Kenny, as he turned his head to Roger. "Hey what's up with you dude, why you frowning like that?" asked Kenny.

"If I tell you what happened tonight, you would not believe me, but here I go," and so he narrated to Kenny the attack by the four hoods. They had not nicked anything. I reckon someone paid them to hit me, but I don't know why.

"Hey, by the way where we going?" he asked Kenny.

Kenny smiled, "You know I told you about those two girls whom I met in the gym last week? Well I fixed us up some action tonight. We are going to meet them at Cleo's and show them a good night, you dig brother."

"Don't do that brother thing on me Kenny. You know I don't like blind dates and especially the ones you pull off. Remember the last one, nearly got my head knocked off by the girl's dad."

"Hey trust me, this time we are going to be okay. So you were saying that those hoods took no money, jumped from nowhere and left you lying in the alleyway." "It's true Kenny, when I got up, there was blood on shirt and my wallet was on the floor.

Something must have scared them off, I don't know, this is all too strange.''

The story that Raj was narrating was hopefully going down, but it was strange. The discussion continued as Kenny joined highway 105 to West Hollywood and Beverley Hills. Cleo's was a young hip hop club that Kenny's Uncle owned, so getting in was not going to be a problem.

From Highway 105, Kenny jumped on to highway 10 and then on to the 405. Beverley Hills beckoned and their blind date was just 10 minutes away. Great thought Raj, how am going to handle this one? Kenny had already turned off the freeway, and now was heading down Wiltshire drive and then up to Sunset Bl, where the Club was.

They parked up alongside the club where Kenny's uncle had a private car park, and entered the club from the back door. The club was heaving with people and the music was rocking away with a 50 Cent and Justin Timberlake single. Kenny was in his element and Roger followed him shaking his head.

"Hey man, there they are near the entrance,'' said Kenny pointing towards two lovely women standing on the far side of the club. Even Raj had to admit that they did look good, and inside he could hear Roger's mind agreeing with vigour. "Come on then Ken, let's go and meet them. By the way, I want the one of the left. She's cute." Before Kenny could reply, Roger rushed ahead of him through the crowds of young party goers towards the girls.

As they approached the girls, Kenny pushed by him and proceeded to greet the girls with his ever so bashful acknowledgement.

"Wow! You guys look crazy, almost good enough to eat." Corny line thought Raj, but looking at the girls close up, he wasn't far wrong. The two girls were both around their mid-twenties, tall, blonde, and beautiful. They had hour glass figures, so no wonder why Kenny jumped at the chance to speak to them in gym. He would love to see what they wore when they worked out. Suddenly he seemed shocked at his thoughts, but then realised, this was the other side coming out. He could never resist a beautiful woman.

"Ladies, let me introduce you to my friend here. Roger meet Katie and Jazz. They all greeted each other. There was a little bit of hesitance on both sides, but the ice was broken once Kenny had brought the first round of drinks. The night started to run smoothly. Kenny had hooked up with Jazz, whilst Raj (Roger) hooked up with Katie. To Raj, Katie looked like a supermodel from his past called Kate Moss. She had long flowing blonde hair, gorgeous pouting lips, and alluring blue eyes that were pulling at his heart's strings. Physically, she was attractive too and certainly stood out from the crowd. He reckoned she was 5ft 9 or 10, hour glass figure, and dressed to kill. Also, what was really surprising for Raj was, then he didn't feel shy around her. Normally when he was younger, he would run away a mile from girls, but to Kate, he warmed up straight away. She in return, was also open and they both hit it off straight away. Raj also felt Roger's energy flowing through him and there was a connection here with Kate. He smiled, "Ok buddy, I understand." Soon he was talking and dancing for most of the night, and as the night wore on, they seemed to get closer and closer.

"This is really strange," Kate said as they sat in quite area of the club, way from the dance floor. Kenny and Jazz were jiving away to some hip hop classics, whilst Roger and Kate were sipping cocktails.

"What's strange?" Raj said, looking back into those beautiful blue eyes.

"This is what's strange", she replied, "This is first time ever in a long time where I am so comfortable around someone whom I just met a few hours ago. This doesn't happen to me. I always seem to scare the boys away,'' she laughed.

"I can see why," he replied teasingly.

"Oh!'' she laughed as she gently smacked his arm with her hand.

"No, I am being serious," she said, "I almost feel like I know you and it feels great."

Again Raj replied teasingly, "Well, I am that sort of person, a lovable old rogue, but once you get to know me, I am a real Casanova, but seriously, I never felt so comfortable around someone for a long time and you're beautiful as well."

She blushed and then smiled at him coyly, and they continued talking over their cocktails.

"You want another drink Kate?"

"Please", came the reply.

At that, Raj got up and headed towards the bar to get some more drinks. As he looked back, he saw the lovely Kate peering after him. "Wow! She is really something, but I don't think I am here to do this", he thought. However, strangely, something in his head wasn't telling him that this was wrong either. "I can't do this. I am leading someone else's life and I am getting hot about a girl whom I have just met." He looked around back towards her. She also looked back and smiled, her eyes did all the talking. "You know she's getting hot for Roger and not you Raj", came the voice inside his head with a chuckle. "I know that boss, just testing you, but she is some catch for Roger", replied Raj.

Once he reached the bar, he ordered a couple of more cocktails and waited for the drinks to come. As he waited, he turned around to look in the direction of

Kate. She was not sitting at the table. He seemed concerned, but then thought that she may have gone to the toilets, so he took no further notice. The bartender had comeback with the drinks and he proceeded to pay for them, and then headed back to the table. Once there, he noticed that Kate had left her purse on the table. That's strange, he thought. Why would she leave her purse lying around in a busy club, where anyone could nick it?

He put the drinks down and looked around the club, being concerned for Kate, but he could not see her. He then proceeded to pick up her purse and wandered down to the dance floor where Kenny and Jazz were still jiving away. The music was really loud, but he soon pulled Kenny away for a minute.

"What's up bro?" Kenny replied hurtfully, "why did you pull me away like that?"

"Sorry Kenny, have you seen Kate, she just disappeared from the table?"

"Hey man, she's probably gone to powder her nose, stay cool", was the reply.

"Why would she leave her purse on the table and look she still not there, something is not right." They both looked up towards the table on the balcony, away from the dance floor and Kate was still not there. They both looked at each other and then both turned towards Jazz. She saw them coming and wondered what they looked so concerned about. Roger then told her that he had lost Kate; he saw her one minute when he was getting drinks and then the next minute she was gone.

For the next fifteen minutes, they searched the whole club, she was not there; Kenny even got the DJ to put out a call, but no one responded. She must have left the club, they next thought, and then all three rushed out first through the front entrance. There was no sign of her, but other people mingling outside the club. Raj then turned to one of the bouncers too see if he had seen this girl, who he described leaving the club. To his surprise, he said that he had seen a girl being, almost, pulled out of the club by a young man. He tried to stop them, but he had to stay at the door.

"Which way did they go?" Raj asked and then the doorman pointed alongside the club where his uncle's car was parked.

At this, Raj started to run towards the car park; something inside him told him that there was trouble. God, he hoped she was alright or someone was going to pay good. As he ran, Kenny and Jazz followed briskly after him, keeping their pace well.

Suddenly, the three could hear a scream and they rushed towards the direction. Raj could see, about 50 yards ahead, a young man abusing and shouting at a young woman on the floor, who he recognised as Kate.

"Oh!" he shouted towards the man, and before the man could realise what was happening, Raj was upon him like a rash.

"What the hell do you think you are doing?" Raj shouted again, grasping his hands around the man's throat in almost a death grip. The man struggled sharply and managed to release himself by punching Roger in the stomach. As he pulled away, and as Raj recovered from the punch, he pulled a knife out.

"Who the hell are you?" he shouted towards Roger. "This doesn't concern you, this is between me and that slut", he said as he pointed towards the very frightened Kate.

Raj had hatred in his eyes, but he knew he had to stay calm, "Look buddy, I don't know what your beef is, but put the knife down and let's talk."

Suddenly the man lunged towards Raj with the knife and in almost a reflex action, Raj jumped in the air and in one swift move, he hit the block with a spinning kick square on the chin, knocking him out cold on the floor.

He turned around to Kate; she was in shock, her arms were badly bruised and she had a nasty cut on the side of her cheek.

"Kenny get some help and call the police for this Muppet", Raj shouted. Kenny ran off to the club, from where he soon called for the cops. Roger scooped up Kate gently in his arms and carried her back to the club, where he was met by Kenny and his uncle, who ushered them into one of the cashiers' offices. Over the next few hours, the police arrived and took control of the situation. They took away the man who had attacked Kate and ushered Kate away to the nearest ER ward in the area. In the ambulance, alongside Kate, went Roger to give her company; she somehow felt safe around him. All the way to the ER, he held her hand and whispered support while the ambulance staff monitored Kate.

The ambulance arrived at Mercy in the early hours and Kate was taken straight into the ER ward, and Roger was told to wait in the waiting room.

The Hospital

Raj had the strangest feeling as he sat in the waiting room in Roger's body. He was here also for another reason; the boy was here. His mind shouted out at him and as he turned his head around to the emergence doors, which slid open, two guys, whom Raj recognised, walked in. These were the guys who had brutally attacked the boy in the park. What were they doing here and where were they going at this time of the morning?

His instinct told him that something was wrong and something was going down, so he decided to follow the two goons. He kept his distant, but followed them keenly around to the end of the ER ward, where the lifts were. There they stopped and pressed the button for the elevator. They looked around nervously and then entered the opening doors of the lift. Raj quickly ran over to the elevators and watched the LED displays to show him the floor at which they would stop at. The elevator stopped on the third floor, and then Raj turned and shot up the stairs through the exit doors to the third floor. Roger was a fit block, and so he reached the third floor quickly.

He had to rush as he could feel the danger now; a voice was urging him around the corner and past the elevators there danger. He clinched his fists and started to run. He heard a scream followed by shouting and then a gun-shot. In front of him, he saw the two men; one holding an automatic 9mm and the other brandishing a knife. In front of them, a man lay dead; it was a policeman who sat guarding the boy's room. As he looked around, he could see where the screams had come from; one of the nurses had also been hit, not by a bullet, but was sliced by a knife.

The men had not seen Roger approaching them, so

the initial hit came by surprise and shock. Roger's momentum had carried him forward and then with a lunging forward flying kick, he had hit one of the men, and in the same breadth, struck out at the other with a venous chop across his forehead. The man, hit by the kick, was the one holding the knife, and as he fell forward, he fell upon his own knife that sank deep within his breastplate, further into his heart.

The second assailant got himself up from the initial shock. He lifted his arm to raise his gun, but it was not there. When he fell, the gun was thrown from his grip to the far side of the corridor. Angry, now the man faced Roger, and taking his coat off, he took out a knife from his waist holder. Like a charging bull, he attacked Roger, and in-turn, like a nimble matador playing with an angry bull Roger stepped aside the charge, and like an elegant matador in return, he hit the man, as he turned around, with a viscous kick to his face. Blood streamed down the bull's face and he then followed that by a forward kick to his stomach. The man sucked for breadth, but he could only cough blood. Roger had to act fast, and as the assailant was still bending down, he brought his leg down hard onto the back of his neck. He heard the distinct crack of his bone as the assailant hit the floor. For a split second, there was silence, things had happened so fast, and now he had killed two men.   There was blood everywhere; Roger was standing above the dead corpse in utter disbelief on what just transpired. As he looked down, blood oozed from the dead man's body onto the white floor. Instantly, he moved away; he wanted to run, but something was stopping. I have got to stay here and help the wounded, he thought. He looked around, the nurse was still alive, he rushed to her. "Hey, you're going to be ok, hold on", he whispered. She looked up, her eyes pleading to him to help her. He looked over her body to see where she had been cut or stabbed, and then he saw a large slice on her arm. The cut was deep, so he quickly ripped over his tee shirt and tied it tightly around her wounded arm. "This is going to hurt", he said, "but stay strong". He then continued to tie the bandage tightly around her arm, and he could feel her pain and anguish, but he could not stop.

Once he was done this, he gently lifted her up and placed her on a hospital stretcher that stood by a ward door. "Stay there", he said, "let me look at the office", as he turned his attention to the shot the policeman. The policeman had been hit in the chest and was dead. Surprisingly, he was not wearing any body armour, which could have saved his life. He looked young as Roger, but had closed his frightful open staring eyes. He didn't have time to take his own revolver out to return fire.

"Things happened so fast", Roger said, and saying a slight prayer, he whispered, "You are going to a better place now."

"Am I?" came the reply. Raj looked up shocked ahead of him. The astral body of the police stood in front of him. "I know you can see me and hear me", he continued, "I have a young family, my mother depends upon me", he cried out.

Raj stood up, "Hey, calm down, if I could have stopped this, I would have, but this was written."

Raj could feel the anger, he could feel the pain, but he had helped. "Look your family will be OK, I promise you and they will know you were doing your job. There is nothing anyone could have done......", his words tailed off; the young man's astral form had vanished, leaving him cold and angry.

In a few minutes, there was police rushing towards him, brandishing drawn guns, shouting at him to get on the floor and put his arms behind his head. He pleaded it was not him, but in the madness, no one listened him, instead, they roughly pulled his arms back and handcuffed him.

What happened after that was a blur; Roger found himself being man handled and bundled out of the hospital and whisked into the back of a police car. He was read his rights by the arresting police officer and was told that if he said anything, it would harm his case. The police drove him to the local Beverley Hills prescient where he was booked on and thrown into a holding cell. He lost all track of time for how long he was there. All he could do was to stare at the empty walls and ceilings. This is what "Hell" must be like, he thought. "No kid, think again", came another voice that he had not heard before. As he looked around, a tall man, dressed in the finest silk suit, stood by him. The man had a striking appearance and looked immaculately dressed. The only thing that stood out to Raj at this point was his eyes; they pierced through like two stakes knifes cutting through a tender steak. "So Kid, looks like my brother has banded you to the wolves, whilst he is off looking after more important things", the man said.

"You're the devil", Raj whimpered, "Should have guessed that you would have turned up sooner or later to claim me." Raj had regained some of his composure by now and looked straight at the man, who had now changed his stance towards Raj.

"Is that what you think?" came the reply with a laugh, "I have got much better things to do with my time then waste my time on you."

"So why you here your evilness?" came the reply.

"Look kid, don't come cocky with me, I could fry you in seconds, but that would not be fun. My brother thinks there is something good in you, and well, I think there's on a bleeding heart of a whimpering little fool

95

there. I have got a wager on you kid, and when the time will come, I will have you in my domain and make you clean out the toilets of hell", and with that he was gone, leaving Raj numb and speechless. Had God banded him? No, surely not. He was the fixer wasn't he?

Before he could delve on this further, the cell's doors were flung open. He was ordered on his feet, and was asked to turn around and put his hands to his back. He was then handcuffed again and was lead out of the cell. From there, he was taken to a meeting room where he sat down on a chair next to a desk. A guard stood by the door, silently staring at him; there was hatred in those eyes, he could tell.

"Can you un-cuff me please?" he pleaded.

"Just shut up and sit there", was the stern reply.

As he said that, the doors to the meeting room opened up and a smartly dressed man, in a suit, walked in. "Un-cuff" was the first word he said to the officer, guarding the room, and then he said, "Leave us". Grudgingly, the officer un-cuffed Roger and left the room.

"What were you doing in the hospital so late?" Came the first question, as the man seated himself in front of Raj.

"Hey look, I came to the hospital accompanying my friend in an ambulance because she had been assaulted outside a club. If you don't believe me, ask the ER ward or the police officers who came to Cleo's."

"So why were you found standing over a dead police officer with blood on your hands and with two other dead bodies lying on the floor?"

"Look, that was not my fault," Raj was panicking now and losing his composure.

"Look, I saw these two guys enter the ER and I got a feeling that they were going to get up to no good. Don't ask me why I followed them up to the third floor.

The next thing I knew, I heard screams and then a single shot, and these two goons standing in front of me. There was a nurse, who had been badly cut on her arm, and so I reacted." He then relied what happened next and finished by saying, "ask the nurse, she saw everything."

For a minute, there was silence and then the meeting room's door opened, and another man entered the room. He whispered some words into the first man's ears. He then left the room and closed the door behind him. CSI Officer, Wells, at this point stood up and walked over to the far side of the interview room. With his back to Raj, he said, "It looks like your story is true. The nurse told the officers on site that you saved her life and even tried to see if the fallen police officer was alive. Your story checks out kid, but I still cannot understand why you followed those two men?"

"Look it was a sixth sense; something within me told me that there was going to be trouble. Don't ask me how, but I knew, and that's why I followed them," Raj cried out.

"OK kid, don't tear yourself up", replied Wells as he turned around. "You want some coffee?" he motioned. There was a simple nod from Raj. Wells pressed an intercom buzzer, near the interview door, and asked for two coffees to be sent through, ASAP.

"Kid, look I still don't understand why you were there, but you saved lives and that's why we are not pressing any charges against you. You are free to go. Do you need a lift home?" Raj simply nodded and continued to sip his hot coffee. Wells got up and left the room for a little, leaving Raj alone, and finally he could breathe a sigh of relief.

When Wells returned, he had Roger sign a statement and then he was free to go. As he was walking out the room, Wells called out, "Hey kid if you need my help, call me because something tells me that you will need it." Roger turned his head and acknowledged Wells, and then walked out of the interview room and followed another officer to the booking sergeant to get his belongings back.

As he stood at the booking sergeant's desk, he looked up at the clock; the time was quarter past eight in the morning. He had been in here for over five hours. What had happened to Kate and the boy? He had so many questions in his head, but he was also tired and wanted to get back to his apartment. When the booking sergeant came back, he handed over Roger's belongings and got him to sign his release form. "Officer Jenkins will give you ride home", the sergeant indicated. Raj looked up and said, "Its okay officer, I will get the bus. I need some air." The officer nodded and then Raj walked out of the building.

As he walked out, Wells walked over the sergeant's desk, "He's either one brave kid or a fool", he indicated, "and that worries me", he mused. "Looks like I am going to have to watch on you kid", he smiled ruefully and walked off.

Walking into the daylight, from the prescient doors, initially hurt, but it felt good. It was nice to be out of the cage, it had brought back a lot of unwanted memories. He knew he was here to save the kid, so why did he feel that he was trying to save himself from himself. As he walked down the stairwell from the prescient, he started to head for the subway, which was across the road.

Before he could reach there, he heard a distant car horn coming from his right hand side. He turned to look and he noticed that it was Ken's car. He stopped and smiled, he should have known he would come and he was relived in many ways that he had come.

"You look shit", was the first words that Ken

uttered.

"Thanks mate, it's good to see you too bud", was Raj's reply.

Raj then started blurring out loads of questions and Ken pulled away and headed home, "Hold on bro, one at a time. First tell me why you got involved with the shit that went down in the hospital?"

"It's a long story Ken and if I tell you why, you would not believe me", replied Roger.

"Try me; you have always trusted me since we were kids. Who else protected your skinny white ass through high school and college?" Before he could carry own on his soap box, Raj stopped him with a laugh, "Alright, I will tell. Pull up at Joe's dinner and we will talk over breakfast, which you can buy."

Ken had a huge smile on his face, "Now you're talking bro", and with that he put his foot down on the accelerator and the V6 roared to life.

The dinner place was close to home, and the guy who owned it, knew the boys well since their college days. He had given them their first job, earning five dollars an hour, cleaning plates and serving food to the dinners.

When they showed up for breakfast, he looked concerned at their be-regaled appearance, though, he understood that the kids these days liked to enjoy themselves partying late, drinking a lot, and wooing the girls, but today, especially Roger looked poor. As the boys entered the dinner, he shouted towards them and they, acknowledging his call, walked over towards him.

"Where the heck have you two come from? You look like I do when I wake up three in the morning to open the dinner."

The boys smiled, they assured Joe that they were fine; it had been a long night. Joe then ushered them to a table in one corner and told them that he would send them across the houses special with loads of coffee. He then smiled, relived, and then turned back to the kitchen side of the diner.

As the guys sat down, Ken then indicated Raj to tell him the story. "You ready are you?"

Ken nodded. Over the next few hours, over a massive breakfast, which they both put away in record time, Raj narrated the course of events. From what he could tell, from Ken's facial expressions, he lost him from the first or second word onwards.

"You serious?" Ken shouted out, as he stood up from the chair. Everyone in the diner looked around. "Ken, sit down and listen. Everything I have told you is true and whether you believe me or not, I don't really care at the moment. With the shit I have been through, my head is spinning and now you don't believe your best friend. When you wanted to know, I had told you that you would not believe me", and at that he stood up and started to walk out of the diner, leaving Ken sitting there, with his mouth wide open.

As he walked out, he thanked Joe for the breakfast and started to fumble in his pockets for money. "It's ok kid. Breakfast is on me. Looks like you lovebirds needed it," Joe said as he motioned towards Ken. "Thanks Joe", Raj smiled and walked out of the door of the dinner. As he walked out, home was a few blocks away, so he turned in the right direction and started to walk. Raj thought, Roger's best friend must think that he was looney with a hairy fairy story about someone swapping bodies. "Thanks boss" he said to himself.

"Hey Rog, wait up", came a shout behind him. "Look, if I would have told you a story like that, you would have told me that I had been smoking pot." Roger smiled, he stopped walking and turned around as Ken caught up. "Look bro, it's a lot to take in at once and a part of me believes you because you have been strange so far."

The two laughed and were about to turn towards the car when they heard a car screech around the corner. Everything happened so fast, two men propped their bodies out of the door windows with automatic rifles in their hands. They cut loose towards the boys. In a split second, Raj pushed Ken towards what he thought was safety, but he saw Ken shot in anguish, as he was hit by stray bullets, a couple in the stomach area and one grassed his temple, knocking him out on the floor with a thud.

Roger too was not spared, and was hit in his left forearm as he fell to the ground.

"Kenn....y!" he shouted as he saw his friend fall, anger swelled inside him and his caged rage exploded. "NO!" he shouted, "I will not let you down." He heard the car screech back towards them for a second run. As he fell to the floor, he saw a broken brick on the roadside and he reached for it. In a quick moment, forgetting the pain, he picked up the brick in his right hand and waited.

When the car was about 20 yards away, he sprang up like a gazelle and threw the brick. At the same time, one of the gunmen fired a shot at him that ripped through his shoulder. As he fell backwards, he saw the brick smash through the windscreen of the car and hit the driver square on, killing him instantly. With the car out of control, it screeched forward into an ongoing truck and burst into flames, killing the remaining occupants also.

His body hit the ground hard. The bullet had ripped straight through his shoulder and was out from the other side. As his body hit the ground, so did his head and slowly he started to lose consciousness He tried to shake his head to clear the blackness and look towards Kenny. He could hear himself shouting, but no one was listening. "No!" he cried, "I can't let you die like this. God help him." With that, blackness consumed him and he drifted away.

"Inspector, he is coming around," shouted the doctor on the ward as he looked at Roger on the bed. CSI office Frank Wells had been at the hospital all night. The kid had been out since they had rushed him and his friend to Mercy. Frank knew why the boys had been targeted and this was over what happened 24 hours earlier.

As Raj adjusted his eyes to the bright hospital light, his vision was initially blurred and he was hurt all over. Since arriving at Mercy, he had no clue of what the doctors had done or how Kenny was doing. His head ached, but he started to focus his vision on the people standing around him. The one he recognised was the CSI officer Frank Wells; he tried to smile, but he couldn't, "You scared us kid," came the voice from the officer.

Raj urged his voice out and asked about Kenny, "Not good kid", came the reply from Frank, "He suffered two fatal shots, one near the heart that severed a large vessel. His body suffered a major shock, due to the drop in blood pressure and the second shot gashed his temple as he fell. Since bringing you guys to Mercy, the doctors have been working all night to save you. Kenny is serious; he is on a life support machine and the doctors are not certain that he will get through."

Raj's emotions were all over the place and he broke down. "Kid, calm down it's not your fault, me the reply from Frank.

"Yes it is," whispered Raj, "if I hadn't got involved at the hospital, Ken would have been okay. Those goons were after me and not him; I got him into trouble." Raj had lost it to the point where the doctor took control and decided it would better to sedate him and let him rest. The doctor then ushered Frank out of his room and advised him to come back on the next day. Frank left reluctantly, as he had wanted to ask more questions, but had decided that then was not the right time. Before he left, he stationed two armed police-officers outside the boy's room, because this time around, he was not taking any chances.

Raj had drifted into oblivion as he was sedated by the doctor and he found himself drifting away from Roger's body and into a place he knew very well. He found himself sitting in the boss's Chamber, and he felt warm and safe, at least for the moment.

"You knew boss, what was going to happen," cried out Raj in reply to God's words," you could have stopped."

"Hush, I did not know this was going to happen, why do you people not understand that whatever happens in your lives, is your own wish and will? Yes I created this universe and I created you and everything on earth, but I do not fix your paths, you create your own destiny with your own actions and deeds. Yes I am the big MAN and I have to be everywhere in different forms, faces and to represent different cultures. Do you think that is easy, do you think you are the only one with issues? When someone dies so do I, when someone is born I rejoice. This is what life is all about Raj, get real."

For minutes there was silence; then God said, "Look Raj I never told you this job would be easy and I also told you would have to face things and you have to face this. Kenny's fate is his own, for the time being he his fighting is own battle in his mind and that is either to release his body and move on, or to fight to stay alive. You or I cannot affect this now and he knows this and it is not your fault. What you have to do is to get Roger's body better by concentrating your efforts on positive thoughts and moving forward. There is still much to do." "Your brother was gloating at me in the cell, God."

"I told you that your demons would want to claim you Raj, and that you have the power to push them away. You remember the time when you were watching that Hindi film called Awarapan. Shivam was trying to save himself at the end of that film by freeing a stranger from slavery, the woman working as a whore for a mafia boss. He found himself, he found his inner power and that came from his lost love. Setting free a caged bird, and giving it its freedom, enabled him to free himself from his own caged and unpredictable life of violence, corruption and deceit. You cried openly after seeing that because it hit a sore nerve, didn't it? Raj, you saw your own rubbish and you didn't like it; its fair to say you hated it."

Again there was silence. "I was Shivam, boss. I didn't commit any murders, I didn't do drugs but I was held in thrall by my own desires and I could not free myself," whispered Raj in low voice.

"You can save yourself now my son," came the reply. "And you can save others by working for me. Don't forget that there are others like you, also working for me. I am everywhere, I can look like the object of your desire, but I am always in your heart. By the way, I don't like being called Danny De Vito and so get that thought out of your mind," He chuckled. "Go Raj, apne Karma dharm kar."

Raj lifted his bowed head up and looked up, and in front of him, saw what his heart wanted him to see, his God, his parents, his family, and they looked all so surreal. His tears turned to joy, his lips started to smile and he brought is hands together to pay homage to them. This time he shed tears of joy, came forward and he started to understand what he had to do.

"Before I go back boss, can I see her once again?"

"She's gone Raj," came the reply. "She has passed through the realms of time, rebirth and is following her own destiny. Anyway her presence will also be in your mind, your heart, body and soul, nothing can change this. It is better to have loved than never to have loved at all. A wise man wrote that once and I believe it is true, but to understand love takes a lifetime, because the emotion gets mixed up with so many different things. Love is one of those emotions that all mankind yearns for, because it makes one feel safe, happy, light, and content. Love can be pure; it can make you feel blind, angry or calm.

"You will meet her and you will understand what love means and then your soul will not mourn, your heart will not ache, but I cannot help you find this path, you must find it yourself."

Waking Up

"Doctor!" came a shout from the attending nurse in the ER ward who was attending to Roger as he lay sedated in his hospital bed. His body was banged up but he slowly opened his eyes. When his vision cleared he could see the young doctor standing by his bed, and realised that he had seen this chap before, but could not remember when. "How long have I been out?" he whispered, and "Three days," came the reply. "How's my friend?"

"Still no change there I am afraid," came the reply.

Raj could feel Roger's physical pain, but he knew he had to be strong and think positively so that he could recover from his wounds. He knew Kenny would want this. "You damn well know I want this," came the reply. Raj suddenly looked up; standing in front of him was Kenny, not in his physical form but in his astral form.

"Ok I believe you now, that wild story you told me in the diner. By the way, you look like shit."

"For a guy standing outside of his body you cannot talk." They both smiled as they shared the joke but that soon faded with Kenny pulling a really serious face. "Hey man, what is happening here? For the first time in my life I am scared shitless, my body is all beaten up and I am standing here watching people walk by, who are like me; can't you see them?"

"What's happening to me, bud?" Am I dead? My body is in the other room strapped to a life support machine and I am standing here in front of you. You know what I have been doing all this time, walking around this hospital. The doctors and nurses can't see me, I have tried calling out, but they walked right through me."

He fell silent for a minute and then continued. "Just a few wards down, I saw an old lady sitting by a bed. She looked at me and smiled and then raised a finger to her mouth and whispered he's sleeping. As I looked on the bed, there was an old man, lying very still, he was asleep and she was waiting for him.

"Have I crossed over?" as he looked towards Roger.

"No, Kenny, you're experiencing an outer body experience but it's not your time yet. If it had been, you would have been long gone. Your body wants you back, but your soul is fighting and that's why you standing here in front on me and not in your own body. I can't help you on this buddy, only you have the power now," replied Raj.

"You know, I saw my mum initially when I stepped out, she was standing my bed and she was crying. She was talking to me Rog, but I couldn't hear her. I wanted to reach out to her, but she kept moving away shaking her head and then she vanished. I was alone again; I sat by my bed for hours, I couldn't move, even when the nurses came in to check on the life-support machines. For the first time in my life, I felt totally alone Rog, and I hated it." There were tears rolling down his cheeks, but he seemed immune to them; his astral form looked like it was trembling and Raj could do nothing to help his friend.

"Ken, you not alone, I am here, we are brothers, right?" "And you're not going to leave me now, I need you," he pleaded. Ken looked towards his friend, who for a tough kid who had grown up in LA, was shaking and crying. "I don't know if I can do this, Roger, there's so much shit out there."Suddenly there were cries from behind Ken.

The nurses and Doctors were running into Ken's room, Raj could hear one of the doctors shout out for a crash unit and quickly.

"Ken you've got to go back, please," Raj pleaded," otherwise you will cross over."

"I have not got the strength Roger," came the reply; "Let me go buddy, ma needs me."

"No, you goof, she was telling you it was not your time," he shouted and it hurt, he could feel the pain in his shoulder and chest area. "That's why she came, but you could not hear her."

Meanwhile in the other room, the crash team were trying to bring Ken back and they were not succeeding. One of the doctors made a comment it was if he had given up the fight. "Come on kid, help us out" the doctor muttered as he inserted a needle into his chest.

Ken watched intently as the doctors worked hard and then he turned his head to Raj, he smiled and then said softly, "I'll be seeing you," and then he was gone.

"No," cried Raj, tears swept down his cheeks like giant boulders but eventually it was the pain from his wounds that made him pass out.

The next few days for Raj were going to be crucial; his mind had already decided that he had lost Ken, so Roger's body started to shut down, the doctors immediately raced into his room to stabilize him. They were baffled because his wounds were not serious, and so wondered about the reason for the relapse. As this happened, CSI officer Frank Wells had just returned to the hospital. He had learnt that the crash team had been busy trying to save Kenny and now Roger's body was giving in. He ran over to the nurses asking, "What's happening in there?" as he pointed towards Roger's room.

"The doctors don't know, Officer, he was fine and all of a sudden his vitals collapsed. The doctors are in there now, we will know in a few minutes." Frank really did not understand what was happening, he could only surmise that Roger had seen what was going on with Kenny and then gone into shock. "Come on Kid, fight it," he shouted internally to himself.

Hell

When Raj opened his eyes, he found himself lying on a wet grassy ground; it was very dark and the air stunk but hot. He raised his body up to a sitting position and looked around, it was really dark and he also found it hard to breadth. The airs tasted like sulphur and stagnant; he was also soaked through, not with rain but sweat.

Suddenly the ground the shook violently and there was a sound of a huge explosion. He was thrown of his feet for a minute, but soon regained them. He looked towards to the direction of the explosion and what he saw shocked him to his core. He now realised where he was standing and that he was on the slopes of a huge volcano, which had just erupted. Hissing towards him at alarming speed was a stream of lava. He turned and started to run away from the streaming lava, though he had no idea where he was going. He was finding it hard to breathe, he had never been good at running because he was always physically unfit. What happened next sent his head reeling and he stopped running instantly. Standing 50 feet away in front of him was Asha. She was wearing a fiery red dress, which sounds really clichéd, but true nevertheless, and she was looking straight at him. For a minute they stood there, neither uttered a word and then things started to change. Asha's facial features started to change into a ghoulish nightmare, she sprang from where she stood calmly and in one leap, her hands were around his neck.

"You killed me," she hissed "and now I am going to make you pay; you made my life hell and now I am going to make yours even worse."

Her wiry fingers started to dig into his neck and he could not release them, "Asha please," he whimpered.

"No!" she shouted at him and then pushed him to the floor. He looked up at her and now her image had changed to something that he could barely recognise. There was no more Asha, but a demon out of the Lord of the Rings, looking down at him. "Run little man, that's all you can do and that's what you always do."

"NO!" shouted Raj,

"Yes, run little man!" and before Raj could react, he pulled out a vicious looking dagger and charged towards him.

Raj stumbled up and started to run, he could hear explosions around him and even laughter rolling towards him. "Please leave me alone; I never wanted this, I was ......"

But, before he could finish the sentence he was knocked off his feet by a large gust of wind. It threw him hard onto darkened charcoaled branches of a burned out tree. He screamed out in pain as a branch buried itself into his side. "Did that hurt Dad?" came another voice that he recognised. As he looked up, he saw himself drifting towards Joy. His face was ash grey and drawn into a grimace, but his eyes were the ones that really caught Raj's eyes, they were on fire.

"Dad, you killed my mother, you killed our family and you left us when we need you. Dad, you were a selfish bastard and now I am going to make you pay." With that he swung what looked like a staff towards him, and the impact tossed Raj clean from the tree and into the open.

Blood was now flowing freely across his forehead and down his face from the impact. "Did that hurt dad? Its only just begun," came Joy's voice in a low whisper. "Run dad, that's what you are good at, run hard. Run!" he shouted.

Raj picked himself up, turned away from Joy and started to run, though his body was beaten up and he was bleeding from his side and head wound.

"Dad,where you going? Why are you leaving us?" came another voice that he recognised. It was Sonya, she was standing some 20 yards in front of him. She looked beautiful in a black flowing dress and cloak.

"Sonya... listens," he whispered.

"Hush dad, the others are right and they told me you would run," she whispered in a low voice. "I told them, my Dad would not leave us, he would always look after us; but no, you ran. Dad, you broke my heart."

"Sonya, listen."

"Hush dad," came the reply; she turned away from Raj and shouted "Enough Dad", and without any warning, she turned around and fire shot out from her out-stretched hands towards him.

The flames engulfed him and he shrieked in agony and fell to the floor writhing. He rolled around on the floor, trying to put the flames out and eventually they died down. His horrified screams could be heard for miles around, but no one was there to hear him. "Please help me," he cried, "someone help me."

"No one is going to help you in my domain and I am not going to let you die this easily. Does it hurt, Raj, does it hurt seeing your own turn against you?

"I told my brother that I would have your soul and then torment it." Raj looked up through his smouldered eyes and standing in front of him was the devil. He recognised his wickedness in his flowing satin suit, as the devil looked at him with satisfaction.

"None of this is real. Satan, you're playing with my mind," replied Raj. "And you know what, Raj I am enjoying it as well. I told my brother in the committee room that you were no good, he pleaded with everyone that you had some good in you. Look now, you are here with me, because once again you could not help another close friend. Kenny died because you stuck

111

your nose in something and he paid the price."

"No!" Raj shouted, "That's not true, I tried to save him, he was my friend."

"Was I?" came another voice and stepping outside the shadows of the devil, it was Ken. Ken moved silently towards him and picked him roughly from the floor. Raj screamed out in pain and Satan was laughing at him. "Why did you have drag me into your personal nightmare? Man I hate you," Ken asked him and then he thrust a small concealed dagger into Raj's stomach.

Raj gasped for air as Ken drove it further into his stomach, repeatedly, until Raj fell to his knees with his arms grasped around his stomach. Several moments passed and everything felt silent, Raj was in pure agony, but death would not come.

"What's wrong, little man, does it hurt, when your own turn against you? I told you when we first met that I would make you suffer and cry for pain, but you would not die. Don't worry you're not going to die now with all your wounds," he laughed loudly.

"None of this is real," Raj hissed "and you're just my imagination playing in my mind, you bastard!" he shouted, as he looked straight up at Satan himself. As he looked, he was hit with a boot to the face that sent him sprawling on the ground. "You stupid fool, I could crush your worthless soul in my realm if I wanted, so don't shout at me. You're just a small little bug under my feet and for centuries and eons I have been killing insignificant things like you slowly."

Raj picked himself up from the floor, the pain from the wounds was excruciating, but he knew he had to. At that moment, he remembered a book he had read years and years ago by Steven Donaldson, about a man who suffered from a crippling disease in the real world, but in a fantasy world he was a saviour and the wielder of very powerful magic. It had taken Raj a long time to understand where that Magic had come from; and that it wasn't from a white ring, but from within himself. He needed to find some similar magic now.

Raj again looked straight at his opponent standing in his evil arrogance in front of him and smiled. "What were you expecting, for evilness, for me to beg at your feet, for me to grovel for my worthless life? Well, enough of that; I am not going to run, I have done too much of that already. You have shown me what my mind wanted to see, I wanted to punish myself for years for what I had done to my family and I always believed that it was my fault. You know," he shouted, "some of it is true, no all of its true and I accept this", he laughed but he was really crying.

For a split second there of silence and then Raj continued, "You see, you humble evilness, I think you are scared of me."

"Ha! Me scared of an insolent little worthless insect like you?" blurted out Satan.

"Yes," came the reply and without any warning, Raj lifted his hands and arched his fingers towards Satan. From his fingers, rays of bright piercing light projected towards the dark one. The light felt warm to Raj and it now flowed from every pour of his body. He could now feel his body being lifted off the ground.

"You see, Satan, I have seen the light or should I say that I have finally seeing the light and understand what I need to do. Your brother was right we human souls do have the power inside us to see the light, even though we walk around, blind to it for years. Perhaps it will still take me many life times to understand, but you're not going to stop me; you hear me?" he whispered.

With that, he urged himself to draw more positive energy from his shattered body and soul and it issued forth and engulfed Satan. Satan screamed in rage,

"Nooooo!" there was a huge explosion and Raj was sent flying through the air. He could hear the shrieks of anger from Satan – "This is not the end yet little man" and then there was laughter.

"Doctor, come quickly, the patient has regained consciousness and opened his eyes." Frank Wells was standing a few feet away from the doctor when he heard the excited young nurse rush out of Roger's room to be where the doctors were standing. Over the next hour the doctors and nurses attended to Roger with diligence until they were satisfied that he was out of danger, only then allowing Frank in to see him.

"Hey kid, you scared us again there for a little while," said Frank, looking at Roger. Roger smiled and said, "I scared myself, Frank."

"Frank, did Ken make it?" Roger asked.

Frank nodded, "barely kid, he even surprised the crash team who worked on him for nearly thirty minutes and they even declared him dead a couple of times, but that kid's a fighter."

Roger smiled, as for the first time he was happy and his heart seemed to miss a beat but he was glad and he uttered quietly, "Thanks Frank" and then he passed out, utterly spent.

Over the next couple of weeks, it was a slow recovery from their wounds but together they understood that they would there for each other. Frank also spent a lot of time asking questions, but didn't get any answers that he liked but he felt that he was gaining their trust. Frank had spent 20 years in the force, and had never taken a bribe or a dive, also had seen some real shit. He had been married for forty years and had three grown up children all doing their own things in life. It scared him shitless thinking about how violent the streets were getting, and how along with drugs the gun culture was killing the City of Angles.

Even his own neighbourhood had its fair share of gang violence and even kids aged five were carrying army knives and using guns. They saw their brothers' gangbang shootouts and they wanted to do them as well. It gave them creditability on the streets and a sense of belonging, as most of them hailed from dysfunctional families. The only problem with that was that the streets were now full of guns, drug lords and mafia dons using the gangs to push their business. The LA mayor could not do a thing about it because the drug barons owned the officials, the courts and even some the law officers who turned a blind eye for thirty pieces of silver. Money talked in LA and the drug barons got richer from the blood of the young innocent kids on the streets.

What changed for Frank, though, happened nearly ten years ago and that experience haunted him even now, when things are starting to make some sense. Frank was working on a stake out with his partner on the south side of LA, when he and his partner where ambushed. His partner was killed outright with two bullets, one to the chest and another to the head. Frank was spared though and he was dragged in by the gang, they were staking out and then experienced one hour of sheer hell.

Frank and his partner were staking out a warehouse in south LA where a gang of Brazilians were using the warehouse to launder huge amounts of money and drugs. They were working with a couple of the local gangs to act as pushers in their respective territories, through clubs, schools, colleges etc. The rate of drug related violent attacks were growing in the area and residents were complaining to their local representative for help. Frank and his partner Joey Fernando were put on the case and this would change his life forever. Frank's partner Joey was murdered during this operation, due to the gangs getting inside information that they were being watched and investigated. The insider had also informed them how many guys were watching them and where they were. So on one fateful day, as Joey took a cigarette break, he was ambushed by some of the gang's henchmen and dragged out in the street in front of the stake house. They called out to Frank to come down or his partner would die, Frank initially didn't and so they again shot Joey, this time in his leg. Frank then rushed out of the building, only to be ambushed himself as he stepped out. Frank was knocked down to the floor, and then hit over the head by a baseball bat. His memories went blank from that point for Frank as he had passed out.

When he woke up he found his hands tied above him as he was suspended from a line attached to crane. As he looked down, he saw Joey tied from one arm to a fork lift and the other arm to another fork-lift.

From behind one of the fork-lifts, a man walked out into the open, in hand he held an automatic pistol and in the other a baseball bat. Looking up at Frank he sneered and then turned his attention to Joey. Frank could see the fright in Joey's eyes but also courage in adversity; the man placed the gun back into his shoulder holster. Then, again looking up at Frank, he smiled and then all of sudden swung the baseball bat into Joeys guts, not once but twice. Frank felt every blow, "you bastard!" he shouted, "leave him alone."

The man looked up again, still said nothing and smiled again. This time he turned his attention to the forklifts and their drivers. With his hands he signalled them to start their engines and to pull away. Again turning to Frank, he said, "You are going to love this next show."

Frank could not watch, but he also could not take his eyes away. The forklifts starting to stretch out Joey, you could see the tension in his face, his eyes. He looked up at Frank, as if, but no words came from his mouth. With gritted teeth, he simply nodded to his partner, who in turn understood the sign and he closed his eyes and wept. The rest was history, Joey died a horrible death; his arms were torn off by the trucks, and Frank was left suspended from the crane unable to help his partner. When help arrived, it was all too late.

Frank would never forget that scene and he had promised Joey that he would find this guy and make him suffer like Joey did. Frank saw Joey every night, asking for justice, the dreams and nightmares were never ending. Something else also happened that day, though all that left in Franks mind was a voice that said, "Frank you are still needed. There will be day when I will call you and that's when the wrongs will be righted." Perhaps helping these kids was that day, as he was drawn inexplicably to Roger, and something told him that this kid needed his help.

The dreams did not end for Raj, it seemed to grow in intensity and it seemed that Dreamscape was another land for him. During the day at the hospital he would lay on the bed and just stare at the blank walls, he could hear voices calling, not to him but to invisible faces in other rooms and wards. The hospital was alive with the dead and with the ones crossing over. He could see and hear them and sometimes they reached out for him to help.

He remembered one day as he took a walk down to the small park near ward fifteen, where he saw a young girl standing by a bedroom door. Raj stopped, he looked towards her and noticed that she was wearing a small nightgown and was holding a teddy bear in one hand. She was staring into one of the rooms; her eyes were glued to what was happening.

As he approached, she looked up at him saying, "do you see, that's my mum sitting near the bed and that's me." As Raj looked into the room, he saw a doctor attending to a patient and that patient was the little girl. Sitting next her holding her hand was a woman crying. He could hear the doctor turn to the women and say, "I am sorry, she's gone," and the woman crying out in anger her daughter's name, which was Susan.

The girl, at that point, turned to Raj and flung her arms around him and he hugged her back. Tears began to trickle down his cheeks as he witnessed a mother losing her daughter at a very young age. "I want my mommy," Susan whimpered, and kneeling down to face Susan, he said, "I know you do baby, but I am afraid it's time to go. You will always be with Mommy in her heart and whenever you're lonely just call her name." Susan clung on to him for what seemed like hours, but in reality, it was just a few minutes. What he witnessed then was truly the crossing over. The air around him started to tingle and he felt his skin feel warm like a soft breeze stroking it on a summer's day. They both saw a glowing white light coming towards them, he could hear the hum of soft music and from the light stepped a young woman. She was wearing a shimmering white silk gown; her eyes showed so much compassion and love that he felt a twinge in his heart. "Come Susan, it's time to go," as she extended a hand towards the girl. Susan initially looked scared, she turned to Raj who smiled back to her and assured her softly that everything would be okay. "Susan," the woman called again and this time she responded and in turn reached out for the woman's hand.

As Raj stood up, he watched the scene in aura and the women looked at him and smiled. "Thank you Raj, Susan is going to be fine," and with that they both walked into the light and were gone again leaving Raj standing there alone. As he turned to look in the room, he could see the doctor pulling the drape over Susan's limp body, the mother was still crying for the loss of her child but these are the pains of life. It is so hard to comprehend the loss of a child and especially one that died so young. Raj stood there for a few minutes totally absorbed, and then he shook his head, rubbed his face with his hands and turned to continue his walk.

As he reached the garden, the sun was out and it was going to be a hot day. He looked around the garden to get his bearings and noticed that this time there were a few people around. He then noticed at the far end of the garden an empty bench and so he made his way slowly over to it and sat down.

"You know Raj, Susan is going to be alright and she told me to tell you thank you." Raj turned around instantly on hearing the voice to notice that sitting on the bench with him was God; in Raj's eyes, Danny De Vito. "She was so young, boss, did she need to go?" "Raj, you know everyone has their own destiny and anyway, her soul has already moved on and she will be happy.

"Something tells me though that you are still experiencing those bad dreams at night."

"They're not dreams, God, they're real and I can feel them, touch them and even smell them in my nostrils. Some days, I think things are getting better and other days I just collapse. On top of all that, I can see and hear everything that happens in this place." God smiled, "this journey was never going to be easy and you will be able to see, hear everything around you that other people can't my son. The dreams will get better all you need to do is master your emotions, channel your fear into positive energy and nothing will harm you," and with that he was gone, leaving Raj sitting alone on the park bench again. Raj sighed, closed his eyes and took a deep breath.

Letting his mind go was an experience that Raj would not forget, as he walked down the wards he could see people that should have crossed over years ago still wandering up and down the wards like they were lost.

He met one young woman, who said her name was Alice and that she was looking for her parents. Raj tried to comfort the young woman who at times looked distraught. Once he got her to calm down he asked her to tell story. She had come to the hospital nearly 80 years ago with her parents; she could remember the events like they were yesterday. There had been a car crash and the emergency team had brought her and her parents to the ER. When they arrived she said, she was totally unaware where she was and where her parents were, she had hit her head very hard against the passenger's chair in front of her where her mom had been sitting. This had left her disoriented and unaware of her surroundings. As the ER doctors worked on her, she literally stepped out of her physical body and stood next to the bed. She watched the doctors frantically trying to save her life but to no avail. The doctors pronounced her dead forty minutes later. She could hear the doctors say that her head injuries had been too severe for her to have survived the crash, the poor kid.

She carried on her tale by telling him that she had heard of out body experiences, where people saw white lights and saw God himself waiting to guide them into Heaven. Nothing like that had happened she said, she had tried looking for her parents but she could not find them and she had been wandering around these hospital wards for decades. She would see other people walking aimlessly around like her, almost lost, though none had spoken to her until then.

"Alice," Raj spoke softly and he reached out for her

hand, which she took gladly, "it's time to stop wandering around and accept that you died nearly 80 years ago."

"No," she cried, "mum and dad need me."

"Alice," he said once again but this time with a little bit of authority, "they're waiting for you but first you must accept in your own mind that you need to move on. Until you do this, my dear, they too cannot move on."

There were tears flooding down Alice's eyes and she wrapped her arms around him, hugging him tightly. "I miss them so much and I am so tired walking up and down these wards searching for them."

"Alice it's time to go, let me help you, trust me, hold my hand," he said.

Alice looked up, wiped her tears away from her eyes and tightened her grip on his hand.

"Close your eyes Alice, and let your mind go and picture your parents' image in your mind. Can you see them?"

"No!" she cried.

"Try harder Alice, let your heart reach out to them and they will come."

Suddenly both Alice and Raj became engulfed in a bright white light. With it came warmth and a sense of safety and from the light Alice's parents stepped out.

"Alice open your eyes, there are some people who would like to say hello."

As she opened her eyes, she first looked at Raj then turned to the front. Standing yards away, were a middle-aged couple, whose eyes shone with happiness and love towards Alice. With arms stretched towards her, they beckoned her to come to them. Alice once again looked at Raj and he simply nodded and smiled. At this point, there were no words spoken and, really, they were not needed because he knew what she was thinking and he simply nodded once again.

She looked towards her parents and ran towards them and after 80 years, mother, father and daughter were together again. They could rest now and carry on with their journey. They looked towards Raj and smiled and then turned away and walked towards the light that enveloped them and soon dissipated into nothing. Once again, Raj was alone, but this time his heart was richer from the experience.

When he finally reached his ward, he headed for his friends room and found him sitting up in bed.

"Hey buddy, how are you doing today? You should really get out of bed and go for a walk."

Ken smiled at Roger and then said, "I heard you again last night talking in your sleep. That's been like that for the last two weeks that we've been here. Today's the first day I have seen you smiling."

"That's because today has been the first day I have been able to let myself go and actually see the world around me. You know Ken, the last couple of weeks have been a blur, all I could think about was, why I was here and why everyone that I loved was getting hurt by me. That day we got shot, I told you all about what was happening, but I still could not stop those bullets, but now I am beginning to understand that I need to get out of this denial stage, otherwise I cannot move on and complete my task and the ones I love cannot move on with their lives. Anyway, I am sure Roger wants his body back in one piece," he laughed and he was soon joined by Ken in his laughter.

For the rest of the day, Raj told Ken everything and he hoped his friend would absorb it and understand, He had to believe that he had found a NEW soul mate and he soon understood why Roger loved him so much like a brother. Never doubt the power of love, it is a wonderful thing and it comes in many different forms but we just have to find it and embrace it.

That day the bond between Raj and Ken grew and together they decided that they would complete this journey together. People say that every human being has an angel on their shoulders looking over them for the first time Raj could see the angel on Ken's shoulder and he smiled. They began to formulate a plan on how they were going to achieve this and the first step was to get out of this Hospital and back out into the world of LA.

Plans

Leaving Ken's room that night Raj was much happier than he had been for some time. Being able to open his mind had helped because now he understood what needed to be done a little and what his role was now. His sleep, however, was still troubled but it was also more manageable. *Deliverance* was not going to be easy; we all go through our trials but Raj has seemed to haunt him. Life teaches you a lot but when you don't listen and learn it seems to get harder. Getting rid of that overnight was never going to be easy and he was never going to get a boon from the Gods with his deeds. He smiled as he sat on his bed and thought that least now he was beginning to understand how people felt; all those years his own selfish mind had never understood how he was affecting others. He could remember Asha struggling in their marriage, caught in the middle with her jobs while also being a full time mum. Was he there? Yes, physically, but mentally he was elsewhere.

How was he going to ask forgiveness for that? Hurting someone who only asked him to carry his weight and not do the things, he did.

"I am sorry, Asha," he whispered between his lips, "I can never mend the fences that I continued to break but perhaps I can make a difference here to Roger."

The following day the friends put phase one of their plan into play and that was breaking out from the hospital with the doctor's approval, of course. Roger had asked to see the consultant and when he came around Roger told him that he would like to go home and recover; there was no need for him to be here. To his amazement, the doctor agreed and said that he believed his and his friend's recovery would be quicker at home. The doctor then turned to the head sister of the wards and gave her instructions to release the boys that afternoon, after their final check also arrange for regular nursing visits to their homes. With that, he departed for his other rounds.

Once the doctor left Roger's room, the delight in Roger's face was a sight to behold and the nurse standing near his bed smiled and then walked out, leaving him alone.

"That was good work, Raj," came the voice he recognised.

"Hey Boss, plan 1 goes into play."

"I felt your pain last night and so I came to see how you were doing."

Raj, turned around, wiping the tears away from his eyes, "I'm fine Boss, couldn't stop myself from thinking about the past."

"Raj, this will only end when you want it to end, my son, but for the time being you cannot let go because in your heart you know what is right and wrong. On the flipside, you cannot keep blaming yourself either because you know which path that will lead you down. Self-pity…"

"Stop, Boss," interrupted Raj, "For me this is not self-pity and you know it, for me it will be *deliverance*, a chance to find myself because I lost that years and years ago. Let me find this please and I will let go when I have done this, now this is my strength and it is my weakness, I understand this. Anyway I want to earn my wings now."

He looked towards his guide and smiled, "21st century Angels don't have wings", came the distant reply and there was laughter, they have Bentleys.

With that, he walked out the room and walked towards Ken's to give him the good news that they could leave today. He also had to find Jose and understand how to help him, there was a lot to do and in so little time.

As he walked into Ken's room, he noticed that his friend had already started to get his clothes out of the cupboard.

"Hey Roger, the doc said we could leave. I was coming to tell you that but it seems you already know."

"Ken, we need to find out where the boy is so we can talk to him."

"Already on the case; I spoke to one of those sweet little nurses and she is finding out for me."

Roger laughed, "You have been hitting on the nurse, you sod," Ken laughed loudly, "Hey Brother I need to see if I haven't lost it yet."

Just before Roger could say anything else, the pretty little nurse that Ken had chatted up walked in. Roger smiled as he watched her walk towards Ken with a piece of paper in her hand. She looked at him and smiled and then handed Ken the paper and walked out of the room.

As Ken unfolded the A4 sheet, it had written on it the details where Jose had been moved to and at the bottom the nurse's cell number, which did bring a smile to Ken is already beaming face. Both friends laughed now and Roger decided to head off towards his own room and get dressed in his civvies.

Leaving the hospital after being there for nearly a month was a great feeling, for Roger could still, with his sixth sense unnamed faces, voices calling out to him to help. He simply nodded his head and whispered under his breath that he would come back. Then he turned to his friend and they both walked out of the front entrance of the hospital and stepped into a waiting cab.

Once in the cab, Roger instructed the cab driver to head towards Beverly Hills and an exclusive housing area. Raj knew this area well because he remembered driving the beautiful 699 down this very road.

"Where we going, Roger?" asked Kenny curiously looking at his friend.

"We going to see Johnny Raja my friend, he can help us and I know he will."

Ken looked at his friend again, "the guy you previously came back in as?"

Roger looked at Kenny, smiled and said "yes. Johnny can help us big time Ken because he has the money and the heart to help us."

The cab pulled up to the gates of Johnny's house, which was an impressive southern American style house. The house stood on a 3.3-acre plot and Johnny's parents had always wished for a lavish open property. It was not to show their wealth but to share with their family and one day for their son. Johnny's mum had dreamed when they arrived in US for the first time in America that they could afford the big houses that they saw in the TV series like Dallas and Dynasty. Her house would have a grand driveway to the front of the mansion and the house itself would be designed not in a modern way but historical western design. She loved the large white-faced house with a lavish large Mahogany door entrance and then huge arching windows opening on to the lawns outside. As you entered the hallway, you first saw marble floors, and then a large winding staircase, climbing to the first floor caught your eyes. The rooms were all lavishly designed around a Victorian theme but also they would also feel comfortable. Johnny's mum did not see the house finished, but Johnny's grandparents made sure that her that their daughter-in-law's dream came true. The house was truly a dream house and no expensive was spared in building it the way she had wanted.

As both friends stepped out of the cab, they were met at the entrance of the house by the butler. He lead both friends through the lavish marbled hallway, just as Johnny's mother had imagined it and Raj smiled because he could feel warmth as someone was smiling above him and around him. She was here he thought and it seemed to lift his spirits. The butler lead the friends through the hallway past the staircase and then through two large wooden Victorian doors. There they entered into the beautifully designed Victorian living room. The room was large and spacious but you had to admire the way it was designed and set up. They were met in the living room by a tall handsome young man, whom Raj recognised as Johnny.

Johnny greeted his guests warmly and urged them to sit down and while he spoke his butler poured tea in three cups.

"Would you like sugar and milk?" he asked quaintly to both Roger and Ken and replies were simple nods and in Ken's case, "Can I have three spoons of sugar please?"

Johnny in the meanwhile addressed Roger, "please do not ask me how I knew you guys were coming here because we don't know each other, but something inside my head told me."

Raj knew, but still he asked, "Who told you we were coming?"

"Look, it's a long story," Johnny replied, "but rest assured I know why you are here and I will help. I have already got a few things ready for you guys," he continued "and if there is anything else that you need you can just call me. All I can say is that, something happened to me weeks ago and ever since then I knew I had a purpose in life apart from help my granddad fulfil my parents' wish. You see, my parents died when I was young and so I was raised by my grandparents and with their help we have built our lives in US like my parents would have wanted, this house was envisioned by my mom and I know she would have loved this.

"Some weeks ago, God allowed me to spend some time with my parents, don't ask me how, but in my heart I am sure you know how," looking at Roger. Seeing my parents was a dream come true and I shall never forget the experience even if it was a dream," he said. He wiped away the tears that were flowing down his cheeks as he spoke openly about his parents. Roger reached out for Johnny's hand, and squeezed tightly and whispered I know.

"This is a really nice crib that you have," commented Ken, "and if I was your mom or dad I would be the proudest ever, man. Look, I know you want to help us and that's why Roger has brought us here, I guess," carried on Ken. "We would really appreciate whatever you can do," he added.

"Hey Johnny, I know your parents are proud of you because I felt their presence in the house as we entered, they are happy and always with you. Just because they have gone, it does not mean that they are not here. I know this when I saw my own standing in this same room with your grandparents…" He had realised what he had just disclosed.

Johnny looked straight at Roger, "I do you know you," he said, "You're Sonya's dad. You crossed over into me and gave me the chance to meet my parents. Now I remember when I crossed over I met a man that I have to admit looked like Danny De Vito." Raj smiled and he could hear the God's voice in him say "Raj!"

"He told me why I was there and who had taken my place. Now I know things happen for a reason and by the way your daughter is beautiful." He blushed and reddened deeply when he said that.

For the next couple of hours the three of them talked frankly about what had happened over time and shared their deepest thoughts with each other. Johnny had asked them to stay there but they declined and said it would not be safe for him or his grandparents.

"Look, at this point let me show what I have for you guys," and with that he urged them to follow him through the vast mansion and through to the backyard. He then lead them to the far side of the property to a huge garage facility that housed all his cars and what a collection he had!

As they entered the huge garage there was some great looking cars parked there and they included a McLaren F1, Porsche 911 Turbo 3, and Hummer H3. As they walked past them, Johnny led them to a black Escalade parked in the corner.

"This one is yours, guys, I bought her three days ago and had the car decked out for you." With that, he opened the door of the car and picked up the keys that were lying on the driver's seat and tossed them over to Roger. He then urged them to the back of the car where he popped the trunk.

In the trunk of the SUV were a couple of suitcases, which Johnny said contained some clothes for the guys because he knew somehow that they could not go home. He reached out for a small compartment to the side of the boot and pulled out another set of keys. He then turned around to the friends and said - these were the keys to their NEW apartment in a nice part of Compton that they could call home. When they switched the ignition on, they saw that the sat-nav already had their address programmed in.

Finally, he pulled out a briefcase from underneath the boot lining. "Inside this case," he said, "is nearly five hundred grand, it's for you because I know you will use it wisely and that you need this for what you are going to do."

Both Ken and Roger could not believe what was happening, Raj shot a question to God mentally, but there was no reply. There was silence were several minutes, "one of you guys say something…" Johnny urged. The silence was broken by a mobile phone signalling an incoming call. "Its mine," said Johnny as he pulled out a sleek looking Nokia phone from his pocket.

Johnny looked at the display to tell him who was calling and then the expression on his face changed and then he looked at Roger.

"Hello," he answered.

"Hey Johnny, I tried to get hold of you the other day, but me and Joy are just pulling up outside your place, you there?"

Johnny's jaw just dropped when he heard this and he answered that he would be there in a minute. After Johnny put the phone down, he looked at Roger, "Sonya and Joy are here, they are just outside."

For a split, minute Raj lost control of his feet and he started to fall back, Ken caught him and supported his friend. "Look after him Ken, I need to go greet the guests," Johnny said.

As Johnny left, Raj had regained some control of his legs and leaned back on the SUV; however, his mind was in turmoil, thinking that 'the kids were here and now. What game was the boss playing with him, was he testing his resolve yet again, or his self-control'?

He looked up towards the heavens, but there was no voice inside his head that spoke to him, instead there was silence. This was going to be his test, he knew this in his mind. After a few minutes, the friends put away the briefcase with the money inside the secret compartment and then closed the tailgate of the Escalade. It was a nice car and Johnny had kitted it out to the hilt. Raj had always like these cars when he was young and the nearest he got to owning one was a Land Rover Freelander years ago. It was a nice car that was until the engine blew up after 32,000 miles. It was a company car that his old boss was contributing to in his car allowance and with hind-sight, he realised that he should never have bought it.

He could still remember when the car broke down at his brother-in-law's work area and then had to be towed to a Land Rover Garage for repair. Was he relieved when it came back under warranty repair!

If only Asha could see him remembering the old times, it's strange he thought that's all you really have left in life, your memories of events, time, places and people that have come in and out of your lives. They say time does not wait, he wished it did, but he knew that he could never change it. "Life really sucks," he said to himself and then sighed heavily.

The Kids and the Party

Johnny had left the friends in the garage whilst he rushed out to the front doors to greet Sonya and Joy. To his surprise, they had not come alone; with them was their other sister and Joy's family. They had apparently had been invited by Johnny's grandparents because they were holding a little party to celebrate Johnny's and Sonya's engagement.

His grandparents had beaten him to the door and they had already showed everyone into the living room. Everyone was there chatting away, Sonya was standing in front of the large Victorian glass window looking out. Johnny walked over and she could feel his presence and she smiled.

"Hey why didn't you phone me that you guys were coming?" asked Johnny softly.

She smiled again, "your grandfather asked me not to say anything and that you needed a surprise. He also said that for the last two weeks your mind has been pre-occupied and you have not been yourself at home and at work."

She turned around and looked at him, her piercing eyes cast over him cutting his defences apart. "What's wrong?" she asked softly.

"Nothing. Hey, I am fine, promise," he replied.

Taking her hand he squeezed it gently and then led her away from the window and then towards the others. As he did both Roger and Ken had made their way to the living room. Johnny saw them and leaving Sonya with the others walked over.

"Johnny, we came to say good bye and to thank you for everything," said Roger. "It's time we left you alone with your family," he continued.

"Johnny!" called his grandfather as he walked over

towards him, "are you not going to introduce me to your friends?"

"Grandfather…" Johnny replied shakily, "this is Roger and this is Ken, they're old friends."

"You know beta you have never brought friends home before and I am so happy you have now." Then turning towards Ken and Roger Johnny's Grandfather said, "Please come in and stay, today's it's my grandson's engagement party and you have to stay. Please will you really disappoint an old man on this happy day?"

They could not say no and they both nodded. "Grandfather, let me go and show the guys the guest rooms so they can freshen up and then come downstairs." His grandfather nodded and said, "Hurry back."

The next several hours seemed to last a lifetime for Raj, being this close to his children was killing him and his emotions were running amok. After Johnny had shown him and Ken to the outhouse so that they could freshen up and change into some new clothes, Raj decided to take some time out. Leaving Ken asleep, he drifted out into the large gardens of the mansion for a walk.

"What's on your mind, Raj?" came the voice inside his head.

"This is not one of my tests, but just the path that everyone is choosing on their own."

"I know boss, but it's a cruel turn of fate; that and the fact Asha is not here to enjoy this. She was the one that raised the kids properly and taught them values that would last them lifelong. Without sounding like a broken record, boss, she was the home maker."

"Raj what did Krishna say to his friend? Lay your worries in my hands and I will deliver you, believe in me and nothing will ever harm you. Raj, believe in me and in your own heart; the reason I chose you is because you have a heart, but you lost your way and now you have to find your way."

For several seconds there was silence, "I know boss, I do believe in you and I have always done, but facing them is hard."

Meanwhile back in the mansion, Johnny's grandparents had organised help for the party and they had arrived. They had already started to put up a large marquee for the party, there were people arriving from all over the place: flower organisers, the guys who were going to do the music, caterers from the Taj hotel from the Campton Hilton. Raj started to walk towards the house and smiled broadly – it was his daughter's engagement. As he walked on, he felt a warm gentle breeze brush over his face. His heart also started to pound hard inside Roger's chest, the hairs of the back of his neck were standing up, and someone was here. He stopped he started to look around like a headless chicken and then he came to a stop, there she was.

Standing near the Marquee and looking into the house was Asha. Her long flowing hair glistened in the sun, but her eyes were transfixed on the house. As he stood and watched her, tears welled up in his eyes; she looked so beautiful. She was wearing a flowing baby pink butterfly saree that hugged her body, with matching bangles on both arms. He started to walk towards her, but then stopped; how could he face her? This is her moment and the kids'. Reluctantly he turned around and started to walk towards the outhouse, tears flowing down his cheeks, but she needed her space. As he turned to go the other way, Asha looked around towards him; she too knew he was there. She understood why he had not approached her, but she wanted him to be there. Her eyes followed him until he disappeared in the outhouse.

On the eve of the party Johnny came to see Roger and Ken; he could not understand how fate could bring all this together, but he was glad that they were here. He then turned to Roger and assured him that everything would be alright; Roger smiled, hugged the young man and sent him on his way. They soon followed him to the marquee outside; Ken could comprehend what Raj must be feeling inside. . He understood why Raj was inside his friend, and he also understood that there was greater good to be done here. What neither of them understood was that this web of lives and stories were all interlinked and their jobs were not just to save the boy, but themselves too. "Life always tests our resolve and understanding, and as humans we are always questioning ourselves and the age old question in most minds is what am I doing here? Both Ken and Roger must push on to the next level where they stop questioning and transcend to a higher mind set."

"Are we ready for the next level if we cannot leave our mortal coils, desires, needs and wants behind? Boss this is so hard."

As the friends reached the marquee dressed in the new suits that Johnny had bought for them, the party was already in full swing. Johnny's grandparents had invited quite a few of their friends and close family. To Raj's shock, they had also invited his immediate family. Mum and Dad would be so happy if they were here, especially with Sonya's wedding. She always had been the special one at home, full of life, fiery character, but always up front. Sonya had matured quickly if you could say that, but she always was a fighter. He smiled, this was so unreal; what weird game was life playing with him. He looked around the marquee to see if Asha was there and she was. Standing in the far corner she was looking on, had she seen him, but he did not know that.

"Come on," said Ken urging his friend into the marquee and especially to the bar and buffet area. Roger laughed; Ken never changed, always thought of his stomach first. Roger turned his attention to Asha, she was still there; he could see her and so he headed towards her. For the first time, she looked up and saw him approaching. Her facial expressions softened and she smiled, he knew she would recognise him even if was not in his own body. As he approached he said, "they look good don't they Asha?"

She smiled, "they do Raj, and you have to look after them now, Raj."

"This is hard for me Ash, remember I was never there half the time. Don't worry, Ash I will not let you down again or myself."

She smiled at him, "I know and who said you let anyone down? That was always in your head, you were there for the kids and they loved you. What you could not control were your own urges."

He turned his head towards the party, they were starting the ceremony. "Go Raj," she urged him to them. "I need you there as well Ash," she smiled again and nodded. Even if he was the only one who could see her he could feel her touch, smell and body. He felt rich when she was around, he felt alive and he whispered, "I do love you."

The ceremony was indeed starting, all the family and friends were present and seated at their tables and Johnny's grandfather was about to speak when Roger made his way to the edge of the tables. They had been set around the marquee in a circular design, leaving a large dancing space in the centre. On the far side of the marquee the DJ was set up and ready to start the music later in the evening.

"Friends" started Mr Raja, "thank you for coming

today and sharing this grand occasion with us. "Today," he continued, "is the proudest day of my old life and that's because as you know my grandson Johnny is marrying Sonya Sharma."

For a minute there was a burst of spontaneous applause and he smiled. "If my son and his wife were here today they would be very proud, because they had a dream to come to America and set up a home for the family. They had a dream not for themselves but for Johnny that would last a lifetime. When they passed away so early, I thought I would break but with your support I pushed on and with my wife's support I stayed strong and with Johnny's hands I created this dream that we call home." Everyone present could feel his pain but also could sense his pride as his chest pushed upwards as he looked towards his grandson.

"Johnny, if my son was here today, he would be doing this and I know he would be proud of you beta; I know I am and I would like everyone here to raise their glasses and take this opportunity to raise a toast for my Grandson and his wife-to-be Sonya."

"Johnny and Sonya," came the reply from everyone present, including Roger/Raj and Ash. What Johnny's Grandfather could not see was his son and daughter in law standing next to him, also proud of this moment? They say when the soul moves on, he will always stay connected and never leave your side, Johnny's parents had always been there watching him grow, supporting him silently with their love. Raj could see them and he nodded in their direction, they smiled in return.

Ash squeezed Raj's hand, there were tears in eyes, and, "I wish I could hold her Raj," she whispered. "You can Ash, go next to her and put your arms around and kiss her cheeks. She's your daughter, Ash and she will know you are here with her. Go Ash, I'll be right here," he said.

She looked at him and then towards Sonya and started to walk towards her. As she did, Ken came and stood by him, "she's here, isn't she?" he asked, Roger simply nodded.

Ash looked back to Roger and he simply urged her on, she smiled like a young sixteen year old and focused on reaching Sonya. Once there she gently wrapped her arms around Sonya and the gently kissed her cheek and then rested her head on her shoulder. The scene was touching but the only one who could see this was Raj with Roger's eyes. There were tears of joy for once in his eyes and they were falling freely. Ken put an arm around this friend, he knew he could see more but was not saying anything, but just absorbing the scene. Sonya, for she felt a warm heat spreading all over her body, the hairs on the back of neck was tingling, "Mom," she whispered.

"I am here, Soni. This is your special day, honey, and I am sorry that I am not here; but I can see you baby, and you look beautiful and you're marrying a really great guy, I know."

"Mom."

"No Soni, no questions, just listen to me because I don't have long. You are my eldest, baby but also the one with the softest heart. Be strong and you know Dad's here and always will be. Be strong because Johnny will need you and I already know he loves you. Your lives have been intertwined for such a long time that your souls had to meet again. I have to go – love you…" and then she was gone.

Sonya's eyes searched everywhere, but she could not see her mum and then she looked at Roger, Johnny's friend. He was standing 20 feet away but the unusual thing was that he was crying, his eyes were so red and his friend was holding him – almost supporting him. She looked puzzled and then she looked up at

Johnny who just winked at her, so she smiled. The others around her like Joy, Ojal, her aunts and uncles were all clapping and smiling, this helped her a tiny bit. She then looked again at Roger but he was no longer there.

Ken had dragged Roger over to the bar area of the marquee and ordered a couple of shots and then together they drowned them. Then it was onto the dance floor to a mixture of rap, disco, Punjabi and Hindi mix. The night had really started and soon everyone was on the dance floor and for Raj it bought back memories of all the parties they used to have all those years ago when his mum and dad were around. His Dad would have loved this, especially because it was Sonya's marriage. Sonya had been spoiled growing up, especially by her grandparents, while the middle one always used to get the blame but she was always the sensible one, while Joy was always given what he wanted, his sports kits, game console, nice new car. All the kids looked happy, Joy looked great with his wife, and so much in love you could see it in his eyes. Ojal looked happy, she loved to dance but not in public, but today she was out there with her hubby.

Roger had left the dance floor leaving Ken to strut his stuff to a mixture of Punjabi and rap music. Raj remembered the old days when he used to enjoy this in another life.

"You miss it don't you?" said the voice inside his head.

"I sure do, boss," he replied. "Thank you for giving me this chance to be with them again."

"I told you Raj, that you helping me weren't about just one person's life but it was about a number of people. You have to be my champion, my friend, but you also have to face the demons, whichever form they might take, like my brother, which is really your doubt

140

in your own ability and how to control your mind and your own guilty conscience."

"Boss, is Ash okay, she was here a little while ago?"

"Raj, she is fine and today you have helped her and she is happy," was the reply.

"I thought you said that Ash had passed through the door onto an*other life.*"

*"S*he has, Raj but her energy will always be here, her soul is still restless because she has never relied on you. One thing though, Raj, today you have eased her mind, her soul is less tortured with worry and confident about the future."

Roger ordered a drink at the bar, it was time they left, and he thought and let the family enjoy their time. The future was rosy and finally things looked up. As he got the drink, Ken walked over, so he handed him a bottle of Becks. Ken smiled because for the first time his friend looked happy but the smile soon vanished when they heard shouting and screams coming from the entrance of the Marquee. Then there was a single gunshot and all the party goers fell to the ground with fright. Three men wearing masks entered the marquee brandishing automatics weapons in their hands.

"Ken, grab that ice pick and hide it, and when I give you a nod be ready to act."

While Ken did this and moved away to one side of the marquee so he could cover the gunmen on the left, Roger picked up a knife that the bar man was using to cut slices of lemon for drinks. He concealed the knife under his shirt selves and walked over through the crowd on the dance floor to the front and

"Keep your temper under control, Raj, this could get messy if you go gung ho into this."

"Don't worry, Boss, no one harms my family again."

The atmosphere in the marquee was tense; the

family were scared and the gunmen had now spread out in a wide arch. The gunman standing in middle was taller than the others. He suddenly grabbed Johnny's grandfather, who was bending down on the floor and roughly pulled him to his feet.

"Hey, leave him alone," shouted Roger as he took two steps towards the man.

"Shut up!" shouted the man at him, and he brandished the 9mm automatic at him. What happened next took barely five minutes.

"No!" shouted Roger, "you listen to me," and with that he lunged forward at a speed that barely gave the gunman a chance to cock his gun. From under his sleeve came out the concealed knife and in one swift movement he had grabbed the hand that held the gun, twisted it roughly and pointed the gun towards the gunmen, standing to his right and squeezed the trigger of the gun in the man's hand.

"Now Ken," Roger shouted, "takes him out." Ken leapt from his place like a cat, and attacked the second gunman with the ice pick and disabled him.

The gunmen in Roger's control did not know what hit him; Roger had dropped his knife deliberately and instead thrust his fist into the gun-man's stomach. Things happened in a flash and as Roger's assailant went down, Roger twisted his hand holding the gun upwards and there was a crack as he broke his hand.

Roger quickly grabbed the gun from the floor and pointed it towards the man.

"Ken!" he shouted, "your man down?"

"He's down Roger and covered." Roger looked up and the third man that had been shot, he was still down but Roger could see that he was still breathing. Turning his head towards Johnny he shouted towards him to call 911 and get help out here ASAP. Turning to Johnny's grandfather he asked if he was okay and he simply

142

nodded, so Roger turned his attention back to the fallen villain.

"Keep still!" He shouted "or I will use this."

It took the police 20 minutes to arrive from the 911 call and they soon had everything under control, It appeared that these three particular men had been targeting the rich and famous along this area and Johnny's place was the third house to be hit in the space of three weeks.

"I suppose they didn't count you two being here and I should have known that you two would be here," came a voice that both Roger and Ken recognised.

"It is CSI officer Frank Wells," as he walked over towards them.

"You know these two gentlemen?"

Frank nodded, "I do, Chris" he replied. Let me take care of this for you. The police officer nodded and walked off leaving Roger and Ken alone with Frank.

"How did I know that you two would here? I woke up this morning and thought to myself I wonder where my favourite two suspects are today."

"Look, Frank this is not what you are thinking, we were invited to this party as Johnny Raja, a friend is getting engaged. If we had not done something someone innocent would have either died or been badly injured," said Roger.

"So I have been informed by Mr Raja senior and he thinks you guys are heroes for what you did, but did you have to make a mess?"

For a minute there was silence, and then there came a chuckle from Roger and he spoke softly,

"Frank, what would have you done if your family were in a pickle like this?"

Frank looked at him, "they're not your family Roger", came the reply.

"Yes they are!" shouted Roger, "Frank!"

Everyone present in the marquee looked at the commotion.

"When you were hanging in the warehouse when your Partner was being murdered and you could do nothing what were you feeling, Frank?" he asked.

Frank's face lost all colour and his eyes showed signs of shock as he looked towards Roger, "how did you know about that?" he whispered.

Roger looking at Frank intently replied, "I know, Frank and I feel what you are feeling Frank, so how could I not react?"

Roger turned away from Frank and started to move away but Frank came charging after him; he had regained his exposure and pulled him by his shoulder to face him. He again demanded to know how he knew about the partner's murder and Roger gave him the same answer and added, "We are all hurting Frank, in your case you are still looking for answers from GOD, questioning why it wasn't you. You want Justice, Frank, and I want redemption formy sins; Frank so you see we are both in the same boat. The only problem, Frank, is that I am dead and trying to change things now, but you're still alive and can change your life."

The look on Frank Wells' face was full of such shock and horror, his eyes were searching for answers in Roger's eyes but he got nothing back. How this kid could know about the incident where his partner was killed, Frank

. He took two or three steps back from Roger and then turned to Ken for answers. He was getting no answers; and he thought that in his twenty years of police job, he had never felt this helpless; and he could not fathom why fate has brought these two kids in.. life. He turned away from them and started to walk away until Roger called out to him,

"Frank, don't leave like this, let me explain please."

Frank turned his head to look back at Roger and simply nodded. For a tough man, he felt like a child now and just wanted answers to the questions swirling inside his head.

"Frank, I am sorry that I shouted, but over the last few weeks I have seen so much and felt so much anger, pain and elation that now my feelings are shot. You won't believe how hard it has been, not being able to tell the people that you know and love what you are feeling. I know in my heart you have known that there was something else happening here and that's why you have not been able to shake our initial meeting out of your head. In a weird sense of the word, you also like the idea of me searching for deliverance from what happened in the past. Time moves on, Frank, and doesn't wait for anyone and with that, our souls move on to other lives," he said. "Frank, I will tell you everything that you need to know but I cannot help you to get past your past; excuse the pun here, but you must do this on your own."

With that, Roger walked out of the marquee and headed to the outhouse, the elation that he had felt during the party had all died away and he was exhausted. "I need to be alone," he whispered, "I can't handle this" and then turning his head towards Johnny's direction, "I will talk to you later."

With that, he walked away, his head bowed down and silent tears running down his cheeks.

As he left, Johnny stood there watching him leave with Sonya and his Grandfather. Sonya turned to Johnny and asked, "Why do I feel that I know your friend?"

"I cannot answer this now Sonya because the answer to that is something that you might not understand." She looked at him confused and then she looked at his Grandfather who just shook his head.

The skies had cleared up the following day though the previous night after he had returned to the outhouse in thunder had been crackling in the darkened skies. Sheets of rain were falling hard on the weathered roof tiles of the outhouse but Raj was immune to the sound. It was almost like he was sitting under the tree again in Hyde Park in the last few days of his past life. Since he had walked out of the marquee he had not spoken to anyone but had just curled up into a ball on his bed, slowly crying until sleep took over. His sleep was restless and he again found himself drifting out from Roger's tired body and into a different plane. This time he found himself standing a well-lit auditorium with rows upon rows of empty seats positioned around the main stage area.

He himself was seated in the front row of the auditorium and he was the only audience member as he looked around the theatre, which sent a slight shiver through his body. The building itself in design reminded him of the Old Vic theatre in London and he was the chief guest. Suddenly from nowhere the theatre came alive with loud music and images started to appear on the stage. The first images that appeared were from his past and they were of his parents bring him as a youngster into the UK. He was so innocent then and he wished even now that he had remained that way. The scene suddenly changed and had moved on to when he was married; he saw himself arguing with Asha in front of the kids. He tried to look away but he could not move his head and his eyes were transfixed on the scene on the stage. It was harsh, he had lost his cool because he had lost another job and he was

146

complaining that it was not his fault.

"That's what you always say," was the reply from Asha and they started to exchange verbal insults. There was no physical contact but the words hurt and dug deep into each other. Sonya had tried to stop the fight but it was too intense and they battered each other with childish remarks. They say that love shows no bounds and it is give and take but this was taking the piss. In the scene that unfolded on the stage at one point he thought the he saw a hand being raised, but nothing happened instead as usual, and he stepped back and then ran out of the house in tears. That was the last time the kids saw their dad whilst their mother was alive because he could never forgive himself for that moment.

As Raj watched in shock horror at his own life evolving in front of him he was helpless, he tried to shout, scream at the images on the stages but no one could hear him. Suddenly the scene changed and as the images appeared one after the other, , he found himself witnessing the funeral of Asha. He had not been there because he was not aware that she had died. After storming out of the house he was so ashamed of his actions that he had turned to the bottle and after that nothing made sense to him until it was too late. His heart ached with remorse but what could he do, like he told Frank he could not turn time back and now he was seeing what he had never wanted to see. His little kids not so little in the scene taking their mother on her last journey without their estranged dad. His heart felt like it was being ripped out of his chest cavity, the pain was unbearable but he still could not turn away from the scene playing out in front on him.

The funeral had started at Raj's old home and he could see all the family members there in hand. Luckily both his parents and Asha's had passed away so they were not here to see this, even though he was sure that their souls were present. The coffin was laid in the middle of the huge living room and it was surrounded by the family. He could see Joy and the girls holding each other tightly crying and looking down into the coffin. Suddenly Raj found himself being lifted from the seat that he was sitting on and now suspended in mid air above the living room so he could see inside the coffin. At the sight of Asha he melted, she looked so calm, like all Hindu traditions they had dressed her like she was a newly married woman. However, she was not wearing a red wedding saree, but a yellow one, which he knew well. His heart was well and truly broken now, how could he had done this, she died too early, she did not see her grandchildren, "Raj," he whispered, "you are a murderer."

The scene began to change again, the Hindu priest had started his prayers and relatives and friends were filing themselves around the coffin, laying flower petals over Asha's remains. Once they had had left the room the family were left alone to say their farewells until the undertaker had arrived to place the lid tightly over the open coffin. Raj had experienced a few funerals now but seeing Asha's was the hardest, but in his mind, he knew that he had to see this.

The scene now had moved on to the crematorium, relatives and family were seated and the Hindu priest was giving his sermon. Once he had delivered his bit, Joy walked over to the pedestal. Joy looked tired but held his composure well for the girls. He was dressed neatly in a black suit, white shirt and black tie. He kept his head held high as he began to speak from notes that he took out of his inside jacket pocket.

"My mother was the sweetest person you could ever meet," he started, still holding his composure, "she never had a bad word to say about anyone and even when dad wasn't with us, she still was strong. She always taught us to respect our elders and to make the best out of any situation. She was committed to her family and she never even complained once. If she ever nagged dad, she did it because she cared. I know Dad loved us and that's why he left because he did not want to hurt us. Mum and Dad were the best, even though they argued like most couples they cared about everyone here today. I know my Mum would have wanted Dad to be here today with us but I know she understands why he is not here today. I am not ashamed to say this here and I don't want anyone else to point fingers or gossip about my parents or the family. Today we are here to release mum and I know she is at peace now and I know she would have wanted us to remember the good times like all the holidays that we had as a family also the hard times that united us as a family. Mum, we love you and we will remember you forever, and this is not good bye. We will see you again in another time and life but for the time being safe journey Mum." And then, he broke down and lost his composure. For a minute, he bowed his head and he said, "Mum this poem is for you, I found it a few years ago in Dad's old things", and then he recited "Never Alone" by Rodney Belcher.

Never Alone
by Rodney Belcher

I feel you in the morning
When at first I awake
Your thought is with me
With each decision I make

You'd been around forever
Since the first breath I took

Now I have to go on alone
But for love, I need not look

Cause by what you bestowed
In our short time together
Will last in my heart
Forever and ever

Although you've left
And now walk above
I'm never alone
I'm wrapped in your love

Enjoy now your long waited reward
Feel peace that your love continues on
What was taught to me, will be taught to mine
Cause you live on in me even after you've gone

Sonya rushed from where she was sitting and put her arm around her brother and together they cried and the curtains came around the coffin and the last journey ended and started again somewhere else.

Raj was numb with shock, he wanted to hold his son but he simply could not move his body. Every pore of his skin was crying for the kids and Asha and all he could hear in his head was that Asha had forgiven him, which was evident from Joy's speech. The words had hit hard, he should have known that the kids had been taught well by their mother. She was her father's jewel, he always described Ash as the perfect daughter because she had been taught right and she was always there. She suffered the most when her Dad died because she was the one who did not see him after he had died. She held the pain inside for a long time after her real hero died early. He was a lovely man but Ash's mum was strong, he often joked with her that her mum was younger than her. He smiled as he remembered that.

The auditorium was silent now, there were no moving images, the visions had stopped he was on his own again. "That was hard, wasn't it Raj?" came a voice from his left hand side.

"You had to see this, it was important so you could see what your actions did. I need you to snap out of this self-denial that you are harbouring in your mind, you need to understand that every action has a reaction. I need you to move on Raj, or she won't, her energy is all over you because you will not let go, Raj.

"Raj, I didn't tell you everything when I said that Ash had already moved on, because she hasn't been able to. At the moment her energy is with you, I know you love her and have loved her through many different lives over the eons." There was silence for a minute and the voice continued, "The reason why you are here, Raj, is not only to help Jose but also to tie up the loose ends that you have left. There are so many lives that are linked here. Let's take for example Johnny, he always longed to see his parents, you helped him and he spent some time with his parents. Johnny and Sonya were always meant to be together and you have helped them. Raj, do I have to carry on, stop this self-indulgence and self-pity, you are bigger than this."

"How do I let her go, Boss?" he asked quietly.

"Close your eyes, beta, and say goodbye and she will be free. She already has forgiven you, she loves you, you big goof." Raj smiled, nodded and then closed his eyes and let his mind go. He started to drift into thin air, he was flying, he could see the earth below him and then he said goodbye but was it really that easy to let this go, because somehow- he knew it wasn't.

As he did, his soul transcended back into Roger as he lay curled up on the bed. Roger's eyes flickered

151

open, it wasn't a dream. Over the next few hours Roger got up from bed, sat quietly in the room, he was figuring out what this all meant. It was not going to be easy living without her but her memories would be enough and he could hang on to those because that is all we are left with. The good times were what he was going to remember and not the bad. His life was far from being fixed but he felt that by letting Ash finally go, he was getting there. Now he knew he had to do the same with the kids and Johnny. He had to move on, that's why he was here, but first he must help someone else.

Johnny and his grandfather were walking in the massive gardens of the estate, it had stopped raining and the sun had broken through the clearing clouds. Johnny looked up at the skies, this weather was strange, and perhaps global warming was now kicking in. His thought pattern was disturbed when he saw Roger walking purposefully towards him and his Grandfather. "Your friend is a strange fellow, Johnny," commented his grandfather as Roger came and stood in front of them. It was clearly visible from the young man's face that he was tired, his eyes looked tired and red and the body was limping.

"Hey, Roger, you okay?" asked Johnny, "How can anyone be okay after undergoing what I have been through over the last few weeks, my friend?" replied Roger. There was an uncomfortable silence for a minute and they absorbed his comment and then he said, "we are leaving today Johnny, there is so much to do." Mr Raja now interrupted, "and you must stay a little while longer please." Roger's facial expressions softened and he shook his head and thanked Johnny's grandfather very much for his hospitality but now it was time to leave. He then added, "I am sorry the party last night was spoiled with what happened but I would like to wish your grandson," and for a minute he stopped and took a few long breaths, then went on, "and your lovely daughter in law the best."

"Grandfather, please excuse me and I will see the guys off."

They shook hands warmly and then Roger did an Indian thing, which completely surprised Mr Raja, and that was to bow and touch his feet. In India this was a sign of respect, so how did a young American born in CA know this? The old man faced beamed and he reached Roger to hug him warmly, "God bless you my son," he said.

Compton

Roger hated farewells but he knew that they would see Johnny again. Johnny had told them that the marriage was pencilled in October this year. Roger simply nodded and said, "Never say never" and with that, Ken started the engine of the Escalade, released the hand brake, and eased down on the gas. The car lurched forward slowly down the long drive way. They could see the huge metal front gates of the mansion open and they went through the gates and were on their way.

An inner suburb of Los Angeles, Compton lives up to the reputation of most inner city/inner suburban areas across the United States due to its high level of poverty and elevated crime rate found in most cities. Compton is rated to be one of the most dangerous counties in US and its population has grown from 100,000 people in 2006 to nearly 250,000 now. The streets in some parts of the city are no-go areas and since the Compton police force was disbanded and the LA sheriff's office took over, resources for policing have been stretched. The local government in Compton had being trying to re-develop certain parts of the city, but it has been slow going. . Corruption is wide spread and local councils have known to be on the take from certain gangs. The city has been broken up into two areas; the largest ethnic Latinos ran the south side while the large Black population ran the north. Most of the white population had moved out to the new neighbouring cities. But, all that said, Compton has many good people living within the city limits, who really try to make a difference. Compton is known as a Hub City due to its geographical position within Los Angeles County. The local councillors have been trying to work hard to help the growing number of residents.

The drive from Beverly Hills to Compton, where the

154

apartment was, is just over one hour or slighter longer in LA traffic. The address for the apartment or house that Johnny had sorted out was East Pint Street, which was off Alameda Street. Fortunately, for the boys this was not too far from the 105 freeway. They were going to be centrally located in a place called Willow Brook, which was good. They had easy access to either West or East Compton. Ken had chosen to drive because he wanted to drive the new gleaming new Escalade.

The 450BHP power all-wheel drive SUV was a dream to drive and being nestled back in the luxurious leather bucket sports seats was a real delight for both boys. The SUV was kitted out with all the extras that you would love to buy if you had the money and Ken especially was in awe of how sleek the SUV was. He commented that a brother could get used to this kind of life and Roger smiled back at him. "Keep your eye on the road," he said teasingly, "we don't want to damage this baby either." Ken laughed and he eased his foot down on the accelerator and the car effortlessly moved through the lanes of the freeway. The DVD integrated navigation, seek-and- scan system guided them towards their designation and as they turned onto 105 they weren't that far away from home. The screen instructions indicated that they were 15 minutes away and so far, the drive had been comfortable. It gave Raj time to reflect on what had transpired over the last 72 hours. There was a lot of hurt but also happiness, you have to bear that in mind, he told himself, when thinking of everything that has happened and the chain of events.

He realised to a certain degree that he was not here just the save Jose, but himself too, and on the way, anyone else who happened to cross his path. His life was intertwined with so many others' that he knew this would be a major task. He needed to release his mind as he had read years ago in a book, so that he would be able to move along the path he must now follow. It sounded easy but clearing your mind of all the lingering thoughts and memories that we gather over the years and then some was hard work. It took learned men years to attain such emptiness of the mind, and he was hardly a learned man. He turned to Ken and asked to re-check the address they were supposed to reach. . Ken handed him a piece of paper left in the glove compartment and it read 2411 East Pine Street, Compton, CA. Johnny had told them that some exclusive apartments had been built in the last year because Compton councillors were spending around 10M dollars re-generating the central part of Compton in a big way. The stepping blocks had been already put in place by the last governor of CA; he wanted the LA County to really tidy its act up.

As Ken turned into Alameda Street, the navigator indicated that they were two minutes away from their destination. Roger had not been in Compton for a long time, he had once dated a girl from Compton but it all had turned sour quite quickly. He was young and having fun and was not ready for a long-term relationship, which was what the girl wanted. Roger's mind drifted now to Kate, I hope she is all right, I want to see her again, Raj. Raj smiled, "you will my friend." Just then, the car navigator indicated that they needed to turn left onto East Pine Street and that their destination was just ahead.

As Ken turned the car, the display indicated they had arrived so he pulled up the SUV on the left. Ken stepped out of the car and asked a passing couple if they knew where the address was. They pointed across the road to a Large Iron Gate and behind them exclusive apartments. Getting back in the SUV, he waited until there was an empty space on the road and he turned the car right and stopped the in front of the gates. On the paper with the address on it was another sentence below the address. It read – "Password for the entrance gate is 2510".

Ken opened his window and then punched in the code on a numerical pad entrance counter. The gates came to life and started swung open, letting the boys drive in.

There were three blocks of apartments and going by the numbers their apartment was in the first block. The large iron gates behind them had already closed, enclosing them inside the apartment complex now. At first glance to the boys, once they stepped out from the SUV, it was definitely very exclusive and very private. The blocks were made up of three well-sized town houses rather than apartments. Roger decided to go to the apartment while Ken got the bags out from the trunk of the Escalade.

Roger climbed up a short couple of stairs and then stopped outside two large wooden doors. He took the key that Johnny had given him, placed it in the lock, and turned the key. The door latch gave with a silent crack and Roger turned the knob and entered the building. As he entered, he was blown away and he had to catch his breath at the opulence. The building was beautifully refurbished in a contemporary style and was very modern. Johnny had told them that he had bought this apartment after talking to the designers who had built it around a loft apartment design. It was two storeys high and once you entered the building, it just astounded you and the interior design was so well done. What really caught his eye was the attention to detail, going from the flooring to the furniture. In the far left hand corner of the apartment, built into the wall was a large 60-inch LED TV. Built into the walls around the TV were Bose speaker enclosures. On a shelf below the

TV was what looked like a slim line media server/PC with a wireless keyboard? On the right hand side of the two-floor open plan building was a beautifully modern kitchen area and again the attention to detail was perfect. There was good money spent here on design, style and functionality. Everything seemed so practical, yet elegant. The kitchen was all designer built and furnished by Buffy, and included a Buffy fridge, dishwasher and service room with water, dryer and extra freezer.

As Roger looked up at the ceilings, he noticed two security cameras mounted in either corner. One was pointed to the ground floor and the other to the upper floor. Johnny, he whispered under his breadth and smiled.

Ken walked in and closed the door behind him, like Roger he could only stand, and marvel at the style, "this place must be worth a bomb," were his first words. Roger had already ventured up the beautiful marble staircase to the loft floor where there were two bedrooms. Both had en-suite facilities and like the down, stairs were beautifully laid out in modern décor. Roger marvelled at the satin quilts and the little touches of detail that only a handcrafted piece of furniture could have. Even the bath taps and handles looked like they were gold plated and handmade. There was so much detail in each of the two bedrooms on the loft floor, that Roger could not take his eyes away. As he surveyed the room, he saw in the corner a glass topped computer workstation. The workstation fitted the room well because it was not one of your DIY store flat packs but a designer one-off piece.

He walked towards it and sat down in the chair in front of the workstation. His hand reached for the keyboard but could not find it. He looked below the table for the PC and it was neatly hidden away, He reached down with his hand and switched it on and instantly the PC came to life. As he did this the glass top of the table lit up and embedded inside the glass was a touch pad keyboard; "OMG!" he thought. Located on the corner of the table was an Apple LED 27" cinema display, which came to life as Roger lightly touched the on/off switch. Raj had to admit that he was in his element, and if he had had the money, this would have been the set up that he would have bought in his time. He loved technology and what it presented and he had been part of the IT industry for the majority part of his life.

As he touched the keyboard very lightly with his fingertips, images on the screen came to life. As he looked intently at the monitor he realised that it was also a touch screen and that he had four options showing on the panel. The first was to open up the internet, the second to music, the third to security and the fourth to normal PC window. Operating technology had certainly moved forward since days of Windows 7 and OS 10, now you have the common synergy of a Microsoft Windows system and Apple's operating system. Built into the monitor was a small key hole CCD camera, so that he could have video conference capability, taking images, etc. "God Bless Bill Gates and Steve Jobs at Apple for their vision", thought Raj.

As he gently touched the internet option on the screen, the PC came to life and opened up a Yahoo web browser. Over the next hour while Ken relaxed downstairs, Roger surfed the web and started to gather information on Compton and where everything was in this city. He had to understand what they were dealing with, especially the gang culture and most importantly, whose turf was where. .

Meanwhile in another part of the city at the Municipal Law Enforcement Services Department CSI officer Frank Wells was meeting local officers who were linked to the gang unit. Compton had been striving for years to control the gang culture in the city and make it safer for the public to live and work in the city. Their life was not made easy by rappers in the earlier eighties like EASY E, DR. DRE, ICE CUBE and DJ QUICK who grew up on the streets of Compton and then wrote musical lyrics and sang about their exploits, romanticizing the gang culture. Gangster Rap made lots of money and it was seen as hot to boast about how many times you had been shot or how many people you had blown away.

The gang team in Compton Police Department though, had been winning the war over the years and even though many good young officers lost their lives, efforts still went on strong to control the culture and educate kids in early school levels. What was really helping the gang unit was that ex-gang members had joined the team and were helping them to reach out some of the younger members of the gangs. This was most notably started by Houirie Taylor and Reggie Wright in the late 80's. They had both come from the south central and Compton area where the CRIPS and BLOODs were formed. They lived the history of what led to the forming of the black gangs. They gave lectures and seminars about the beginning of the gangs that many of today's experts have adapted to teach.

Frank had come to meet Oscar Reynolds, he had been part of the gang unit for the last 10 years and he was also an ex-gang member from East Compton. Oscar had been in many gangs from a young age and came from a broken family. His father had walked out on his mother when he was two and his mother could never support him and his two sisters properly. She had been addicted to crack for a number of years and even though she had tried to get herself off, the damage was already done. Oscar used to cry himself to sleep because his mum was so high some nights she did not even recognise him. Oscar was the eldest of the three and he had had to grow up fast. Joining the gangs was an easy way to make money for the family and once you were in it was a blood oath. Saying this Oscar did get out, and what made him change was when he saw the birth of his first son. He knew then that there was more to life than this. He had also spent his young life messing around with the gangs listening to the local rappers sing songs about their harsh lives and making it big on other people's misery. Things had to change, it was not easy leaving and other gang members had tried to kill him but he made it through sheer will and grit. That was now nearly 20 years ago and was just a bunch of distant memories. His biggest regret was never seeing his younger sisters growing up because they had been killed in gang led shooting by a rival gang. Their faces were etched in his mind and some nights he would still wake up screaming from his own nightmares.

"Oscar Reynolds, my name is Frank Wells from the LA PD," and he stretched his hand out to greet the man. The first thing that struck Frank about Oscar was his size; he was six and half feet tall and looked like he built like bull for his age. Frank reckoned Oscar was in his mid-forties and by the look of his face had seen a lot of shit. Oscar stood up from his desk and greeted Frank warmly and ushered him to sit down on the spare chair next to his desk.

"Thank for seeing me at such short notice," Frank started off saying, "but I need your help in identifying a particular gang in Compton." Oscar looked at Frank for a minute, told him not worry about disturbing him and said he would help as best as he could. He carried on by saying that he had heard about the case that Frank was working on. "Before we do this Frank, we cannot talk here, let's go and sit down in one of the meeting rooms."

Oscar led Frank to his boss's room on the far side of the office and then closed the door behind him. Once seated, he apologised for moving them here but explained that the office had a leak somewhere, especially over this case. The case was high profile because it had been one of the biggest shootouts on Compton's streets for quite some time. It had left nearly 20 people killed and another 10 hospitalized. Three of the people who were hospitalized were innocent bystanders who had been walking by.

The LA Sheriff's office had put them under some pressure to solve the case but all the leads and gone quite. The only suspect was a young kid who was in hospital but after the attempt on his life, he had gone missing. Frank knew all about that because he had moved the boy after the incident at the hospital. Jose was the key in solving this case and others.

"What if I told you that I have the boy and I moved him to a safe house?"

There was a long uncomfortable silence, "you have the boy, where and why," demanded Oscar in a cool calm voice. Frank smiled, "because there is more to this story and there is someone in my department and yours here in Compton who is leaking information. The boy had not told me a thing; he was so beaten up after the shooting that he ran from that he was luck he survived. The bastards even raped him, that's how sick Ramon's brother was."

He stopped for a minute to let his words sink in and then he carried on, "If that was not enough, the officers, they tried to come back to the hospital to finish him off. The boy was in luck that he had a guardian Angel looking after him or he would be dead by now."

Frank stood up, his anger over this whole business was affecting him, and he was not sleeping at night, wondering why he was so closely linked to this case and why both Ken and Roger were involved.

Frank walked over to the far side of the office and stood by the window, "Look Oscar, I need your help to get this Ramon character and lock him away, and it's not going to be easy because he has people inside but I need your help, man."

Before Oscar could reply his mobile started to ring, "excuse me," he said and then answered the phone. After a couple of minutes Oscar put the phone down and looked towards Frank who had now returned to the table and seated himself down.

"Looks like someone at the LA PD do not want me to speak to you, Frank; that was my boss on the line telling me to humour you."

Frank smiled ruefully at Oscar, "well then I should take my leave and work on this myself. Hey wait a minute, Frank; I never said that I was going to listen to my boss. I want this guy as much as you do because he had my wife killed nearly a year ago. He was trying to send me a message so he paid for a hit on my wife."

"I am sorry Oscar, I did not know," replied Frank.

Oscar managed to smile and then looked up at Frank, "you know when I joined this gang unit I thought it was going to make a real difference. For a few years things moved smoothly,   and then things started to happen that didn't make any sense and now this phone call," he finished.

With that, he stood up and ushered Frank out of the office and back towards his desk so everyone could see them and not suspect. He then handed Frank a business card, which was his. On the back of the card, it read that I will call you later, people are listening. Frank got up, shook Oscars hand and walked out of the office.

Once out of the building and out in fresh air, two things happened. Firstly, his mobile rang, it was Roger and then a gunshot rang out and he felt a searing pain in his left shoulder as a bullet ripped through his shoulder and out the other side. The phone call and saved his life, otherwise that bullet would have gone straight to his heart.

He fell backwards with the force of the shot and he could feel himself blacking out with the pain but he focused his thoughts on staying awake and keeping his eyes open. He tried to focus on where the gunman was but he could not see him. There was now a crowd of cops rushing to his aid, one of whom was Oscar. Frank reached for his phone and pushed it into Oscar's hand, and said, "Call the last number". With that, blackness consumed him and he passed out with the pain.

As Frank passed out, Roger hung up the phone. He had heard the gun shot and he knew something had happened. "Rog, you better come down here buddy and watch the news." Roger rushed down the winding marble staircase, he could see on the large LCD on the wall CNN news channel on, and they were reporting a shooting of a police officer in Compton.

The police officer was identified as Frank Wells of the LAPD and it was reported that a Gunman from a moving car and taken a shot at Frank as he was coming out of the Compton police station. The reporters were not certain if Frank had survived but they knew he has been rushed off to Compton General. Both men looked at each other trying to read each other's thoughts, on one side they had to go to Ken, but on the other would it expose them. The hit on Ken must somehow be linked to them. Suddenly Roger's mobile came to life and started ringing – it was Frank's mobile.

Roger picked up the call and said hello, the caller on the other line identified himself as Oscar Reynolds of the Compton's Sheriff's office.

"How can I help you, officer?" Roger answered in a cool voice, his heart was racing but he was keeping control. Raj told himself that he had to do this and not panic as he used to years ago in another lifetime. Oscar then narrated to Roger that he had been asked to call him by Frank Wells who had come to his offices asking for his help. Frank had told him that the boys needed his help. "Look," he carried on, "I know this is strange but I think we should meet." There was silence for a minute and then Roger asked about Frank. He had taken a 38mm in the chest and had been rushed into Compton General. Doctors prescribed his chances as 80/20 but they were trying their best.

"Look officer; let's meet at the hospital as it's a public place." Following that Oscar told Roger where Frank was and which ward he was in. He also told him that when he got there ask for him and he would let him in and then he hung up.

Roger put the phone down and then looked towards Ken, "you're staying here buddy." Ken protested but Roger would not listen, he simply stood up, and picked up the keys for the 4x4 and walked out the door.

Oscar had told Roger that Ken had been taken to the LAC/Martin Luther King JR general hospital. He had also given him the address, which he tapped into his Sat Nav. The hospital was not far away according to his guidance system and indicated it would take those 15 minutes to drive to S Wilmington Avenue where the hospital was. As Roger drove out of the private car park, his mind was a mess and was working overtime. The boss had sent him down here to save a boy but was that what it was really about. There were too many other lives involved now, they all linked into this end goal, and they even included his own kids from his past life. Who was he trying to save, "I am trying to save you my son," came the reply in his head.

"It's not fair, boss, that you have linked so many lives into mine, I might hurt them," he replied.

There was silence for a moment as Raj turned onto East Pacific coast highway.

"If I thought you would that then I would have left you with my brother, Raj. You know in your own heart and from what I have already shown you that life is but a game and now you must play it to save yourself and the people that come into it. Your heart is telling you that is right and that's why you are here and don't let despair creep into your mind."

It was warm outside and Raj was sweating so he turned the air-conditioning up to try to cool down. His stomach was churning, something was not right but he had to go to the hospital. Traffic was light and his Sat Nav indicated that they should be at his destination in eight minutes. Concentrating on his driving he turned the 4x4 onto N Avalon BLVD, the hospital was now just around the corner. Traffic on N Avalon had come to a stop at a set of traffic lights and Raj eased the big 4 x 4 to a stop. The traffic lights were taking a long time to change so he switched on the radio. The radio was automatically tuned to Hip Hop channel 102.3 FM and the music started to rock the car with DVB quality sound.

The traffic signals changed and he eased his foot down on the accelerator and the 4x4 came to life with ease. A few hundred yards later, he saw signs for the hospital and he turned right into Wilmington Avenue. As he drove down 50 yards, he saw the entrance to the hospital on his right. He turned in and drove to the visitor car parking spaces where he parked the car. Switching of the engine, he took a deep breath and looked through the windscreen towards the hospital. His stomach was still churning with nerves but he had to go inside and meet this Oscar Reynolds. As he stepped out of the 4x4 something strange happened, it was the same feeling he had when he had left the hospital with Ken after the shootings.

He could hear voices some asking for help, others calling out names of loved ones that they were still looking for. There were images of faces of people shooting in his head and for a split second, he staggered in his footsteps. For a minute, he could not move his heartstrings were being pulled and the voices did not stop. He turned towards the SUV and grabbed the door side window for balance and he had to stay there for a few minutes longer. Once he had gathered his composure, he again turned towards the entrance of the hospital. He then nodded his head in acknowledgement to all the voices that he could still hear and in his mind, he said he would help, but at this moment, he had to meet Oscar.

LAC/MARTIN LUTHER KING JR GENERAL HOSPITAL

Martin Luther King JR general Hospital was located north of the city of Compton and south of Watts Originally, the Hospital was closed in 2007 due to substandard conditions and steady decline over several years, but it was given a face-lift and re-opened in 2012. This took the local authorities and the local people a long time to achieve. Now they had a hospital that could cater for the public with 1000 odd beds and a new research wing. The Federal Government had to concede that the residents of Compton needed the hospital and awarded several grants for this to happen. They also advertised for more doctors and nurses and soon the hospital was receiving acclaim from the local community and beyond. The biggest winner was the community of Compton – they had a hospital they could be proud of and it carried the name of Martin Luther King and that stood for something.

Roger walked through the main entrance of the hospital, and the first thing he noticed was the large presence of Police officers. They were checking people coming in and that meant he had to go through security too. After a physical search, he walked up to the reception desk. A young woman was on duty and he could only describe her as cute. She looked up at him has he approached the desk, fluttering her eyes at him she coolly asked him how she could help him.

Roger smiled, he wanted to reply something else but instead he asked her where he could find Office Oscar Reynolds from the Compton Sheriff's office.

"Please wait," she replied politely and getting up from the desk, she walked over to one of the police officers. Roger could not help himself as his eyes followed her movements away from the desk. He smiled; some things never change and she did have a nice behind under that tight nurse's uniform.

A few minutes later, she came back, followed by a uniformed officer. The officer was a stocky built black person, which was a little dimidiating, and as he approached Roger, he smiled and asked how he could help. Officer Oscar Reynolds asked me to meet here, do you know where I could find him please. For a second the police office thought for a minute and then asked Roger to follow him. As he followed the officer, he turned his head to the nurse and winked at her, causing her to blush and turn her eyes away.

As the police officer led Roger around the reception area and then to the elevators, Roger could hear the voices again. They were now coming from all directions but he had to focus. Once inside the lift the police officer with the name Larry on his badge pressed the fourth floor button. The evaluator doors closed and they started to move up towards the fourth floor. Roger could sense the police officer looking at him intently but he did not utter a word. Roger kept his head towards the doors and did not stare back and when the doors opened, there was a huge sense of relief. As they stepped out of the elevator, the thing that struck Roger was the huge presence of police men on this floor all armed and looking warily at everyone. The officer asked him to follow him and he lead Roger from the elevators to the front desk of the fourth floor ward. There he asked Roger to wait while he went to find Oscar. As Roger stood there he looked around – the ward was busy with doctors, nurses and police officers, but there was something else. Standing at the far end of the ward stood a man, a tall man from first glance. Roger could not take his eyes off him, there were images blurring inside his head of this person. At this point, the man turned his head towards Roger. His eyes were drawn and he looked tired. From first appearance, the man was not dressed in modern clothes – more of early 1970.

Roger found himself walking towards the gentleman, as he felt that there was something that he had to do here. As he got nearer to where the man was standing, the image of the man started to change – instead of sad faced individual, his facial images contorted into more of to what resembled a skull with deep eye sockets. Roger took a step back and fell backwards as the image in front thrust an arm at him. He could feel the impact of the man striking him in his chest and the pain was incredible. It felt like someone had just stabbed him and then left the knife there. Then there was laughter in his head and that is when everything went black and he collapsed to the floor.

As he came around from the black out, Raj realised, he was no longer standing in the hospital where he started out. Instead, he was standing in a bleak baron mountainous valley, the ground was full of ash and there was no life. Suddenly he felt movement behind him and he quickly turned but there was nothing there. He could feel eyes upon him but physically there was no one there. He then heard laughter ringing in his head. He stood his ground closed his eyes and focused his mind on happier things. The laughter stopped and there was an eerie silence and then came the voice, which he recognised straight away.

"So Raj, we meet again – and this time in my surroundings. Your soul is deeply tortured and is mine to devour and now I shall reclaim it."

"NO!" shouted Raj from deep inside – every bit of his body shouted and brilliant light radiated from every pore of his skin. "NO," he spoke more softly this time –

"this soul is not yours yet, Satan. I have things to do and lives that I must save and you shall not have me yet. I am not scared of you anymore because you are me – and I will not succumb to thee. Know this Satan, that when the time comes we will meet and I promise you this: that we will then decide where I go. Now be gone and leave me be, your darkness, because there is no place for you here."

He could hear a scream of anguish and could feel the air burning around him but the light kept him safe – his heart kept him safe – for once, his faith kept him safe and then it all stopped and he opened his eyes.

He found himself lying in a bed and as his eyes focused there were people around him, he was back in the hospital. Someone was asking him if he was OK, he turned towards the voice, it was a young female doctor, pretty he thought, he smiled. "I am fine he said", lost my balance for a minute, I am sorry I caused a fuss". He sat up and looked very sheepishly at the people around him. "Are you Roger?" came a booming voice from his side –from a towering well-built man in his early forties, Raj thought. Roger nodded and the man extended his hand, "my name is detective Oscar Reynolds, I believe you are looking for me."

Once Roger had regained his feet and balance – Oscar urged him to follow him out of the room, and he did. Together they silently walked past a maelstrom of activity, until they arrived at an observation room. There Oscar stopped and then turned to look in the room. Roger also stopped a few feet away from Oscar and turned to look into the room.

Frank Wells lay on a hospital bed unconscious, linked to heart monitoring units, glucose/medicine drips, and were keeping him alive. He looked so peaceful to the naked eye but Raj could see and feel different. He could hear Frank's voice inside his head asking for help and the one question he kept asking was, "can you see me?" To the naked human eye all that was visible was the lifeless body lying on the bed, but Raj could see, standing next to the bed, Frank in his astral form. The Astral form moved closer to the observation room window and stared directly at Roger, – "you can see me can't you? I knew you were different," – he smiled.

Roger, for an instant, took a step back; he looked at Frank and then turned to look at Oscar who was staring at him intently. "They say he is fighting but they cannot be sure how long it will take him to regain consciousness," said Oscar. "As he lay in my arms he continued he asked me to seek you out, why would that be?"

"Frank thought there was a connection with the shootings that took place with me and my friend and what is happening now. He believes there is a link to all this and that me and my friend are part of this," replied Roger – "and are you?" quizzed Oscar. Roger turned to look at Oscar for a minute; he did not answer immediately, he considered what he should say but before he responded he looked deep into Oscars eyes, wondering if could he trust him and something inside told him yes.

Roger nodded as an acknowledgment to Oscars question and added that he was looking for a boy that was involved in a Latino gang. He had been brutally beaten up and left for dead. "I need to find that kid and try to help him," he continued. There was silence for a minute and then Oscar blurted out, "Are you his guardian Angel?" mockingly; Roger looked up, and simply replied "Yes."

Oscar was taken back with Roger's response but he could see that this kid was serious, and there was something in his face that told him that. This would

172

also answer his questions, like why Frank came to see him in the first place. Gangland violence was on the up again and there was a turf war going on, especially with the Latina gangs. To back this up the FBI were looking into drug barons from South America being involved somewhere.

Roger

After standing around the ward for an hour talking to Oscar and giving him a recap of what had gone before, Oscar understood a lot more, like how and where the Detective Frank's relationship fitted into this. Oscar tried to question Roger on his comment of being the guardian Angel for the boy but he would not answer that one.

They carried on their discussion further in a private room that Oscar had arranged for his use. Roger explained how he first met Frank and why he was here now. Frank thought there was a connection with everything that had happened in his lives and they were all connected to gangland action in Compton. "Are you connected to all this?" was the question that came back from Oscar, Roger looked up at Oscar and simply nodded but did not say anything else. After a few minutes, Roger indicated that he needed to use the men's room – Oscar called one of the officers outside the room to show Roger where it was.

As Roger Closed the latch on the toilet, he could sense there was someone standing behind him. As he turned around there was Frank standing a few feet away.

"You can hear me can't you?" he spoke, "you can see me as well – I knew there was something different about you."

"Hold on Frank – yes I can see you and yes I can hear you but no one else can. If I go out there and start talking to empty space, they will have me in a straight jacket. Anyway you should be in the room where your body is and slip back in."

"Slip back in!" Frank shouted, "I am dead and you're not telling me. You are not dead yet, Frank because you have not crossed over yet. That means it is not your time or you have something on your mind. Frank, I can hear voices inside my head all over this hospital and like you they are all asking the same question, can you hear me?"

"It frightens the shit out me but you want to know why I can see you? Because in this young body lives the soul of a guy who was born in 1965. You see Frank, my name is Raj Sharma and I am standing before you. I am co existing in a body that belongs to a young man who was left for dead in an alley way and while that young man's soul recovers I am using his body."

There was silence for a minute – Frank's facial features seemed to change and soften – he seemed to be losing his composure.

"You see Frank, as I waited to die in alone in Park—feeling sorry for myself – I felt like I was lifted out of my earthly shell and then carried off to another world. I thought I had crossed over but this was not the case, instead I was offered another solution – I was shown a way to redeem myself and do a job. I chose the job – because Frank, I needed answers and I needed to find myself. Everything that is happening now has been written Frank and we are just passing through that Time Phase – Yes, we can change it but the question is will we change it? For Fuck's sake Frank, what am I supposed to do?" he turned away because he could feel tears starting to form and he did not want to cry.

He then turned around to open the toilet door and walked out. Frank followed Roger out and as he did he shouted out, "stop! Roger." Roger turned around startled by Frank's voice and call.

"Frank, what's wrong?" he asked, "that man Roger in the Doctor's coat – he is not a Doctor – he was there when my partner was killed."

Roger turned to look – the man ahead of him looked up and Raj could feel what Frank was saying and suddenly Raj saw Frank's ex-partner standing next to the man.

There was instant action from Roger; he pounced forward and shouted out, "Stop that man." As he did this the man reached within, his coat and pulled out a semi-automatic Heckler & Koch .45 calibres and started to fire bullets at anything that moved. There was uproar, chaos, and cries of agony and terror from all directions. Several police officers were caught off guard and were cut down by stray bullets. However, Roger did not seem to care when he leapt forward his momentum carried him forward and with a leap in the air and angling his body into a flying karate kick stance, he hit the gunmen in the chest knocking him backwards and forcing him to drop his weapon.

As he fell the semi-automatic fell from his grasp and crashed away from him and before he could react, a volume of gunfire aimed at him hit his chest and ripped him apart. He did not move again, there was blood splatter all over the walls of the ward. The scene looked more like a war zone than a hospital ward in Compton, there was confusion, people were shouting and doctors and nurses were streaming into the ward to help the wounded and shot. Roger had landed like a cat, his Karate training helped him and he had hit the gunman square on the chest, and as he looked straight ahead, he could see the man's bullet ridden body lying on the far side of the blood-splattered ward. As he looked on, he also saw more

The man's soul stepped away from his body, his eyes were in shock as he looked down at his broken bleeding corpse. He then looked up towards Roger but before he could do nothing he felt his soul being dragged down into the floor. He was screaming but no one apart from Roger could hear. Roger was transfixed, he could not divert his eyes from the scene. The terror in his eyes would haunt him for a while – as the gunman was fading and above him appeared another creature's face and that was one Raj recognised in the form of Satan. "I am coming for you Raj, and like this soul I shall devour you piece by piece," and with that he was gone. Something else caught Raj's eyes and that was the form of a woman. She was standing at the far end of the ward – she looked so beautiful dressed in a white flowing silk gown. The most striking feature was her face; she looked like a model, with high cheekbones and lushes lips.

Roger started to move towards her but there was someone else also moving towards her and that was Frank's ex-partner. He looked to Roger and smiled and then looked towards the woman who stretched out her hand to him.

"Wait," called Roger, "what do a tell Frank?" The man looked around and said "tell him I am going home, don't worry." He then quietly turned towards the blond lady and reached for her out-spread hand. Once she had touched his hand, his facial expressions changed, he had a huge smile on his face, his eyes brightened up and the tension on his forehead was gone. He turned his head back towards Roger and waved.

"He's free now," said a quiet voice next Roger, it was Frank – Roger nodded and said, "He is going home my friend." With that, also Frank vanished as well, leaving Roger standing alone assessing the carnage around him.

Roger did not know how long he stood at that spot and he was only disturbed when Officer Oscar Reynolds came around. "You okay, young man?" he said. Roger looked up, nodded, and looked towards Oscar.

"What happened?" asked Oscar, "My officers told me that you shouted out something and then hit a man brandishing a gun with a flying kick."

Again, Roger nodded, "the man was part of the gang that killed Frank Wells Partner. I shouted and he pulled out a .45 and started firing." Before he could go on a young officer interrupted the conversation and handed a piece of paper to Oscar.

"Oscar looked at the paper and then with head bowed he urged Roger to follow him. They headed directly towards where Frank was. While the chaos was occurring in the other ward someone had slipped into Frank's room and killed him."

"How had this happened?" cried Roger to Oscar – "apparently from the accounts given a man dressed as a male nurse approached the officer guarding Frank's room and caught him by surprise and stabbed him in the neck. As the officer fell, the man slipped into Frank's room and finished the job that they had started. Before the man could escape he was approached by two other officers and was shot, he was killed instantly."

Raj Looked into Frank's room, he could not see Frank or hear him and all he could see was Frank's earthly body. Frank could not have crossed over – surely not, he thought. Raj was in despair – things were all happening too fast and nothing made sense. This whole thing was getting messy and complicated and he was no super hero like the one you see in Hollywood films. He admitted that he was in the body of a young man who was physically Fit and a martial arts expert but he still was no a super hero.

"Don't despair Raj," came in the voice inside his head, "you will find the answer and remember that all the lives that you have come in contact are linked. You need to work this out and I know you can do this."

"That's because you had already written this boss," came the reply from Raj.

"Raj, remember what I said to you before – the

paths are not written; they are what you make of them and you have the power to change this, open you heart and mind my son."

"Look, we have tried our best here, Roger, to look after Frank Wells. My Officers have paid a heavy price today so get off our backs," retorted Oscar." Roger looked towards him and then back to the other ward and then again to face him. His face softened and he replied "I know, but there has to be leaks in your office – how else would these guys know where Frank was and what your security was." With that, Roger turned and walked away towards the elevators, he had to get out and back to Ken and safety.

The elevator doors seemed to open automatically as he approached them and he got in. He did not look back at Oscar who just stood there and did not know how to respond. He pressed the button for the ground floor and the lift sprung to life. His mind was running 100 miles an hour, Frank was gone and he was still back at square one. All he wanted to do was to get back to the house, gather his thoughts, and try to formulate a plan to find the boy. He knew now that Oscar's offices had been comprised and it would not be wise to work through this route even though Oscar was a good man. The doors of the elevator opened and he stepped out. There was a hive of activity on the ground floor, extra police officers were filing into the hospital and were locking it down, while Roger slipped out quietly.

Roger had lost all track of time so he looked at his watch as he walked out the Hospital. It was nearly mid-night in Compton so he decided to hurry along where the SUV was parked. Reaching the SUV, he fumbled in his pockets and pulled out the keys. He aimed the small key receiver towards the car and pressed the remote control. The door locks clicked open and Roger opened the driver's door and slumped back into the seat. His body seemed to relax a little as he closed the door and he felt safe. Satisfied that everything was ok in the SUV he turned his thoughts on getting out of the car park. He turned on the ignition and the SUV came to life. He then pressed a voice control button for the built in computer and went the commands for Sat NAV. He set the details for home and then put the car in drive.

The Escalade lurched forward and he slowly winded the big car out of the hospital car park and then to the main road. At this point, the Sat Nav came to life and started to command him to follow the directions set to his destination. Once on the main road his phone started to ring, he remembered that he had left this in the car. The Bluetooth system kicked in and answered the call, "Roger where the hell have you been?" came an angry voice over the microphone: "I have been calling you all night." Roger smiled, as it was good to hear his friends voice again; "hey Ken, calm down, I left the phone in the SUV when I went to the hospital." After a pause, he continued and the narrated the story of what had happened.

"You okay?" came back Ken.

"Physically buddy I am fine, mentally and emotionally I am all over the floor. Frank's dead Ken and I could not save him."

"Hey that's not your fault, how did you know that killers were going to be there? "Someone knew, Ken."

"Hey look, we will talk more when I get back but please make sure that you check everything is okay? I get the feeling that someone knows we are here. Hey Ken," he continued, "Call Johnny and make sure they are okay, but don't tell them anything else. I will see you in a while," and with that he hung up the receiver and the call ended.

His emotions were all strung out and he started to cry, tears rolled down his cheeks and he could not control them. He had to pull the SUV over to the roadside and take some time to regain control. He placed his heads in his hands and wept.

Meanwhile in a different part of Compton there was a meeting being held. Around the table, sat four men and one sat at the head of the table. The men sitting around the table were all dressed in dark black woollen mix suits and all but one was smoking heavily. The man at the head was shrouded in darkness and was not revealing himself but from the looks of the other men, they feared him. There was tension in the air and no one spoke – they were all too afraid of what may happen.

The silence was broken by the headman, "gentlemen" he said quietly but sternly – "I believe our two operatives were successful in getting rid of the cop. However," he continued, "I believe from these photographs that I received their job was nearly comprised by the interference of this man."

He then proceeded to throw across the table images of Roger. There was silence again for a minute and the man started to speak again, "is this the guy who Ramón has been tracking and trying to kill and if so what was he doing at the hospital? You guys realise that there is a lot hanging on this business with Ramon and that he owes me money.

I do not want any complications, so find this person, kill him, and then find me Ramon.

"I want my money or you guys will pay and so will your families back home."

With that the meeting ended and the group of men hastily left the room leaving the head man seated at the table. He stood up from where he was seated and walked over to one of the large windows and started to laugh.

"I will have you Raj," he said, "this game we play

together will come to an end soon and then my brother will give me your soul."

There was pure hatred in his eyes and fire and he clenched his fists tightly and as he did so flames burst into life in his hands, "you will not embarrass me again, Raj, and I will have my day with you. I told you that I exist where ever there is evil," and with a rueful smile his form started to fade away and completely vanish from the room.

Roger drove through the gates of the exclusive apartments that they were staying at and then pulled the SUV over to their allocated parking area. Once he stepped out of the car, he locked the doors and started to walk towards their apartment. Before he got there, the front door opened and Ken greeted him with a consoling arm around his shoulders. Roger was grateful for his friends greeting, his eyes were red from where he had been crying and emotionally he was drained. He knew things were happening for a reason but now he had no idea as to why they were happening, also no control over the events.

They entered the apartment and Ken allowed Roger to stumble into his room and go to sleep for a little while. Ken understood this was not the right time to quiz his friend. He recognised that Roger was all over the floor emotionally and what he needed now was to rest and sleep.

Once Roger hit the large king, size bed his eyes closed straight away and he drifted off into a deep sleep. However as his body rested his mind drifted away into a different time and a different place. He found himself sitting in a huge arena that resembled the Roman amphitheatres of the past. He was part of a large boisterous crowd watching gladiators fight to the death. He could feel his heart beating hard and being been drawn into the heated excitement of the moment.

The crowd was cheering and jeering at the gladiators on the arena floor. He looked around the huge amphitheatre and he was in awe of the structure. There must be over 20,000 people crammed in, watching the barbarity below. On the opposite end to where he was seated was where the emperor and the VIPs sat. They were heavily guarded by rugged stocky looking men dressed in Roman designed armour. Raj was drawn to the man taking centre stage, he somehow knew this man, even from the distance that he sat from him he could feel the man's eyes staring at him. The man smiled ruefully and the stood up and addressed the crowd.

"My friends and countrymen, today we celebrate a great victory against our enemies and I thank you for coming out today. What you are going to witness are our finest Gladiators performing for your delight. There may be some among you who would call this barbaric and reel at the sight of blood in my arena and to you I call out," he commanded. The man then looked directly at Raj and then raised his arm and pointed towards him. Raj recognised the man; it was Satan, in a different guise of a bloodthirsty Roman style emperor. Before Raj could react to what the man said he found himself being seized by armed men and then being manhandled down steep stone steps to the arena floor. There he was carried to the middle of the arena and dumped to the sanded, hard, dusty floor.

The noise in the arena stepped up a notch and the bloodthirsty crowd were hysterical and baying for blood. Satan looked on and was pleased at his audience reaction as he stood in defiance on the platform above the main arena floor. He now smiled broadly and his devilish eyes blazed with fire, "you cannot escape me Raj and let the games begin."

"Give him your sword!" he shouted to one of the

men who had brought Raj down. The man bowed and then withdrew his sword from his side. He then dropped this on the floor next to Raj and then moved away. Actually all the men that had dragged Raj down had moved away.

Raj looked towards the sword and reached for the hilt, it was made of Ivory and felt cold to the touch. At the end of the handle was a wood pommel. Ingrained into the ivory were ridges – these were there for gripping with fingers. Gladius is the Latin word for sword and early Roman swords were not much different from Greek versions. The swords were dual edged around 20" in length and diamond tipped. Essentially designed for cutting and thrusting the roman sword was described as the one that conquered the world. The well-tempered blade gave the swords their strength and for a Roman solider this was important when going into battle. Raj now remembered the scenes from the TV series Spartacus; he visualized the violence of the thrusting sword and the site of blood everywhere on the arena floor. Raj was not that person and the graphical violence shown made his stomach curl but now he was here.

Something strange happened once Raj gripped the sword's handle, his body started to tingle and he felt sparks of electricity rippling through his body. He then raised himself from the floor, stood upright, and pointed his sword arm towards the man that had spoken. For some strange reason Raj smiled, there was new energy rippling inside of him and he seemed to have lost his fear. The sword in his hand also felt like it was a part of him, an extension of his arms and it felt right.

The eyes were set and he addressed the man that had him dragged from the crowds.

"Your darkness," he started, "I have told you before

that it is not time for you to play games with me, I do not fear thee and I will not be slain by thee. Hear me Satan, today I stand in front of your hordes holding the sword of God and as he is my witness, I swear that if you will come in front me I will strike you down."

For a minute complete silence fell across the arena but this was broken by the man's laughter. As he stood up there was a transformation in his appearance, he no longer resembled a man, but his original deformed body of Satan. "I play no games here little man, we are destined to dance and I will have your soul, it is written he shrieked"

With that, he commanded his gladiators to enter the arena and commence battle. As he commanded so it was done, from the far corner of the arena entered several heavily built armed men dressed in Roman armour. Each Gladiator carried a different weapon of his choice and it would take strength and guile to beat these guys down.

Kneeling on the floor Raj remembered a line in a Christian Palms that read, "Though I stand in the Valley of Death, I will feel no evil, for thou are with me and shall deliver me from Evil." He then stood up, raised the sword in air a whispered a silent prayer – as he did so he was enveloped by a shining light, his physical being started to change and he felt stronger. He looked down upon himself and noticed that he was now dressed in full Battle armour, which consisted of a heavy chain mail shirt and over it shiny metal breastplate. On his head, he wore a typical legionnaires Helmet that would protect him from sword thrusts. In his left hand, he now held a shield with a crest embalmed of the sun. In his right hand, he held the sword but that too had changed to one that he had seen held before in Satan's land.

There were three well-built men walking towards

him, each armed differently but each looking menacingly towards him. On his far left, the first Gladiator held a Small Net in one hand a large evil looking Trident; they called this guy Retiarius on the other. The Gladiator, next to him, held a small round Shield and in his other hand a Roman Spear called a Pilum. The third Opponent held two evil looking Curved Arabian swords. The men started to fan out around him in a semi-circle preparing to strike together or individually, strangely Raj smiled he thought of all the old films he had seen and shared the same scene as now, the only real difference was that this was somehow real – can you call dreams real?

As Raj stood his ground he waited for the first strike he concentrated his mind and thoughts on this situation – he almost felt like in a trance because he could feel his opponent's breath, hear their heartbeats. Then suddenly the first attack happened – it was by the opponent with the trident and net. His opponent was fast and sleek and with manual armour on, he could be. Swinging his net in one hand and preparing the Trident in the other he attacked. Raj reacted instantly as well, side stepping the initial swing of the net and the trust of the trident he arced his sword in a sideways move and sliced through the mid rib of his opponent. As his Man fell, he moved with the speed of a cat and brought is sword down hard across the man's neck, slicing straight through. Not looking back at his falling assailant, Raj steady himself towards the other two opponents. This time they attacked together and fast. In a split second the opponent with the Pilum thrust forward, Raj reacted by using his shield to protect him and bring his own sword down hard on his opponents shield. The second Gladiator also attacked and Raj just managed to avoid the menacing swing of the swords towards him.

As the clash progressed, the attacks came faster and

harder and each time Raj counter-attacked, but his resolve stayed firm. He could hear the blood lust chants of the crowds and the shrieks of laughter and delight when each attack happened. He drew upon his belief now on the big boss man helping him and that gave him strength. If this was another test, he wished he could wake up and end it. This was all too real for his liking. He knew he liked the film 'Gladiator' all those years ago now but he never wanted to be part of the barbaric spectacle.

For a minute, there was breathing space for Raj before the next attack and this gave Raj his chance. He could see the man with the swords relaxing slightly and then he attacked. His attack was unconventional in terms of the roman term and was more like that of a Japanese Warrior. Shedding his shield all of sudden he leapt forward like a leopard would strike and arced his sword through the mid rib of his opponent, the man was caught by surprise by the attack and fell to his knees. Following up on his attack motion and without the second opponent reacting Raj thrust his sword into his side causing the man to drop his spear. With both assailants down, Raj stood up and took stock of the situation. He then faced Satan and shouted, "enough!" and, "you have had your fun," and with that, he scooped up the fallen spear from the floor and threw it like a javelin straight at Satan in one swift motion.

The spear, which was like Arjuna's arrow, the famous archer from the Mahabharata, hit true to its target, which was Satan's chest. Silence fell across the arena as all the crowds turned to see what had happened. The man standing on the raised alter looked down with shocked eyes to his chest, the Pilum had driven through his breastplate and lodged deep into his chest. As he fell to his knees all hell broke loose, from the man's body smoke and flames rose, and within the

187

smoke and flames came the shrieking sounds of a hideous creature that resembled a dragon. The whole aura of the arena had changed now, the skies became dark and red and the air smelt of rotting bodies. The actual arena had vanished and Raj found himself standing on a barren ash-filled ground, but this time he did not stand alone.

Standing next to him was a man that he recognised as God and not Danny De Vito. He moved ahead of Raj and as he did so, his bodily form started to grow and radiate with light. "Enough, Brother!" came a booming voice; "you go too far with your charades and games and this shall end now," he commanded; "go back to your realm."

"The soul you save is not clean and so he should be mine brother," came the reply.

"NO!" commanded the voice of God, "this soul is clean and it is you who would afflict it would worry, doubt, misery. I am the creator, I am lord do not challenge me or you will feel my wrath."

With that, the light grew brighter and stronger, Raj had to close his eyes, and all he heard at the end was a loud cry.

Ken came running into Roger's room when he heard the cry from his room and as he entered, he found his friend sitting up on the bed drenched in sweat. His face was ash white but his eyes were the most striking appearance that hit Ken. There was swelling around the eyes and the pupils were heavily diluted. As Ken reached his friend, he gently gathered him in his arms and held onto him, "You okay buddy?" he whispered and there was no response.

They sat in the room for what seemed like hours but in reality it was minutes – no one spoke. Then Roger finally spoke – "Ken do you believe in me?" he asked, "please say yes," he pleaded. Ken held his friend hard and said, "You know I do, no matter what happens."

"We have to find the kid Ken and finish what we started and save whoever we can on the way. The boss believes in us and he will protect us and now I have no more doubts about this, Ken."

His friend looked at him bemused, he wanted to ask questions but looking at Roger, he could not. Instead, he simply nodded and accepted what his friend told him.

Roger did sleep for the rest of the morning and Ken stayed by his side and when he woke up, he showered and started to plan how they were going to find the boy. They knew that the Compton Sheriff's office had been comprised and there had to be a connection. They were also sure that the people who had had Frank killed were involved here. It was funny why two lads from a different life were now involved in doing this but you could call it *kismat* (Path); whatever it was this was real. They had to see this through.

It was late morning when Ken shouted towards Roger to join him in the living room. Ken was excited; he had found something and wanted to share his news. What's up said roger as he walked down the stairs from the Bedroom, Ken looked up and said that he had hacked in the Compton police force network and he thinks that he knows where the boy is. Roger did not want to know how Ken had hacked into the network but looked keenly at the big monitor on the wall. As he took in the information, he noticed that the police reports stated that they had moved the boy twice after the initial attack at the hospital. He was now in a private clinic in Compton called Trees cape.

Trees cape

Dr Raymond Garcia had been working at the private and exclusive Trees cape clinic in West Compton for more than ten years now. He specialised in trauma cases and in understanding how to help victims of severe trauma cases. Before coming to the Clinic, he had spent 10 years working in LA General Hospital in the ER. He had found working in LA General hard, the hours were long and there was never a dull moment. He has seen a lot of gang related trauma cases come through the doors of LA General and he decided then that this was his calling. He could remember growing up in a poor run down area of LA where it was easy to get into drugs and gangs. He was the youngest son of three boys and an elder sister. His parents were originally from across the border, a small town in Mexico. They had smuggled themselves into the States for a better life. His father had worked hard, he took jobs on board that you and I would never consider doing but he had to feed his family. When US state offered an Amnesty to all illegals for a month, his father took the opportunity to declare himself and when that happened life got a little better. He could send his kids officially to school and claim some benefits. His wife took small cleaning jobs whilst she could to help pay the bills. For all their good work, they lost their eldest son to gangs, one day he was walking home from school with his sister and he was shot. He was caught by a random bullet in a drive-by shooting and died instantly. This had affected the family badly but Raymond's Father decided that he would not give up on his American Dream.

As Dr Garcia stood drinking his coffee in his office thinking about the old days, there was a knock on the door. The door opened and a pretty little nurse came in, holding a brown folder. She smiled at him, and handed over the folder to him. He smiled in return, took the folder, and thanked her, with that she left him alone again. Taking the folder, he walked over to his desk and sat down. He placed the folder on the table and began to open it. He then looked up towards to a picture frame that sat on the far end of the desk. He smiled; it was a photo of his wife Kelly and their sons Rafael and Andrea. He wished his father were here to see him today; he had died before he had fully qualified.

He looked down at the open folder and his look changed, he was deeply affected by this case because it involved a minor. Gang violence was still ripe in Compton and the victims were still the young and vulnerable. The police had brought this young kid to the clinic some weeks ago, but his condition had not changed. He was still very heavily traumatised and had not responded to anyone. As he flicked through the pages, he studied carefully for the 100th time the conditions of the boy and what he had suffered through. The beating up was vicious and then the rape by two grown thugs left their scars, both physical and mental. The worst things were that these men had tried to comeback and kill the boy at Compton General. Fortunately, a guardian angel had saved him at the hospital and that is when the police had decided to move him here under the strictest possible secrecy. The boy had now been here for a number of weeks now and had made no progress; Raymond was disturbed by this. His own sons were of the same age and he had always tried to keep them sheltered from the bad things in life. He had a promise made to his father to uphold, that his grandsons would have a better life. This boy also needed a break and he had to find a way to break through to him.

191

As he pondered over this, there was another knock on the door. Looking through the window panels, he saw the nurse who had brought in the original folder to him. He nodded towards her to enter and she entered his office, but she was not alone. Behind her followed two young men who were intently looking towards him.

Raymond rose from his table, and greeted the two young men and asked them to be seated. Raymond was confused as to who these two young men were, because he had no meetings booked for today, but he was courteous and asked how he could help.

"Dr Garcia, My name is Roger and this is my friend Ken and we need your help, please. A few weeks ago, Compton police department very quietly admitted a young patient to the clinic. This young guy was a gang victim and we believe that you may be looking after him." Raymond now concerned also uncomfortable – the young man who spoke carried on after a brief moment, "Dr Garcia, I know we have come to see you without an appointment booked and are asking you a very sensitive question, but I do not want to place you in a difficult situation. The reason I am asking this question about the boy is because I was the person who helped him that night in Compton General. I need to help him now, Dr, and we need your help."

Raymond tensed and looked towards Roger and then towards to Ken. They both looked like decent young men but Compton Police force and warned him to be careful. "Look," he said, "I cannot give you any information concerning about any of the patients in the clinic." Roger looked dismayed, and pleaded, "Dr, this kid is in real danger, the men who beat him up in the park will be back and you know why Doc, because this kid took something from them. Doctor Garcia I know you are bound by your rules and I know we are random strangers who have walked into your office but I am asking you to trust us." Roger let his words sink in for a minute and then continued. "Earlier this afternoon at the Martin Luther King Hospital a good friend lost his life and he was a cop. We need your help Dr, please," he pleaded.

Raymond pushed his chair back and rose from his table and walked over the far window to his left, he felt tense but there was something in this young man's tone he believed. He turned around to face the men, he took off his glasses and said, "look I want to help you but how do I know you are straight up. The police warned me not to trust anyone." Roger rose from his chair, "look Doc, we have seen what the guys who beat this kid can do and it is important that we help him now. I know your dad would be proud Dr Garcia." Raymond looked up his eyes showed emotion but again he sensed no malice in the words but reassurance. "Dad," he whispered under his breath and he could swear he could hear someone in his head saying, "it is fine my son, I am proud of you." There were tears in his eyes, for years he had been waiting for his dad to speak to him and for someone reason his dad spoke to him in his head. His head went down and he quietly nodded towards Roger and said "okay."

Looking back up at them Raymond took off his reading glasses and started to speak, "guys I will help you with this, but you have to remember that we are a private psychiatric hospital and I have to follow procedure. Most of the people that come to us are all private patients and most of their relatives pay very good money to us. In the case of this boy, the Police department brought him to us, because they wanted somewhere quiet and that would not be looked at. Also we specialise in severe trauma cases." There was silence for a minute and then he carried on by saying that helping them would go against the Clinic's policy and especially the police department's. "However something about this tells me that it is alright to help you."

Looking straight at Roger, Raymond stretched out his hand and said that, "you must promise me to be straight up because if you are not my heart is telling me there will be big trouble for everyone."

Roger stretched out his hand and once again shook Raymond's hand but this time he held on, as if to say do not worry, we are here to help, doc.

The hospital itself was like most other psychiatric institutions, and varied widely in its goals and methods, as Raymond described as they walked out of his office. Some hospitals might specialize in the short-term or outpatient therapy for low risk patients but we are slightly different from them. We mostly cater for high-risk cases where there is a high risk that the patients will be a threat to themselves or their immediate families. Most of our cases have been brought to us by their relatives, who simply cannot handle them at home, and are willing to pay privately for our care and assistance. You may not like to hear this because you may think we are driven by only looking after the rich – but the government wants it this way.

The boys listened as they walked down the halls from Raymond's office to the lifts at the far end. Once there he depressed the button to call for a lift and then turned to Roger. "I don't know why I am helping you guys – but something feels right here; but please tell me how you know about this young lad and how you propose to help him."

Roger smiled and then looked at Ken and Raymond. He was just about to reply as Ken jumped in and started to relay how they were involved. Roger could feel Ken's hand gently push down on his arm as if to indicate, let me do this. Roger understood and let his friend take over the lead and he started to give Raymond the full rundown while they waited for the elevator to come. Roger looked up at the indicator lights of the elevator, it was still stuck on the ground floor, and they were on the third.

Roger looked at his friend and Ken was in full flow in narrating their story but movement to his left distracted his attention. The voices inside his head were now also quite audible and someone was calling him. It sounded like a woman, he could not recognise her voice but she was asking for help. There was movement again towards Roger's left and as he turned, he could clearly see a woman standing a few yards away looking at him. She was dressed in the style of the earlier 19th century and was in her early twenties. She was looking at him intently and he was drawn to her to the extent that he turned away from the other two men and faced towards her.

"Please sir," she pleaded, "can you help me, they have taken my children away from me." Roger's face softened but he started to shake his head and whispered, "I cannot help you;" "but they said you could," she cried turning around and pointing her arms to the far hall. They said you had come here to help us all, they lied," she shrieked at him. Before he could respond, he suddenly felt his legs collapse underneath him and he fell hard on the floor. As he fell he could still hear the women above him shouting at him, "they said you would help me, they lied they lied." He could hearing her sobbing as he hit the ground and then as he hit the floor hard he also felt someone kicking him in his stomach and face. He started to curl up to protect himself but they would not stop until he passed out.

"Doctor Garcia, he is coming around! Please come," one of the nurses called out to Raymond and Ken.

When Roger had fell to the floor and apparently hit his head he had passed out. Raymond immediately had him taken to a private room so they could treat him.

As Roger came around his head was thumping and he opened his eyes slowly. For a minute, his vision was blurred and as he focused, he could see a concerned doctor and Ken standing beside him. He tried to smile but his body hurt all over – it felt like someone and thrown him in front of a car and he was hit at speed. "Hey guys, I am sorry," he started – Raymond interjected and told him to relax everything was okay.

"What happened, Roger?" asked Ken after a few minutes, Roger looked towards him, "I don't know, one minute I was standing there listening to you speak to the Doctor and then next minute I felt like someone was beating me up." He then looked at Raymond, "Doc this may sound like a really weird question but what is the history of this clinic – as it also served the clinical insane." Raymond was taken aback by Roger's question and asked "why?" – "Doc you are not going to believe me but for a minute up there I swear to you that there was a young women dressed in 19th century period costume asking for my help and then shouting at me and that's when I fell." Roger was looking straight at Raymond when he said this – he thought he would get a different reaction to the one he got.

Raymond, looked like he had been hit by a rock, his face had gone all white and his eyes were transfixed into a wild stare. It took him a few minutes to regain his composure and then look back at Roger. "What you have told me has been described very quietly by some people who work at this hospital. They say when they are alone or walking in some of the halls that they hear voices calling them and one or two have described exactly what you say you saw today. The management here has always killed any rumours or stories like this because they don't want to get this hospital noticed like this."

As he continued, he narrated to the boys the background of the hospital and when a man called Robert Davies founded it in the 18th century. "The story goes that Robert Davies was a wealthy land owner around these parts and he decided to open a psychiatric asylum after the mysterious death of his young family. It was said that his first wife lost her mind and butchered their young children in a wild rage and then took her own life by hanging herself. Robert Davies was so grief stricken that he decided that no one else must suffer like he had and that he would devote his life to helping others, which was a very noble thing to do. Therefore, he was the very founder of this hospital and he spent his entire fortune on building the hospital and gathered the services of the best medical professionals in his time to work here. The rumours would have that this place is still haunted by Robert Davies's mad wife and that Robert Davies himself still walks the corridors at night."

The boys looked stunned, Raj knew that since he took this role on board for the big man that he would be different and he could feel things, hear things and see things. The story sounded brutal but things like this happen even today. Raj could recall one very close to him when he was younger and a local neighbour who police claim killed his three children and his wife in a blind rage because his wife had left him. "I need to see him then," he said quietly, and both Raymond and Ken looked towards him; "what?" asked Raymond, stunned by Roger's words. Roger looked straight up at Raymond and said, "I need to find Mr Davies and help him or otherwise this will not end."

The words totally stunned Raymond – "are you mad?" he said aghast, "they will lock you up in here

197

and throw away the key as mentally insane for believing stories like this. Plus the media would have their books full of a laughable story of a modern ghost whisperer in one of the TOP LA hospitals."

"Look Doc," said Roger – "you said you could feel something about me and I can see this in your eyes; well, it's true; there is something different about me and call it what you want but I have a task to do, but the only way I can complete this is by helping others. I can heal myself as well, in the process Doc – I know in scientific language everything I am saying to you is rubbish and none of it can be explained, but trust me when I say that I am here for a purpose. This is no Hollywood B movie script but the real deal."

"I could feel your own father, Doc back in your office trying to get through to you and that has not happened since his death. You blame yourself because you were not there when he passed away; you were on the wards working with patients."

Raymond was taken aback with the last comments, he almost stumbled but he knew this was the truth. How could he know this – not even his wife knew that he blamed himself for not being there in the end, he idolized is dad, hung on his every word when he was a kid growing up.

"Doc, I am not trying to pull a fast one on you or a magician's trick by reading your thoughts – it's the truth and I want to help, I have to help or these will haunt my sleep. Doc, give me a chance, I am not mad, I promise you."

With that, he raised himself from the bed under protest from Ken and started to walk out of the room. He did not look at Raymond at all.

"Stop", when my father died I was working at Compton General. I was covering for another doctor and I could not pull out. My father was taken ill and was dying but I had to be somewhere else saving other patients. I could have saved my father, I could not say papa I love you and thank you for being there when I need you. I could not say Papa again or hold his warm hand or feel his breath on me."

Roger stopped, turned his head back towards Raymond who had his back towards him, he could feel every bit of his pain and it hurt so much.

"Doc, I am sorry, I had no idea this was going to happen and it was not my intention to come here and hurt you, but there is so much you don't know here, and most of it you would not believe if I told you." Raymond turned to face Roger, his eyes were red and his cheeks were wet, "my father was a good man and I don't understand what is happening here but you know things that are very close to me and your right I am sceptical but I will help you."

Robert Davies

Dr Garcia took the boys down the elevators to the administration offices; there was a specific room in the hospital that he wanted to take the boys. The room was located deep within the basement area of the hospital and it was only open to some hospital personnel, but Raymond had a pass, for he had worked hard enough to reach a senior position within.

As Raymond guided the boys to the basement, the temperature around them had significantly dropped. Raj felt it the most as they entered the basement area, the hairs on the back of his neck were all standing up and he could feel goose bumps all over his body. Someone or something was present here and they had been waiting. Raymond stopped as they approached a large heavy oak door with large round brass door handles. "Guys, this is the only original part of this building that still exists," he said, "what do you mean Doc?" asked Ken. "In the early 70's there was a fire, no one knows who started it but most of the old building was burned down and over 100 people lost their lives in the fire. This apparently is Robert Davies office and the fire fighters were amazed that the fire did not touch this part of the building, so they kept it.

"The building was rebuilt but they never forgot Mr Davies."

Raymond then drew out from his white coat a swipe card and ran that through a card reader that was located by the side of the door. There was a re-sounding click and the door opened. Raymond entered the room, followed by Ken but Roger for a minute just stood there, his feet would not move or listen to his commands.

The two other guys stopped and looked behind, "Roger what's wrong?" asked Ken concerned. Roger shook his head, "I don't know why but my legs won't move, just give me a minute."

They waited and then he tried again, this time he was able to move and he entered the room slowly. The lights had automatically come on when Raymond had swiped his security card. The room was huge – resembled more of a library than someone's office, there were rows upon rows of oak bookshelves crammed with books of all shapes and sizes. The most noticeable thing in the room was a huge period style globe set in a large wooden frame. Next to the globe was a magnificent veneered desk – everything in the room looked like it was period furniture and very beautiful, if not airy.

"Someone must clean this place regularly," said Ken, "there is no dust anywhere."

"The Governors do keep this clean because they get paid heavily by Mr Davies' relatives who carried on funding the hospital project after his death," replied Dr Garcia.

Raj looked around the room, there was definitely a presence in this room, and he could feel it. He walked over to the main desk area and then he stopped in his tracks. Sitting at the desk looking at some files sat a man. He was engrossed in looking at files in front of him and he did not seem to have noticed the visitors who had entered. Raj looked around to the other guys, they were still looking around the room, and they had not noticed the man sitting at the table. Raj looked back at the man; he was still engrossed in the files. The man like the woman that Roger had come across in the main hospital was dressed in a late 18th century to early 19th century suit. The man was in his late sixties but looked amazingly good shape.

"Young man you have been staring at me for the last five minutes and what are doing in my office at this late hour?"

To Roger's astonishment, the man looked straight at him, his steel grey eyes piercing him sharp daggers, but there was also kindness in his face.

"I am sorry I rudely entered your office sir," Roger replied, "but I needed to meet you and talk to you."

As he said this, his other two friends looked around and they understood what was happening, and so neither of them spoke, but quietly looked on.

"What is your name young man? And please come closer, I do not bite, you know. They may have locked me away in this office now that I am nearly seventy years old but I still have my senses," he laughed. Roger seemed to relax but he sensed that there was someone else in the room and that entity was not as kind.

"Come young lad, please come sit down, it has been such a long time since anyone has spoken to me," he smiled generously at Roger. Roger walked over and pulled the chair back from under the desk and seated himself down, "now what brings you hear to see me?" the man asked.

Roger looked nervous initially but then he spoke openly, "Mr Davies I was sent here to help you sir."

"Help me?" asked the man curiously, "Young man, I am more than capable of looking after myself," he replied.

"I know sir," replied Roger quickly, "but my boss thinks that it's time, he says that you were not to blame for happened so many years ago and it's time to move on and rest."

There was silence for a minute and then out of nowhere there was a loud shriek. As Roger looked around, standing ten yards away from him was the young woman he had met earlier. This time her eyes were on fire and in her hands were covered with blood.

"Don't believe him Husband, he has come to take

you away from me, I need you," she pleaded.

Mr Davies at this point stood up from his chair, "Hush, wife, I have been protecting you for eons and never have I asked you for anything, even though you in your madness would have killed our small children. I devoted my whole life to trying to figure out why you would do such a hideous act, so vile that I cannot live with myself at times, but still I have stayed here and protected you."

"No!" she screamed, "it was you who killed my babies, when I came home that day they were already dead." She now broke down and fell to her knees and sobbed, she looked up at him, "It was you who killed them.

"I still remember that fateful day, I had gone out with my sister into town to meet our mother and when I returned that afternoon the house was quiet. I thought the babies were asleep, they must have had a tiring day, but instead when I went to their bedrooms I found that their necks had been ripped open. There was blood everywhere, I slipped on the floor, and my clothes were covered with their blood. I shouted for you, Husband, but you did not come, and you know why - because you were in our bedroom with your slut, your mistress, after you had killed my babies. When you saw me there, you flew into a rage and knocked me out. The next thing I knew felt was a rope being tied around my neck and me sitting on one of your horses. You were standing there, Husband."

She stopped for a minute and looked at him ruefully speaking once again, "You were standing there next to the horse with that slut laughing at me.... and then there was blackness."

Roger was stunned, he felt like he had been hit by a sledge hammer, what he thought was the truth about this kind old man was a lie and the wife had been haunting him ever since.

"You do not scare me anymore, Husband," she said, climbing back on her feet and as she did her demeanour had changed, she was now dressed very smartly in a beautiful flowing dress.

"You don't scare me anymore, Husband," she said again, "because someone here believes me," and she pointed towards to Roger.

"I told you, Mr Davies," she said in a more polite tone that one day the grim reaper will come and today is the day."

She then looked at Roger, "I am sorry for earlier on, but it was the only way I could get you to stay." Roger smiled, "It's time, Laura for you to go."

She looked stunned, "you know my name?"

Roger was surprised that he did, but someone chuckled in his head. With that, she was gone only leaving the original actors in play. Mr Davies' persona on the other hand had changed; he no longer looked like a kind old man, but one full of rage and confusion.

"How dare you come into this hospital, which is mine?" he shouted.

"Is that why you burned it down all those years ago?" Roger retorted. "Yes, you Mr Davies, I know you were not around in your physical body but you were in mind, and overcame a helpless young boy to do the deed because you wanted a legacy and to bury the truth. You see, the reason I know this is because I am here to save that same little boy in this life because the boss feels that he has already paid the price too heavily. It is time to put right a wrong and unveil the truth behind the kind and generous Mr Robert Davies, and instead label him as the cold, calculating murdering heel he is."

With that, Roger turned to one side and behind him stood a man that everyone will see in some form, depending upon your creed, colour and religion and that was the grim reaper.

All the anger in Mr Davies just vanished, his face went paler than the white walls in the room and his eyes were transfixed in a death stare.

"NO!" he shouted and then his life force was sucked out of the room from where it stood and was no longer anymore. At the same time, the reaper had vanished leaving Roger and the guys alone.

Roger turned to face both Raymond and Ken, "It's finished," he said quietly, "there will be no more haunting or ghosts walking the halls."

"You knew all the time that Robert Davies was the real killer of his children?" asked Raymond.

"No," came the reply, "Like I said to you, Doc, there is a lot you don't understand here and it will take me too long to explain. All I knew when we originally felt the entity in the main hospital was something was wrong and someone was hurting. I did not know that everything was related to our quest but I should have guessed. You see, Doc, everything in our lives are interlinked with each other and we go through eons searching for the answers. Some of us," he continued, "are lucky and we find the answers quickly; however people like me and you we don't."

He walked over to the two men and placed his hand on the doctor's shoulder, "you too have to let go of your pain and there is someone here who wants to tell you something but first you must open your eyes to see," he said softly.

Stepping to one side standing behind him was a man that Raymond recognised straight away, his father. Tears streamed down his cheeks and he did not know where to look, Roger simply nodded and stretched his arm towards Raymond's dad and said, "Go, say goodbye."

Raymond looked up at Roger; he did not know what to say, because in front of him stood a man he had loved all his life and was his hero, Papa.

"Is this really him?" whimpered.

Roger simply nodded, "open your heart and eyes. Your father is here because he too has not moved on because you are still holding on; he will always be here doc, and you need to make your peace." Raymond smiled, nodded and walked towards his father.

Jose

The time spent in the basement stayed with Raj for a very long time, it was hitting him hard and his own emotions were everywhere. In his life, Raj had always worn his emotions on his sleeves and he was quick to react and could never play the game of keeping things close to his chest. This was in his working life and in his home life and it always got him into trouble.

Watching the doc bond with his father pulled at his heartstrings and he wished he could go back into time and space and do a few things differently to make his family proud of him and get a second chance. That's the real problem; we do not get a second chance. His thought pattern was disturbed by Ken nudging him in the stomach, "Hey, where are you?" he asked his friend gently. Roger turned to Ken and smiled, "Sorry buddy I was lost seeing the Doc and his father."

All three men left the basement together; no one spoke, too much had just happened to comprehend. Raymond had gathered himself up after the meeting with his Dad and he had been able to let go, his papa wanted him to be happy and that he was proud of him. He needed to rest but in his heart, he will still be there. The ambience in the hospital seemed different once they were back up in the main building, the black cloud and the suffocating sense had vanished, nurses and doctors were smiling, the ghost of the previous owner vanquished. Raymond smiled, he took a deep breath and another and for the first time it tasted nice.

Raymond led the boys up to the fourth floor of the building and the last private room on this floor. The first thing the boys noticed was the presence of armed guard outside of the room. This was very unusual but Raymond had told them that this was being funded by the Compton sheriff's office. The hospital had to agree or there would be problems and they would not be responsible if anything happened to the kid. In 2007, there were over five million cases in US of severely traumatised children. Almost fifty years on that figure has doubled and trebled. "It's normal and expected that most children will experience some symptoms of acute distress, like shock, crying, anger, confusion, fear, sadness and grief. In Jose we have seen all these symptoms and it's almost as if he has shut down said Raymond."

Before they reached the room, the Doc ushered the guys into an adjoining room. This was a therapist observation room. The Glass wall was the same type the police would use but much more sophisticated now. This Glass wall had built in optics that could monitor any changes to the boy's health.

"God," said Roger, "Science has really moved on – is this shit for real?"

Raymond smiled, "yes, this is for real and not out of the fifteen series of CSI."

Jose

Jose was in a world full of hurt, his physical scars had healed but the mental trauma that was still there had shattered him. He was confused, almost paralysed because the only functioning part of his body was his brain. Everything else seemed to freeze and not want to move or listen to commands that the brain was sending. The computer inside his head had broken down and the only messages being sent out were "I am hurt, I am scared and papa I need…"

The images of his parents had been flashing by on a daily basis, his father calling his name haunting his every breadth. His ma was crying, he could see her tears rolling down her soft weathered cheeks. He wanted to reach out but his arms would not move – "I am sorry," he said in his mind, "I need you."

Jose looked like a normal teenager on the outside, but when you looked at his open staring eyes, you knew there was something wrong.

Sleep came gradually for Jose but even when he slept, his brain was active, reminding him of the chain of events that had led him to that night. The nurses could hear him cry every night, sometimes uncontrollably, but they could nothing. Dreams and nightmares haunted his sleep every night and he constantly woke up and fell asleep. When he was awake, his active mind would ask questions but there were no replies, he was alone and he felt cold. He had been exposed to what children should never be, and then protected and comforted, but still his mind was experiencing those fears and that evilness. As Raj looked, he moved closer to the glass wall, he could feel Jose's pain; he could feel his emotion, as they were his own. There was a growing ache in the bottom of his stomach and he could not stop it but still he was drawn to him.

"Raj, I did not say this was going to be easy but if you believe in me then we can help him," said the voice inside his head.

Raj nodded, he urged every sense in his body to expel any signs of evil or despair; he had to be strong, not the old Raj that would start crying at the smallest of arguments.

He turned to Raymond and asked if he could go in the room with him, Raymond looked unsure at first but then he remembered what had happened in the basement and agreed.

"Roger, only five minutes – it's getting late now," he said whilst looking at his watch. Roger nodded and he followed one of the nurses that Raymond had had asked to show him into Jose's room.

From the observation room they watched Roger enter cautiously and then wait until the door closed behind him. Raj then very slowly inched closer to the bed and then sat down on the floor next to it. As Raj sat on the floor next to Jose's bed, he remembered sitting beside Joy's bed every night. Joy had not realised that his dad would sneak down to his room from the loft once he was asleep and simply observe his young son sleeping.

"Joy, I miss those days when I could do everything with you and there were no worries."

Looking at Jose now, it brought back sweet memories and tears to the eyes of Roger whose body Raj was in.

Jose at first did not notice the stranger coming into his room and did not react, but a split second later, he did, and instant fear set in and he started to pull himself away from the man. Almost a minute later fear had been overcome with fright and danger. Jose started to be agitated and then started to scream. He was standing up on his bed now, not tearing towards Roger but trying to push his fingers and nails into the wall. Roger reacted too and calmly moved away from the bed, his arms and hands were spread out in front of him aiming towards the floor as if to calm Jose but it was not working. "Hush Joy," he whispered, "Daddy's here and nothing is going to harm you."

What was he saying he thought and he shook his head and concentrated on Jose. The saner idea here would be to retreat out of the room and then gradually build up the trust and with slow movements, he retreated from the room.

Once back in the observation room he looked back through the glass, Jose and regained his composure and sat quite on corner of the bed.

"It's going to take some time, Roger, in getting

through to the kid, there are a lot of mental scars," said Raymond. Roger simply nodded and then indicated to Ken that they should leave and comeback tomorrow. As they turned to Raymond, he had ideas of his own and insisted that they come back to his home for a meal with his family.

"That's nice Doc, but we could not. Whoever is still after the kid will be looking in all corners, we cannot risk them finding you and harming you family." Raymond protested but Roger reassured that when everything was over they would have some drinks and talk in more detail.

Saying their goodbyes and telling Raymond that they would be back tomorrow the boys left the hospital and headed for home. Ken was driving the SUV home, while Roger sat back in the passenger's seat. A few minutes later Roger's cell phone started to ring, he did not recognise the number but he pressed the answer button. "Hello."

A woman answered back, "Roger its Kate."

Roger smiled for the first time, "Hey how are you? Sorry I had to rush off and leave you but there were things that I needed to do," he said and, "there's me thinking that you were not interested."

They both laughed and exchanged sweet small talk, and then Kate said that she really missed him.

"I know we only met that night but it left like that I have known you all my life, is that strange?"

He chuckled, and said that he felt the same. Inside Raj knew that this was Roger's conscience talking and he knew that his was another task that he would need to seal before he departed.

They talked for a long time while Ken drove home with a big smile of his face. It was good to see his friend smiling he thought. One hour later, they passed through the gates to the apartment and then parked up.

Behind them, the gate closed and they felt secure in their surroundings. The hassle over the last couple of weeks had been tiring and now they seemed like they that they were reaching their goal. As Roger got out of the car, things changed however. Three or four gunshots rang out and one of them hit Roger in the back, whilst the other two broke the car windows narrowly missing Ken.

The bullet that hit Roger was serious however, the pain was excruciating, he could feel the bullet tearing through muscle but the surprising thing was that it had missed the most important key areas. As he hit floor, Roger hit his head hard on the solid concrete and passed out. The shots had come from a gunman in a car that had been following the boys from the hospital and as soon as they had fired the shots, they sped away into the early evening.

While Ken was ducking behind the side of the SUV, he had not noticed Roger going down. Once he heard the car speed away, he lifted his head out and then he noticed the blood and as he walked around the other side of the car, he saw his friend. He was not moving, there was blood everywhere on his shirt and there was blood underneath his head.

"Roger!" he shouted and he quickly knelt down beside his friend. He panicked and was too scared to turn him around in case he made things worst. Suddenly standing up he fumbled into his pockets for his cell phone but his fingers would not type of the urgency number. In some way he did not have too, he could hear police sirens and as he looked towards the gates, a crowd had gathered.

He bent down to his friend again who had not moved, was he dead, he couldn't be they had come so far and in Ken's mind there were things he wanted to ask him. He went down with his hand to find a pulse in

Roger's neck and it was still there, but was very faint. "Hold on buddy, help is on the way, don't die on me I need you."

A minute later the gates behind opened and there were police officers everywhere, with them arrived the medics. The quickly rushed to aid Roger and they pushed Ken out of the way. They gently attended Roger, checking his vitals and then getting some fluids in him. They had to be careful picking him up because of the head wound, the medics were shouting instructions to the police about getting people out of the way, "this man is serious and losing blood."

When the shot hit Roger, his whole world turned upside down, he felt a sharp stabbing pain his back and then his legs crumbled beneath him. As he hit the floor, his forehead hit the concert floor hard and that's what knocked him out. Raj really did not know what was happening, part of him wanted to step out but he could not, he had become attached to Roger and he liked what he saw. The kid's mind was refreshing to listen to and clean of dire thoughts, he was always positive. Raj could hear words in his head saying be strong, I am here. Raj forced open Roger's eyes so he could see what was happening and gave the medics hope that he was still alive.

He could feel the drips they were putting in and running through Roger's veins.

"Hey Roger," he said, "We can't give up buddy. I won't on you..."

As Roger's eyes opened, Raj, kneeling beside Roger's body, could see Asha. She looked concerned and reached to touch his forehead. He smiled; this action confused the medics around him who had now gently lifted him up onto a stretcher and onto a waiting ambulance. Ken went with his friend and when he saw Roger open his eyes and smile, he knew what was happening but he was troubled about the shooting. Someone must have been following them and this was alarming news. What Ken did not know was that things were going to get even more hectic as the days go on.

The ride to the hospital was an arduous one, the pain from the bullet wound was burning into Roger's flesh, and the painkillers they had given had not kicked in yet. Strangely, Roger's eyes were transfixed towards a blank space next to him, it was Ash, and she had followed him into the ambulance and sat by his side. There was deep concern in her eyes but also so much love.

"I don't deserve this," he said in his mind, "but thank you for being here."

She shook her head gently, gosh, she looked beautiful he thought, "Why was I so stupid Ash?"

"Its life," she said, "you had other things on your mind, and your parents chose me because they knew my parents back home in India. Don't you remember that you always said that all you were ever looking for was love? I am not sure that was me, Raj."

"Ash, it was you," he replied, "It took me too long to recognise this, I was the one who made the mistakes, I know it takes two to tango but if I hadn't pushed things too far you would still be here with the kids. I don't think Sonya was ever the same, yes she was strong on the outside but inside I destroyed her, Ash, by taking you away."

Again, she shook her head, "no, Raj, we both did this, I never moved an inch when you needed me to, perhaps I did not support you when you needed me to," she replied. "We were both wrong Raj, I know you loved me in your own way, I know you cared, everyone knew it and I loved you too. You remember before we got married how we used to meet and once you did not like my new hairstyle, but I changed that for you, even though I looked like a drowned rat that day."

She could hear him chuckling, "Hey don't laugh, you know how long it took me to get those curls out of my hair? And now…" she laughed.

There was silence for a minute, "Hey, you look beautiful today," he said and then blinked in Roger's eyes.

She laughed, "Are you making a pass at me?"

At that moment, the ambulance came to a sudden stop and the doors came open, the paramedics then rushed Roger into the waiting ER team in Compton General. Over the next four hours, the doctors and nurses worked on Roger. Roger was lucky apparently that the bullet did not hit an important organ otherwise; he would not be here now.

Roger was rushed into surgery and Raj found that he was unable to step out of his hurting body. Raj also found that Asha had not left either, and she was standing in the operating theatre, watching the surgeons at work. Even though Roger's eyes were closed, Raj could see Asha standing there, with her hands held together in a prayer. There was love in her eyes, also concern, "What had he done to deserve this?" he thought.

"Boss, I need sometime so I can talk and make my peace because that's why she is not moving on with her life, either."

"Raj, I know you need to do this and you are right she has not moved on and I have tried. You both need to talk so go and I will look after Roger. By the way, Raj, I think you finally understand what is happening."

They say, love is made up of a number of emotions but no one could really define what it really means, Raj had always believed this and today as the surgeons operated on Roger and as he looked at Asha, he knew different. Love meant, passion, love meant affection;

love meant you were warm at night, and love meant you would never be alone or feel the cold. The meaning of love had stared him in the face and he had never recognised it until now. "Pleasures of the body were not love," he said, "but being beside you and feeling your hair against my skin and knowing you would be there is love."

The operation took over two hours and when the doctors were finished, they were happy that Roger would make it. Outside in the waiting room, Ken waited and there were two other people who were waiting with him. Police officer Reynolds and a beautiful young woman called Kate. Kate had found out that Roger had got shot through the news and she had rushed down to Compton General. Ken had identified her as a friend, so they let her in.

Officer Reynolds however had been asking a lot of questions that were not easy to answer but Ken made it through and explained to Oscar that they were not involved with gangs. Kate sat by herself on the far sofa in the waiting room; she had dropped everything to be here. Something was really strange, she thought, this guy whom she met in a night club had saved her life and made her feel safe in his strong arms, and was now fighting for his life. She was drawn to him and again she did not understand why this feeling was so strong, all she did know was that she had to be here when he woke up.

While Roger was recovering from the surgery, two lost souls walked in hand in hand along the hospital corridors towards the exit to the hospitals gardens.

"Was I really that bad to you?" Raj asked with his head bent downwards but still holding Ash's hand tight.

She turned to look at him as they walked and smiled and said "no, but ..." she stopped for a minute and then said, "Initially I knew who the real Raj was, but other days the real one didn't turn up. He was so engrossed in his own thing that I believed I was second best."

At that point, they walked through the doors that led to the hospital gardens outside and there, they sat down on one of garden benches.

It was a pleasant evening; there was not a cloud in the sky over Compton. Ash looked at Raj and continued, "you know when we got married I was so young, I had been working since I left school in a job that I really enjoyed. My parents used to say that I was their prize daughter because I had all the sense and could look after things, but I *'was'* happy Raj," she emphasised.

"You know our families knew each other and we attended the same functions and family events and in some way I knew our paths were linked."

Asha continued, "So it was not a surprise when marriage came up but now that I look at it perhaps it was too early for me. Raj, I gave you everything when we got together and when we got married. I accepted your family, I accepted who you were and initially things were great if not pressurised. Raj, I know I had my bad habits, we all do, and that is what makes us who we are. I could blame you for a lot of things but I won't because I know now that I was also to blame for not understanding what you needed and wanted. I took it for granted that we would grow to love each other without any complications or hang-ups but I was wrong. When the kids came, we were close and you were always there with me to bring them up. The girls worshipped you and still do, and Joy, well you spoiled him but he turned out to be a great kid. But I feel that somewhere along the line you were not there."

Raj felt it was his moment to speak, "Ash, I can truly, hand on heart can say that I loved you and the kids and I agree that I had a funny way of showing it. I could also sit here today and make a dozen excuses on what went wrong for us but I cannot because I need to be true to you. You are right, I was lost in my own little world and I used to jump out of reality and live a life that I thought would bring me only happiness at times and not share. You can call me selfish or someone who doesn't think of consequences, but as time went on, Ash, my life became a big lie. I would sit back on one side and give these great lectures to other people about how they should run their lives when on the other side I was throwing mine away."

He stopped for a minute to let his words sink in and then he continued, "You are right about me, you always were, and that I was spoilt by my parents. I always used them, and abused their kindness and love but in some way, that is how everyone in my family viewed me. Inside though,, Ash, there was this kid who was insecure about his own feelings, insecure about how to come out, insecure about life itself."

This time it was Ash's turn to squeeze his hand, she could feel his pain now and perhaps for the first time in over 50 years she could feel him.

"Ash I always loved you and everyone around us, I always wanted to be close to you and hold you and feel warm." He looked into her warm brown eyes, "I just didn't know how to show you Babes, I treated you sometimes like meat not as my soul mate. We developed this love-hate relationship because we could never talk. It was obvious that you lost your faith in me, you know what, so did I, and that's why I continued to fuck up. I was so caught up in my own self that I was lost, it was too hard to come out of it, and that's why I have not succeeded in any of my jobs. Ash there was never anyone else in my life – it was just you, my parents and our kids and me."

Tears were now flowing down his eyes but he didn't

break up for once and just looked straight at her. "I now realise how much I love you and all I have ever wanted for everyone is to be happy. There were times Ash I that wanted to kill myself and take the easy way out – but then I was a coward, who would look after the kids, what our families would say."

His head went down and he could not look at her, "Ash I cannot ask for your forgiveness because I don't deserve it and that's what I told my God every day of my very existence. It's really strange Ash, when I think about things are now, because everything is so clear, my judgement is not clouded but the only axe to grind is on me. I am being haunted by my own demons and these are the ones that I need to address."

He stood up and walked to a fence support that looked over the grounds of the garden, "You know I used to dream about retiring to a home in Malibu years ago," and then looking back her, "When we as a family were out here that was my dream come true."

Turning around to face her he smiled and continued, "I don't blame you for this – years ago I thought I did because I thought that you did not support me and that I lived in a dream world. You were right, I didn't realise that my own actions would haunt me or hurt me years later."

He smiled again and then walking towards her he seated himself down next her.

"It's so strange remembering these things now, I even remember listening to a Frank Sinatra song that went like this:

Call me irresponsible
Call me unreliable
Throw in undependable, too

do my foolish alibis bore you?

Well, I'm not too clever, I
Just adore you

So, call me unpredictable
Tell me I'm impractical
Rainbows, I'm inclined to pursue

Call me irresponsible
Yes, I'm unreliable
But it's undeniably true
That I'm irresponsibly mad for you

Do my foolish alibis bore you?
Girl, I'm not too clever, I
I just adore you

Call me unpredictable
Tell me that I'm so impractical
Rainbows, I'm inclined to pursue

Go ahead call me irresponsible
Yes, I'm unreliable
But it's undeniably true
I'm irresponsibly mad for you

You know it's true
Oh, baby it's true"

Bending his head he started to cry and whispered out,
"I have carried this all through my life Ash, I blame
myself for a lot of things and I used to put these down
to "Man Things" or you only live once what the hell,
but I never understood how my actions hurt other
people, especially the ones who I loved. Ash you know
I would never hurt anyone. The stupid thing about all
this is that I have always wanted to love but I never

understood. I never understood that loves means that you give yourself completely and unconditionally to someone, yes there is hurt but there is also is happiness. We all go through life, Ash, wondering if we did the right thing but we could never define what the right thing is and I never understood. Even when we had the kids – I loved them with all my heart and I would die for each one everyday but that's the closest time I ever came to unconditional love."

"Why didn't you tell me this?" she said softly.

He looked up, "How could I? When I looked at you I could feel the bond between us, but there was always a wall of mistrust, which I had built. I just couldn't because you would have never understood and would think that I was being a big baby."

"Was I really like that?" she said coolly. He smiled now through his tears and simply nodded. With that, he pulled her forward into an embrace, clinching her tightly so he would never let go.

They talked through the rest of the evening into the early hours of the morning and for once, it was civil. They walked back together through the ward towards where Roger was and once there, they turned to face each other. Holding both her hands, he smiled and leaned forward and kissed her cheek and smiled at her.

"It's time Ash, I have to let you go, but we will meet again in another life. First you go. Hey, look they are waiting for you," as he pointed towards the corridor behind her. As she looked, she saw a bright light consuming the corridor and coming towards her. As it reached her the light stopped and from it emerged someone Ash knew, it was her father.

He smiled at her, he looked so young she thought and immediately hugged him.

"Dad…" she whimpered.

"Yes," he nodded.

She then looked back towards Raj, he was also smiling and there were tears as well. She walked over to him and gently wiped away the tears from his cheeks and kissed him.

"This is not goodbye, Raj," she whispered.

"I know," he said quietly.

As she pulled away she touched his chest and said, "I forgive you," he smiled and with that she was gone, leaving him alone once again.

Sitting in the waiting room Ken stood apart from all the others, he couldn't bear to think that he would lose his friend now after all they had been through. He looked up towards the ceiling and whispered a silent prayer to anyone that was listening. To Ken the last couple of months had been a rollercoaster of a ride and it was hard to comprehend what they were going through and how much of their lives had changed.

He remembered when they were growing up – they did everything together and got into some hot water. When you are young that sort of shit happens, he smiled now and his thoughts turned back in time when they received their black belts. They both had worked so hard and they were recognised to be one of the most talented martial artists in LA. Their Karate Master took most of the credit; he had spent the majority of his life in the army and had been based in south Asia for most of that time. He had been based in Korea and a place called Camp Castle. It was there he had perfected his skills in the martial arts and earned the highest rankings outside of Japan." Martial arts have been practiced in Korea for more than two thousand years but little is known about the country's early fighting methods." Japanese martial arts like judo, karate and kendo were introduced to Korea during the occupation or brought by Koreans who had studied in Japan. Native Korean martial arts were banned but survived through

222

underground teaching and folk custom. After the occupation, ancient books like the Muyedobotongji became popular study material for Korean martial artists, and influenced the development of many modern Korean fighting styles.

Ken remembered his master telling them that Karate would give them belief within themselves and if they learned properly, they could control their mind and actions. Ken remembered that they would be at the dojo every day after school, sometimes practising and sometimes watching the other students. Their master was also keen that the students observed their peers in action and learn from them. The day came when the boys were going for their black belts, the dojo had been cleaned out properly the night before and everything was in place in the morning. Master Roberts followed everything by the book, his army teachings were ingrained in his head and this came across so strongly. On the morning of the testing Master Roberts had five students going for their first degree black belts and he had a further five today going for their brown belts. The younger kids had already gone through their tests and grading days. Today was special –the dojo had being open for nearly 20 years and some of the highest-ranking masters were coming today to watch the grading. Sensei Roberts had great hopes for Ken and Roger who were his prize students. The US Olympic team manager was here today as well to add some pressure.

Ken was lost in his thoughts, nothing around him mattered and he drifted back to that grading day. It was the only time that his parents had been out together to see him and he was eager to impress. Sensei would say to the boys, "it's not about showing off out there, but about how you have mastered the basics and principles.

"Before you go out on the grading floor, I want you

to follow my art of mediation and condition your mind and focus. You should feel this seeping through every bit of your body, then open your eyes and come out."

They both then bowed to their sensei and walked off to prepare. Master Roberts watched them go, as it had been a long time since he had felt like this. Over the last six months, he had pushed both boys hard in their preparations of the exam to come. It was important that both Ken and Roger were ready and were disciplined enough in their studies. They had been coming to his dojo for more than six years now and had worked hard. He bowed his head to the dojo and walked off to finish his own preparations.

Ken looked up from his thoughts because he thought he heard something, but it was nothing a nurse had dropped some papers and a police officer was helping her picking them up. As he looked around Kate was sitting down on the furthest sofa, she was reading a paper but her eyes were elsewhere.

As he looked around further, he had noticed that Dr Garcia had arrived and he was busy talking to some of the medical staff. The doc was a good man he thought.

Drifting back in his thoughts both him and Roger walked out to the competition dojo floor. They had to wait a little because the lower belt students had been going through their first stages of their exams. Once they were over, Roger and Ken had been called up. Even though both boys had gone through their meditation warm up and focused their minds on the task at hand, they were nervous. The ambience in the Dojo was electric; they could feel the tension, excitement and other feelings of elation and expectations. They could see seated in front of them the special VIP guests and the examiners. Master Roberts had invited some people over from Korea to the event; there were invitees to the head of the Karate US

Olympic team who was an old army friend and some local government officials from Compton.

The boys bowed to the examiners, VIPs and their sensei. They were then requested in Japanese to take up their stance for the first part of exam. The test started with the basics (Kihon), this was to demonstrate some basic techniques of Kata and to do them correctly. The boys excelled. Their movements were crisp and precise, and their eyes were focused. The initial nervousness now was gone and replaced by positive energy that just simply oozed from all their movements. It was like watching two synchronised swimmers performing. Every movement that they were asked to perform was effortlessly done, their kicks, punches and blocks were crisp. The years of practice was now coming to fruition in from of their peers. After fifteen minutes, the guys were asked to sit down and take a rest, while the lesser belts now commenced their second stage tests.

The second stage of the exam was called Sanbon Kata (three point fighting).This is the first kind of fighting the young students learn and it involves the attacker making three attacks forward and the defender blocking three times and then counter attacking. When each attack took place, the attacker would announce his attack so the defender knew how to block correctly. The points are awarded if you have used the correct movements properly and well. You would be asked to team up with a partner and then demonstrate strong technique and discipline. The partner was usually another brown belt partner but in this event Sensei Roberts and asked another couple of second-degree black belts to partner up with both Roger and Ken. This added extra pressure on the boys and they knew they had to be strong here.

Again, both Ken and Roger walked through the second phase without drawing too much energy. Their kicks and punches were precise and their blocks were accurate. At no stage of the test did the boys feel fazed by their experienced attackers. Instead, their movements were graceful, quick and effective.

Once this part of the exam was over, they were again allowed to rest whilst the judges conferred. Throughout the event, the boys did not talk and were totally immersed within themselves in concentration. The next part of the exam was the free sparring stage but this would be different from most Karate schools – this would be full contact sparring so the boys would need to wear special head guards and chest guards. Their opponents this time would be first-degree Dan holders. The scoring for the free sparring would be normal traditional tournament scoring; this meant that points were awarded for kicks to the head, to the body and hand techniques. There were also points awarded for sweeps.

First up for his bout was Roger, he was going to spar with a first degree Dan student who stood just over 6FT tall. He was one of the fastest martial artists in the Dojo. Roger got up, Ken remembered without any fear or trepidation, put in his teeth guards and walked onto the competition floor. He then turned to face his sensei and bowed with respect and then to the examiners and VIP's. He then faced his opponent, tapped on his hands and bowed but always keeping his eyes on his opponent. The referee started the bout and immediately Roger took his usual South Pole stance and watched his opponent carefully, who also mirrored Roger's action but he was a little bit more nervous. This young man in front of him was doing nothing and just looking at him, this annoyed him, and he made the first fatal error and pushed forward.

Roger's actions were fast and crisp; as his opponent attacked so did Roger with a front kick to his opponent's mid rib. The kick was sharp and his opponent felt it and fell to his knees. The referees announced the first point of the match. The atmosphere in the dojo was tense; even the young students who were invited on this day were quiet. Ken watched his friend; he could see the concentration in his eyes but also the confidence in his actions. The two opponents bowed again in front of each other, the next point were crucial to the match. This time the men circled each other, Roger's opponent had regained his composure and was thrusting a few attacks forward, which Roger blocked and dodged easily.

Then it happened in a split second, the man pushed forward again with a round house kick to Roger's head, Roger side-stepped and then proceeded to sweep the other leg and dropped the other man to the mat and quickly followed this up with a vicious arm blow to the chest. The men regained their feet, Roger still in total concentration mode, his opponent however was totally broken to be on the losing side – he knew what was coming. The main referrer conferred with the examiners and then walked over to Roger and shouted out "Ippon" and raised Roger's hand. Roger bowed to the examiners and then to his opponent and shook his hand.

Ken smiled, thinking about the event now, as he stood in the waiting room, they were both so proud of what they achieved for their master. A couple of years later both him and Roger were chosen for the All American team trials, which were held in New York. They won those in style and they were chosen to represent US in the Olympics to be held in Tokyo, Japan.

Ken smiled, thinking about the past, Roger had always been part of his life and he could not lose him now. As he looked up he saw someone else walking into the waiting area of the ward, it was Johnny and his grandfather. They saw him and walked over towards him, their faces were filled with concern. It was Johnny's grandfather who greeted him first; the old man's face showed natural concern as he took hold of Ken's hand.

"What happened?" he said and with that, Ken narrated what had occurred a while ago. Both men listened intently and asked many questions, Ken took it in his stride and told them not worry – Roger was going to pull through.

Johnny's grandfather nodded, "I agree he will pull through; there is something about that young-man."Just then the doctor appeared.

Ken excused himself from the Rajas and greeted the doc who was looking after Roger. The doctor looked tired but relieved – he said, "Roger came through the surgery well and they had removed the bullets."

"The bullets?" Ken asked.

"I thought Roger was hit only once," the doctor shook his head.

"No, he was hit twice and he was lucky that the second bullet did not hit a vital organ."

The doctor then explained that Roger was sleeping at the moment and needed to rest. They could talk to him tomorrow morning and with that, he left them alone.

Raj found himself drifting back into Roger's body after his meeting with Ash. The boss had told him that she was now on her way and that this was meant to be.

"Roger now needs you Raj so be strong."

Raj agreed and his soul once again drifted back into Roger. Instantly Raj could feel the body's pain and so he started to fight and think about positive thoughts. As he did so, he could feel a warm glow spreading out from his soul and into every blood flowing vein in

Roger's body. Soon the whole of Roger's body was glowing like a white candle, Raj was thinking positively and he was channelling everything he could must into healing Roger's wounded body. Raj felt good, for once, there was no self-pity or remorse and that was replaced by happiness, strength and well-being. "We will win buddy," he said; "and my boss will deliver us from evil, I believe now and I need your help for a little while longer, so stay with me." Roger's soul may have been sitting elsewhere but his body still retained his conscience and his brain.

As the early morning sun broke over Compton, the first rays of light hit Roger's face through the large Hospitals windows. The sun felt warm and offered him hope as he lay there with eyes wide open. He had been awake now for over two hours now and he felt no pain; either the pain killers were very strong or something else had healed his body. Raj could feel Roger's sub conscience asking him questions even though he was not here but somewhere else. Raj could only give him a few answers; "but in the end, my friend, things will be set right and you will be back here and I am not going to let anything happen to you."

"Hey you're helping me remember all those good looks, martial art expertise and look; I even hooked you up with a drop-dead gorgeous woman."

For once Raj felt at ease with his own pain. He remembered what Ash had told him before she left and it was true. She had said, "Life is too short to wake up with regrets. So love the people who treat you right and love you. Love the ones who don't just because you can. Believe everything happens for a reason and if you get a second chance grab it with both hands. If it changes your life, let it. Forgive quickly, my Husband; God never said life would be easy. He just promised it would be worth it."

When he thought of that and last night's miracle he smiled inside – "Roger," he said, "everything is going to be alright."

Ash was right and this is the message that the boss was trying to tell him all the time but he had not listened and now he understood what it meant.

"Ash, I love you with all my heart and life is too short and you should enjoy every waking day and be true to yourself. Hey boss, I think I am finally getting this," he thought. Raj could swear he could hear someone chuckling in the back of his head. Getting back to reality, Raj had to start to think positively now and quickly because Roger's body had to heal quickly. "Boss, I need you for this," he said.

"No you don't, Raj," came the reply, "you have the power, reach for your heart."

Outside in the waiting room no one had gone home, they all waited silently until they were given the green light to see Roger. Ken had now sat down with Raymond and asked how the kid was doing.

"No change," came the reply from Raymond; "he still just sits there in his room on his bed. It's almost like he is in a trance and his world has stopped, the nurses say at night time they hear him talking to himself and then he would start to cry and then sleep a little. The sedatives that we are giving him are not working so I have advised the nurses not to give him anymore. "

Suddenly the door to Roger's room opened and Roger stood in the doorway, in his blood-coated civvies; everyone was surprised and shocked to see him, how could this be?

He had just come out of a serious operation, he should be in his hospital bed recovering from serious gunshot wounds, and there would be no way that he could be walking – impossible. Roger was taken aback when he saw how many people were waiting for him and he felt a bit embarrassed.

"Hey guys," he said weepily at which point the nurses and doctors converged on him with concern and ushered him back into the room and onto the bed.

Over the next fifteen minutes, the doctors and nurses checked him over and they were astounded that all his wounds had healed completely and there were no marks. They could not understand this - how could this be he had just been in an operating theatre for the last four hours?

Eventually they had to give in and let him be. As soon as they did the waiting friends came into his room, all but Ken and Raymond were astounded by his instant recovery. Roger winked at Ken and said, "I am still here buddy." Ken smiled in acknowledgement

In addition, there to see him were Johnny and his grandfather who was especially happy. There was some deeper connection; Johnny's grandfather understood this. His Indian upbringing told him that this man was connected to them in some way and Raj knew he knew.

Next to meet him was Kate, Roger looked embarrassed as Kate flung her arms around him.

"You scared me," she whispered in his ear as she held onto him.

Raj chuckled and said, "Hold her you fool! this is what love is and she loves you," and Roger smiled and for a minute he also put his arms around her and held her. Roger's soul might be elsewhere but his subconscious was still inside his body and Raj felt a connection to Roger and he liked it.

The next hour drifted by slowly; everyone was asking so many questions that Roger could not answer and it was up to Ken to step in and help his friend. They had all moved into one of the bigger private counselling rooms where they could talk. Ken had now stood up

231

because questions were flying, which Roger could not really answer at this moment in time.

"Look guys, can I get your attention please?" Ken said loudly.

Everyone looked towards him and his or her faces showed confusion.

"Look guys, I know you have questions and I know there are things here that no one understands. At this moment, we cannot give you all the answers but what I can say is please trust us, there are things here that even we do not understand. Look guys, today has been a really harsh day and seeing Rog walk out of his room with no scars from his wounds has even surprised me but now I know that there are other powers helping us and driving us at the moment. All our lives in this room have been affected but for the better and we all know this."

At this point Roger stood up, "What Ken is trying to say is, guys, there is another force working here and you have to trust us. What I can tell you is that this force is on a mission and on the way we are fixing lives and in some way it is a personal journey of redemption."

He paused for a minute and then looked around the room, Raj through Roger's eyes could see how many lives he had affected and it hit him. The boss was right all our lives were intertwined together and our souls just moved on. He looked at each face and it told a different story, but it showed so much love. He smiled, perhaps what I am doing is right, perhaps I am on the right road and I cannot let these guys down.

As Roger sat back down, Kate squeezed his hand as she sat next to him and smiled and whispered, "I love you." Roger looked up and there were tears in his eyes that trickled down his cheeks. "Raj, what do I do?" he asked.

"Grab it with both hands and never let go and when this is all over and I am gone you both will enjoy your lives together. When love hits you my friend never let it go and Kate is the one, trust me I know. By the way she is blonde, 5ft 10, great figure…"

"I get the picture, Roger," said in his mind laughing.

For the first time after a long time Raj also laughed, "I am glad some things in life have not changed."

There were questions for the rest of the night and Roger and Ken knew that they would not be able to get away. One person who had stayed quiet until the end was Oscar. Once the friends had all gone, Oscar approached the guys, he had been listening carefully to their explanations and story, which he knew, held a lot of gaps.

"Guys, we need to talk so I suggest we sit down before you go anywhere also I cannot risk you guys going back to your apartment. Whoever came after you earlier, will try again?"

The boys acknowledged Oscar's request and sat down on the sofas.

"What's on your mind Oscar?" asked Roger.

Oscar smiled before he responded. "I think you know what's on my mind, first of all I have a dead cop who asks me to look after you guys before he is shot and then I have another shooting that does not make, sense, especially in the terms that you use to explain them, Sir."

Oscar pointed at Roger, "not only he gets shot but then walks away…" He stopped, as he did not know what to say.

"Look Guys, I do not know what is going on here but I know I need to get involved because otherwise someone else will come and this time finish the job. So start by telling me the truth, I can take it," he said.

Roger stood up, walked over the large window of

his hospital room and looked out into the darkness.

"I don't know how I can explain to you what is happening because; even for me it has been a lot to absorb. My whole life has been turned upside down and I am fighting with my own emotions but also sharing someone else's. I know you won't understand this because it is a long story and I am not sure how bellevable this is, but it is the truth." Turning around to face Oscar and then took a deep breath and narrated the story.

"Oscar, when I sleep my dreams are filled with someone else's dreams and that's because my soul is sitting some were else and Raj's soul is within me. Raj has all my knowledge and my sub conscience is still partially here but Raj is leading me. I trust him Oscar because there is a higher authority at work here and we are all on a road of leaning and healing. The reason you are drawn to us is because you know what it is like to lose someone close to you. Raj feels your hurt and he knows that you have never let go and it is time to let go because it will kill you. Your sisters need you to move on and your mum wants your forgiveness. It was not easy for her Oscar – she tried hard but once you are addicted it is so hard buddy, and now she is remorseful because she feels that she has damaged you. She needs your forgiveness, because she cannot move on."

Roger walked over towards to Oscar and placed his hands on his broad shoulders, Oscar looked up he and he was overwhelmed with emotions.

"I used to sit in my room when was I little and I cried myself to sleep when my young sisters were asleep. I wished my mum would come up and read me a book like my friends used to tell me their mums did.

"The only comfort I have ever got was from the gang bangers that I got mixed up with – I hated myself but I got drawn into the culture and did shit that I really hated. Then one day it all changed, my sisters were walking home and they were shot in a roadside shooting. The boy who shot them from a moving car was only ten years old.

"My mom blamed me for their deaths because I was part of a gang, but it wasn't my fault. I had left the gang; I didn't want to be part of it in the first place." He stopped and looked town and there were tears rolling down his cheeks. I loved my mom and when the girls were killed I was broken and it took me over twenty years to recover and when my son was born I swore he would never get mixed up with the gangs."

He sobbed and his head fell onto Roger's shoulders and Raj could feel the pain so badly in his chest. "It's time to move forward, Oscar, and there are some people here who want to help you." Oscar looked up, "or should I say something," made him look behind him.

Standing feet away from him were Oscar's mum and two young sisters. Oscar could not believe his eyes, they looked so beautiful and they were smiling at him. For a big beefy man Oscar was reduced to a dwarf and grief and happiness overwhelmed him. He looked towards Roger, "is this real?" he asked and Roger simply nodded. Looking back towards is family he slowly walked forward, first the girls met him. They flung their arms around their big brother and hugged him. He could feel a surge of warm energy flowing through their bodies into him, soothing his weary bones and healing his wounded heart.

"I am so sorry," he said to them, "it was my fault that I was not there."

"Yes, you were big brother," replied one of his sisters.

As Raj watched on, his own heart strings were being pulled, he could remember having fights with his sisters

235

and then blaming himself for them. He was always a soft target but he took it and then moved on, he knew the big man was watching him.

Oscar's mum stepped forward, "I am sorry my son," she whispered, "I let you down, I was not strong enough Oscar but you have to be now. I have a lovely grandson who needs you to stay alive."

Oscar looked astonished, "you never met your grandson."

"Oh I have," she replied.

"Children are very receptive to seeing things when they are young and we had a chat."

She smiled, "forgive me, my son for not being there but I am here now."

She put her arms around him and held him for several minutes as he sobbed and said, "Mom I love you and that's all I ever wanted."

"I know," she whispered, "I know."

As he pulled away from her arms, she said that they had to go but one day they would meet again.

"Mom…" he wailed.

She smiled and shook her head, "bye son."

For a big man tears rolled down his cheeks, but they were tears of joy and happiness rather than sorrow. He turned around to Roger and Ken. "That was real, wasn't it?" he asked. Roger nodded.

For a minute or two, no one spoke and it gave Oscar enough time to recover his composure.

"Oscar, we have gone too far now," said Roger and "I need to find the boy, it's important that you trust us on this."

Oscar looked up, his demeanour towards the boys had softened and he nodded. "Are you okay and well enough, Roger?"

"Yes," came the reply, "Gather you stuff and meet me downstairs and make sure you don't attract attention. Whoever took the pot shots at you will be waiting."

With that, he left the room, leaving the boys alone again.

Whilst Roger got his stuff ready, Ken popped out of the room for a couple of minutes. When he came back, he held in his hands a white plastic bag. He emptied the contents out on the hospital bed. The bag contained two green surgeon outfits – he had nicked them from a trolley outside the surgery theatres. Roger smiled, and both guys slipped on the clothes and got ready to leave the room and head down. They slipped out of the room without much notice, for some reason there was no police guard outside of the room. Oscar thought Roger must have arranged it; quickly the boys rushed down the main ward and towards the stairs. It would be too dangerous to wait for the elevators to come up. Once they were in the stairwell, they silently and quickly went down the stairs to the ground floor.

Once there Ken put his head out first to check the way, it was relatively clear and he urged his friend to follow. Reaching the exit they noticed a car waiting outside the entrance, Oscar was in the driving seat.

Once in the car Oscar quietly moved away without drawing any attention, well that's what they thought. As Oscar pulled away, another car followed them from a distance.

As the car pulled away, Raj looked back at the hospital through Roger's eyes, he could hear voices asking him questions in his minds and he could visualize faces but he had no time to help them. The voice inside is head told him not to worry, they will understand but that didn't help because Raj had always been too sensitive. He would cry at the smallest thing but he never turned anyone away from help. This was hard for him but he understood that he had a job to do now. He once remembered reading his hand online and on a YouTube demo. The lady in the demo quoted that everyone had a guardian angel he hoped now that there were a few now in the hospital watching over the distressed souls. It was strange remembering this now, but there is a purpose in life; the only thing is that we have to find out.

His thought pattern was cut short by Oscar asking him where they were going. Roger turned and replied Trees cape. Oscar nodded and he eased the car out of the hospital grounds. The drive to Trees cape was uneventful; no one had spoken since leaving the hospital. They were all lost in their own thoughts. For Roger it was now simple, he had to get to Jose and nothing else at this time mattered a lot to him. Was he Jose's guardian angel? Perhaps but something was drawing him to the boy now.

"Hey guys," called out Ken from the back, "there's a black sedan following us – it seemed to pull out the same time as we did."

"I noticed," said Oscar. He then turned to Roger, "open the glove compartment please and take out the gun."

Roger opened the glove box and he instantly saw the colt 45. He reached for and drew it out in front of him. Oscar looked towards him, "you know how to use it?"

Roger replied "yes."

In an instant, Oscar rammed his foot down on the accelerator of the car and the big V8 of his Mustang came to life and leaped forward like a sleeping panther. The growl of the well-tuned engine roared as Oscar pushed harder.

Meanwhile the Sedan kept pace as they weaved in and out, meandering around the slow moving cars in front of them.

"Oscar, when you get the chance pull over somewhere and let me out; carry onto Trees Cape and I will meet you there."

"Are you crazy?" came the reply from Ken in the back seat to his friend, "No buddy."

Roger looked back at him.

Their eyes met for a minute and Ken understood. To Raj's surprise, Oscar did not question the request and with his eyes focused in front, he weaved the mustang in and out of traffic. Suddenly he swung the car into a sharp left, he was too quick for the sedan because it shot by and was totally caught by surprise. Meanwhile Roger pushed the gun into his coat pocket and as the car came to a stop, he bailed out and Oscar sped away.

"Raj what are you doing?" he asked himself.

"I know," he answered himself back, "I know."

"Raj this is dangerous," came the voice inside his head.

"I know boss, but I have to get to the serpent's head before I can save the boy."

"You know who is leading the serpent, Raj?"

"I know boss, that's why I am doing this. Like you said, I am facing my demons now head on, let him know that I am coming."

With that Roger pulled up the zip of his jacket and walked out the alley way. He had lost track of the time and day, but he was focused on the task ahead. As he reached the main road, he stopped and reached for his cell phone from his pocket. A new generation android phone that had GPS built into it. He touched the screen and the phone jumped to life. The first thing he noticed was the time, it was nearly 2.00am in the morning and LA was still buzzing with life. Second thing he noticed and this hit him hard was the date, the 26th June.

Raj stopped for a minute, today was his birthday, if

he was alive today his kids would be calling him to wish him happy birthday – however this was a different life and he had no time to waste, the end game was near.

He then flicked through the icons that led him to the built in GPS system and got his bearings. He knew that he was not that far from the hospital, and so realised he was in downtown Compton. His objective was to find out where the homeboys' territory was, because there he would find the head of the snake. He quickly flicked the icon to the web explorer and then on the search engine. After a few minutes, he found what he was looking for – south Compton. Putting the phone away, he looked up the road for a night cab.

He started to walk further up the main road passing some shops on a small parade. Most of the shops were boarded up bar one, where he stopped. It was a Japanese gift/ food store, but they had a lot of other things like small ornaments and others. The thing that caught his eye was a sword – it looked like one of those ornamental samurai swords you would see in someone's house but this one called out to him. In the small amount of light on the road he could make out the bright red scabbard it was sheathed in. There was ornamental writing running down it, which he found he could read. The words read "little Tiger we love you" The handle looked like it was made of white whale bone; it too was carved all the way through it. This was no ordinary sword; visions flashed through Raj's minds of battles of old, a young boy covered in blood but standing proud.

He looked around – things were quiet so he quickly steered towards the doorway of the store – he pushed at the handle to gauge the weight and lock strength. To his surprise, the door was not too heavily locked. One big push he thought, it would open, and that's what he did.

The door gave way and he fell through the door with a thud. He waited for the alarm to go off but nothing happened. Getting to his feet, he closed the door and then edged towards where he saw the sword. There was some light coming through the window from the outside streetlights and that was enough for him. He was completely focused on holding that sword – it was calling to him now in his head. With a few more silent steps, he reached for the sword with his stretched hand. As he grasped the handle something happened, he found himself falling into darkness, he could not feel his feet as he fell. The air around him grew foul as he fell and soon he landed with a thud on his bum. As he cleared his eyes he found himself sitting in the middle of a large arena, he had been here before and the boss had given him strengthen to overcome Satan.

As his eyes became accustomed to the light, he could hear the cheering and roaring of a large bloodthirsty audience. He then looked at himself, his complete physique and outfit had changed, and there was no longer the body of Roger or Raj but that of a young Japanese youth. He was dressed in what could only be described as a white ninja style suit and he had red chest armour. On the armour was a crest and that was of a tiger. With further inspection, the young man looked and felt tired and there were many bruises on his body, including cuts from swords across his left arm.

He noticed hanging from his waist/hip were two swords, a small short kaftan and then the sword that he recognised as the one in the Japanese store. Looking around the arena, he could now understand why he smelt the horrible smell, because they came upon the corpses of dead warriors, children and animals. It was a blood bath, and the sight revolted him. Standing to his left stood another man, dressed similarly, with, his hair tied back in a long ponytail and holding a long wooden staff. The man looked at him and Raj could feel his pain and anguish. There was blood dripping from small cuts on his arms but he held firm. He nodded at Raj and then looked forward.

To Raj's right there stood another man, this one was stockier in build and his expression was stern. This man had seen some wars and he bet he had won some. He also looked sideways at Raj and said

"Hiruko, are you ready?"

Raj nodded, smiled, and then looked forward.

"Where am I, boss?" he whispered.

"You are in Japan, 250 B.C. my son, and in an earlier incarnation of yourself. A young lad called Hiruko – his parents were killed at an early age and he was brought up in a very old Japanese temple. The monks of this temple were famous for their fighting prowess but also known to be very gentle and wise. Hiruko was saved by the head of order when he was visiting his parents' village as they were being slaughtered by a gang of men from a local warlord."

"Hiruko always vowed one day he would avenge his parents' death, but he was also a very gentle boy, he loved nature, he had a pure heart and he longed to belong. Then one day the temple was attacked by the same warlord and his old master was killed trying to save him. Hiruko and some of the other monks were rounded up and brought to the arena of death and this is where he faced his final moments."

"Why show this to me now boss?"

"Because I want you to understand that your lives in every re-incarnation are intertwined and you have always been working for me. Every strand of your DNA, Raj, I have made and so I understand you very well. I know what makes you tick, Raj and I know you are my follower. Sometimes we fall out like good

242

friends do, but you will always come back to me."

"Let go, Raj and feel Hiruko's heart and be one with this pure soul."

Raj looked out into the bloody arena through Hiruko's eyes, there were tears of sadness but also great strengthen within the boy. Yes, he was still a young lad and he had matured fast under the monks. His master called him his little tiger cub because he was always inquisitive and getting into trouble with the other teachers.

That boy they said, he is the bane of our lives, but they did not mean this, because Hiruko was of pure heart and mind, he loved being around children and he was always seen as a guardian figure to the younger ones.

As Raj looked up, he saw sitting on a throne a man dressed in the finest silks that the ancient world could provide. There was something odd about him because he did not fit the time. Everything Raj had read about Japanese history because he had always been a fan of Japanese fighting skills, especially the handling of the kaftan. He remembered he had bought a Kaftan years ago from a mail order company for a company party – the event was fancy dress and Raj went as an Asian Raja.

The man on the throne now stood up, he was tall and lean but his facial features were hidden by a large hood on a flowing red cloak. In his hand, he held a wicked looking staff with a pointed metal spike at the end. Raising the staff he banged it hard on the floor three times to grab everyone attention. There was hush silence in the arena, faces from all shapes and sizes had turned their attention towards him.

"My People..." he addressed, "Today you have seen my enemies put to the sword in the arena for your sport. I have been very lenient towards these menaces but now I will finish this quickly. Bring out my finest warriors and bring me the head of that young man to me. I also want his heart, still warm from his chest in my hands!" he cried.

He had been pointing towards Hiruko who in turn just stood and listened – he did not seem fazced by this man at all. He was resigned to the fact that today was a good day to die and so he said a silent prayer. Raj knew who the man was, it was obvious that it was Mr Horn himself and it was time to do battle again.

Hiruko turned first to his left and then to his right and addressed both men. "Masters it is not your time to die; please stand down and let me face these demons alone." The two men smiled and did not move away from him and instead raised their arms for the coming fight, "With Honour we serve," they said, "and with honour we die in battle, we are not your masters, young one; you are the master. You have always been the one – but no one told you – not even your master before he was killed."

Tears trickled down the young man's cheeks but he dare not show any weakness even though his legs felt heavy.

Suddenly there was a crunching of metal and as they all looked forward, they could see ten or twelve very heavily armoured men coming towards them. They were circling the three friends with assorted arms, drawn to strike. Hiruko, like a Cheshire cat, sprung to his feet, he placed one hand on the hilt of the kaftan in a drawing position and waited. All three men waited patiently in there fighting stances, each man in his own style. The Man with the wooden pole stood with his red leg slight spread out and left leg back. The pole was pointed downwards the length extended to the ground and waiting. The stocky man also stood quietly, his left hand gripped his long kaftan on the side of his hip, legs closed and right hand poised to draw. The movements would be so quick that the battle would be over in minutes. Their art was refined to the T.

Hiruko also waited, he had moved his own sword to the side, it felt warm to the touch and he was ready. His master had presented him with the bone-handled sword when he became the youngest master and he was very proud of this. His master had also told him that his late father had been his village sword maker and this was one of his weapons. Now it was his son's. As the assailants drew near, the three masters did not move, which was very disconcerting for the men coming to attack them.

Without warning and with movements so fast the three men struck in tandem. The ten / twelve men around them stood no chance and the fight was over in seconds. All that was heard in the battle was the cries of the victims and the Whish of the swords. Hiruko, however had not stopped moving, there was surprise in his attack as he moved gracefully through his opponents. His eyes were homed upon his victim, that was the man on the throne, and as he sliced through his last assailant, he also threw in succession and with deadly accuracy shurikens (Japanese Throwing Stars). The shurikens that Hiruko threw were six sided chromo stars laced with a high toxin that would insure a quick death in reality he hated using these things but his master had always said know your opponent. His aim was perfect and with extra strength coming from Raj his speed was phenomenal.

The man sitting on the throne pedestal did not see this coming, three six sided stars entering into his cap and burying themselves in his eye sockets and forehead. Hiruko landed on his feet with, his sword back in his sheath on his side, and there was a deathly silence in the arena as the crowd could not believe what they were witnessing. Hiruko looked up as the man on the throne toppled of the pedestal and onto the arena floor with a thud. Hiruko's companions quickly rushed to his side and pulled him up and whilst there was confusion they successfully made an escape from the arena. Raj's heart beat fast as he ran in Hiruko's body out of the arena; they had timed this perfectly because no one knew what to do in the enemy camp. This was not the plan, in their eyes and the loss of their leader was very hard to fathom.

The three companions were now out of the arena complex, and they had stolen some cloaks and concealed their identity as they mixed with the crowd outside. News of the events was filtering through outside and panic was setting in and the crowds were getting restless and loud.

The men still rushed away in stealth until they reached the far gates of the city. They had travelled the distance fast even though they were tired and exhausted from the earlier events. Self-preservation was the key driving force here and supporting each other, the other. The gate was not heavily guarded and they easily overcame the lazy guards.

They were out of the city and they slipped into the dark night and the forest, however they did not stop moving. They drew on all the energy reserves they had and kept on moving. If one man stumbled, the other supported. That night they covered amazingly over five miles, until finally they had to rest.

They found some cover in deep forest woodland and if luck would have it some fresh water from a small stream to quench their thirst. The gods were on their side but they knew they had to keep moving until they reached the mountains and then safety. After resting for thirty minutes, they were back on the move and they travelled all night, no one spoke about what had just happened over the last few hours, for it was not time yet. Raj had let himself go within Hiruko and he could feel the boy's heart pounding like wilding stallions racing on open wild plains. The boy had indeed a pure heart, all he could think about was his family and his master, and he shielded his mind from black thoughts. What had happened in the arena was his duty, his karma, his kismat but something was wrong. This was all too easy – how could a powerful warlord expose himself so easily?

When dawn broke, the men had reached the edges of their mountain range and they recognised where they were. There uneasiness eased a little but until they found the hidden entrance to the temple complex, they could not rest. Suddenly they heard a thundering commotion behind them; they stopped and turned to look behind them. What they could see with their own eyes shocked all three men. Heading straight for them at speed was a black flying serpent; the devils steed was chasing them. Its body must be about thirty foot long and it was covered head to toe in armour like scales. Riding on his back, a man dressed in Red flame fighting armour and carrying a sword that was burning in flames.

The devil himself was chasing them; Raj knew this was the reason why he was here. His fight with the *dark one* had been going on for eons and now he was determined that Hiruko would not loose. Raj turned Hiruko around, he whispered into the boys sub-consciousness not to worry, that this was his time.

Hiruko would not run now – the boy knew his path and turned to face his opponent. He then turned his head towards his friends and told them, "keep on moving and I will meet you there." They initially protested but Hiruko insisted and told them that this was his destiny. "Go!" he shouted. The companions turned reluctantly and ran, leaving him alone to face the dark one.

Raj summoned up his own energy and closed his eyes in a silent prayer. As he did this Hiruko withdrew the kaftan but this time as he did he found that the bone handle was too ablaze. The heat however did not hurt him or burn him, it was pure. The blade too was burning and radiating a brilliant white light. The Serpent had now slowed down towards the boy; the sword had done its job of warning him.

"I am with you Hiruko," Raj whispered again, "this time we will face him together, and our parents will be proud."

"Yes," was the simple reply, "yes" he said again. Hiruko looked up towards the heavens and could have sworn that he could see his parents and his master looking down upon him. With his head bowed, he felt a renewed energy surging through him. Raj's soul also could feel the positive energy flowing through every blood vessel, the boss was right, he had been here before. The Dance with Satan would happen repeatedly – "let's dance," he whispered into Hiruko's subconscious mind.

At a good distance, Hiruko's companions had stopped and turned around to watch; the scene unfolding before their eyes would live with them for the rest of their living days. They were in awe as well as shock as a young boy should get ready to do battle with the Akuma himself. The story of Hiruko will live forever.

Hiruko, took a deep breath, exhaled slowly, letting his body and senses become one with his surroundings. Spreading his legs in a solid stance, he raised the sword above his head and waited. His master had taught him that when using the kaftan, be one with the sword and everything will follow. The Serpent was nearly upon him and the man on his back commanded he pick up speed. The serpent obeyed his command and came straight at the boy, his eyes fixed on his query. The man ordered his steed to let out the fire and the serpent obeyed. He opened his mouth and streams of hot smouldering flames shot out towards Hiruko.

With their emotions in one, as the serpent's breath reached Hiruko, he too responded by leaping 12 feet into the air and burying the burning white sword straight down upon the beast in front. To the onlookers this sounded like a huge earthquake had suddenly hit the land and that they were doomed to die. Instead, an intense battle had commenced between right and wrong. The sword cut through the flames and glanced off the serpents head, causing the reptile to veer off to the right. Hark and landed on his feet with the grace of a Russian ballerina, his eyes were intense and already thinking of his next move.

The man on the serpent was angry; he turned his steed around in a wide arch and moved back towards Hiruko. Raising his staff in the air and he pointed at Hiruko and out from the end shot out bolts of lightning that caught Hiruko by surprise. The first one hit him, sending him reeling back on the floor, the pain was intense but he had to be strong. Raising himself up, he shimmied to one side just in time before the serpent was upon him. This time Hiruko ran the blazing kaftan through the underside of the creature. The soft belly just carved open as the sword cut a huge gash. The dragon, lost control, it was screeching in pain and he hit the ground with a thud. There, like a wounded animal, it thrashed for minutes and then it was still.

The rider on his back had jumped off in time and now he stood in front of Hiruko. Hiruko could not see his opponents face but he knew now this would be a fight to the death. His assailant twirled his staff in the air and was ready to attack. For a split second, nothing happened and then in a flash both men attacked at the same time, their moves were lightning fast in real time and both men attacked and counter attacked. The movements were sharp and crisp and no one had the edge.

The samurai were regarded as the most skilled fighters in history and Hiruko remembered his master's instructions, feel the force around you and focus your energy in one with your movements. With this in mind, he waited for the man to attack again and then he reacted with lightening reflexes. There was an art to wielding the sword and he brought the kaftan up so fast he sliced straight through the attackers mid rib. His attacker's body collapsed in two pieces and as it fell, there were flames that erupted from it burning the body to ashes and dust.

Hiruko stood there for a minute and then calmly he sheathed his sword, bowed respectfully towards his opponent and turned to run off towards the hills. As that happened Raj felt himself swept from Hiruko's body and back to the shop where he found the kaftan.

Was that real? It had to be real, he felt the pain and he had been there before. His thought pattern was disturbed when the store lights came on and an old man stood with baseball bat in hand. "Put that sword down, and why are you in my shop?" he shouted.

Roger, still griping the handle of the thirty-inch kaftan turned and faced the man. He suddenly realised that he was back in the real world. He also realised that he was still holding the sword close to his waist. He looked up the man, who Raj guessed was in his late sixties, small in stature and Chinese/Japanese of origin. There was something else though that caught Roger's eyes and Raj felt it straight away, a soul. Standing directly behind the man was a tall young man, and he

250

was dressed in Samurai style clothing. What really caught Raj were the young man's eyes, they were proud, but yet, they showed concern. The young man looked towards Roger; he left the old man's side and walked over to Roger.

"私を見ることができます。" (You can see me), Roger simply nodded and replied yes. "Who are you?" Roger asked back in Japanese, "私の名前は和子だし、私は 1 年 370BC the great 家の Koan で生まれました (My name is Kazuko and I was born in the year 370BC in the great house of Koan)." "What are you doing here, Kazuko San? You should have moved on;" the young man's eyes softened, "I stand guard over him as he stood guard over me when he was alive in my life time. In the great battle under the great emperor Koan, I fought with honour also died with honour. This old man you see in front you worked for me; he was young and wanted to be a samurai but he was not born into a samurai clan. He begged me to take him and so I took him in and on the day of the great battle he died trying to save me. I could not stop the young fool from charging into the battle – I should have been there….." he tailed off. "The great gods allowed me to stay with Maki through many different life's and I stood guard. Many a time I would hear my name called and windows of light opening for me but I could not leave him."

How long have you stayed guard over him, Kazuko san?" "Eons," came, the reply. Kazuko noticed the kaftan in Roger's hand; "you hold the kaftan well my friend. You are Samurai from birth," he said, "and not an ordinary one either. The katan you hold was first held eons ago by a man ………" he did not finish the sentence because Roger finished it for him, "Hiruko. The katan has found its master my friend and that is why I am in this place. We are destined to meet again

251

and perhaps fight our on-going battle with the dark lord, but for you Kazuko san, you must rest and move on." "NO!" came the stern reply, "I have to stay……" The young samurai moved away from Roger to stand again by his old friend.

The old man's gaze had now softened, he had been listening to the words that Roger had spoken, even though he could not see Kazuko sen, he had always felt his presence around him. "My master," he spoke gently, "I know you are here with me, I have always known this. God has let me remember my story in my old age and it was my fault, not yours. I wanted to be a samurai like you, feel a katan in my hand but I was not good enough……." "No," replied Kazuko, "you were good enough and you are my friend and I am not your master." "You must go, Kazuko san and when you are with our forefathers, wait for me," there were tears in the old man's eyes. Kazuko, bowed his head and then removed his own katan from his waist pin. He then bent down on bowed knees and then holding his sword in stretched hands he bowed his head for a minute. He then placed his katan on the floor in-front of his old friend and bowed his head.

When he rose, he turned his head towards Roger and he was about to ask something but Roger stopped him and said, "it is already done my friend. You must go, your brothers are waiting for you on the battle grounds." Kazuko smiled and bowed his head and then he was gone.

Meanwhile the old man looked down in front of him, his eyes brightened and opened wide, there on the floor was Kazuko Samurai Battle katan. Its long 30 inch blade sheathed in a whale hide hardened sheath. It was a thing of beauty to behold, Maki San fell to his knees, tears were streaming down his cheeks and he picked up the katan in both hands out of respect and bowed his and uttered, "I am not worthy, master, of such a gift. I will hold this to the day we meet again on the battle grounds." He then looked up towards Roger and bowed his head and mouthed 'thank you.'

Roger stayed with Maki san for a little while until he had settled down and then he took his leave, but before he left the man gave Roger a few other things that would help him in his forth coming battle. The small velvet bag contained Japanese throwing stars (Shurikens), Maki told him that these very ones were eons old. Also in the bag were a set of three throwing knives. Before the old man let him he go, he spontaneously hugged him and wept a little more but this time he said they were happy tears. He also made Roger put on a long coat so he could hide the katan in his hands.

As he left, Roger's cell phone went off, it was Ken, him and Oscar had reached the clinic and were getting ready to move the boy. "You alright?" he had asked his friend, who replied, "yes, it is a good day to be alive. Take care of the boy, Ken, and I will see you soon, Ken; where is Oscar?" "I will put him on." For the next ten minutes Roger asked him where the Homes territory started from. Once he got the information he put the phone down. His mind was focused now on what he had to do and there was no turning back. "You have to be sure, my son," came the voice inside Raj's head; "I am boss; just as Hiruko was ready for his dance with the devil .Its time, boss, to pay the fiddler," and with that he waved down an oncoming taxi and got in.

The Homies

Compton gang culture was pretty wide spread and gang members made sure they covered their territory well. No one liked another gang to come in to their back yard or there would be trouble. Compton had seen its fair share of that in the past. Where Roger was going now, it was where it all started in some way with the original homies – Rosewood. If you looked on Google there were over 95 gangs listed in LA and each had their sign. What made this different was that the Columbians had come in with their drug money, armed gang members and started to own the streets.

Roger instructed the taxi driver to take him to Rosewood and Alder street. The Taxi driver was a middle aged black man and he gave Roger a peculiar look. "You want to go to Rosewood at this time of night, are you mad, son?" he asked. Roger simply nodded, and replied, "if you are not comfortable, then drop me off a few blocks before." The man did not ask the question again; maybe he recognised the look on this guy's face and he realised that he was serious.

"Alright Son, please put your seat belt on – the police around here are quite strict." (Which actually sounded quite funny?)

The drive to Rosewood took around fifteen minutes, but it gave Roger time to think about what had happened so far. Other bad things were going to happen tonight and he should be prepared. He took out the velvet bag that Maki san had given him and gently untied the strings –and he removed two five inch stainless steel throwing knives. The blades were razor sharp, so he had to be careful and respect the weapons. He then removed one of the Shurikens, The throwing star looked deadly and wicked. Its design fascinated him, it was a five pointed star – 99% stainless steel but the tips were blackened out.

He then tied back up the velvet pouch and put it away. He placed the two throwing knives under one side of his utility belt and the star under the other side. This was going to get messy, he knew this but he had to have the conviction to see it through. Raj was speaking to him all the time, reassuring him that this would be all over in a few hours. "This is our 24, Roger, and we have to do our thing," and he also joked that Jack would be proud of him. Roger laughed for a minute, 24 was one of his favourite programmes

The taxi driver had pulled up the cab a couple of blocks before Alder street. "How much sir?" asked Roger – "that's ten dollars, son," came the reply. "You need a receipt with this." Roger laughed, "No thank you boss, I don't think I can claim this back as a company expense." "Look after yourself son, these streets are rough," and with that he took off into the morning darkness.

The walk to Alder street was not that long but in the dark, it was a bit scary, but Roger had his mind set on his task. As he walked up Spruce Street, there were tell-tale signs of gang activity. There was graffiti painted on some walls telling people that you had stepped in Homies territory and then a few minutes later, the first signs of gang members.

When Roger saw them, he quietly slipped behind a wall and watched them. There were three young Latino kids swaggering towards him on the other side of the road. Their dress design was distinctive to what Roger had already seen before, the black leather jackets and the red bandannas under their baseball caps.

Roger was totally hidden in the shop doorway from the Homies who were in deep conversation, so they walked on by. Once they were at a safe distance, Roger moved out of the doorway and started to move further up the street. He had walked a few hundred yards stopping frequently to look behind but he was safe. As he turned around the corner, walking towards him was another member of the gang. This guy was younger but he was carrying a pistol in his hand. Roger quickly darted to one side and waited for the young-man to come towards him.

Once he passed by, Roger pounced like a sleeping panther out of the darkness and formed a strange hold around the young-man's throat. Roger remembered from his Karate lessons, to apply a wrestle type sleeper hold and he applied this now. He gently squeezed tighter and felt the man go limp and pass out. He then dragged the young man into a dark shop window and laid him down. Before leaving him, he took the young-man's automatic pistol and put it into his outer coat pocket.

He ventured on up Alder street, his mind focused on the task in hand, there would be much blood split this evening, he could feel this. He did not want this to happen because that was not in his nature but tonight was going to be a long night/morning. He had travelled another fifty yards when he heard shouting from behind him, the three gang bangers had found their other member. They were now running up Alder street in pursuit. Roger had to find somewhere to hide or things could go drastically wrong here, even before he reached his goal, and that was Ramon. He quickly darted into a darkly lit ally way and hid behind a large dustcart and waited. As he waited, he removed two throwing knives from his utility belt in anticipation.

As he waited, he heard the men approach, one of the men suggested that two of them look in the alleyway and he would walk further up.

"Shout if you see something. That bastard could not have gone far," he commented.

Sweat streamed down Roger's brow as he waited patiently for the first strike. His Karate master had taught him to be patient and then strike hard. Knife throwing was new to him, but for some reason he just felt comfortable with these tools. This was Raj, he thought he could hear a voice inside his head saying don't worry, let your body flow like the wind and strike like a tiger.

The men approached now the Dustcart and Roger made his move in lightning speed. Darting out from behind the cart before the men could react he threw the knives in quick succession and hit each target precisely. The first man was hit in the neck, he immediately dropped his gun and grabbed for his throat. The second man was hit deep in the forehead between the eyes, he stood no chance. For a minute, Roger froze but Raj urged him on. It's not the time buddy to freeze on me – even though it was only Roger's sub conscience inside the body.

Roger moved to the body of the man hit in the throat, he was dead; he pulled out the knife and wiped the blood from the blade on the man's clothes. He moved to the next and did the same but he needed to apply a bit more force to retrieve the blade. He put the knives away and headed out of the alleyway. At the corner, he looked around to see where the third assailant was and he saw him running back towards him. He turned around, waited again, and pulled one of the knives in readiness. As the man was upon him, he stepped out and literally clothes-lined him like a wrestler would do in the ring and he fell on the concrete floor with a thud. Quickly Roger crawled over him and pressed one hand over his mouth and the other handhold the blade across his neck.

"You make one sound and I will cut your throat." To push the point home he applied some pressure on the neck. "You're going to help me here buddy," he said, "you're going to tell me where your boss is, if you don't I am afraid I am going to have to kill you."

The man was shitting himself, Roger could tell by the glazed frightened look on his face. When you get one of these gang members on their own, they lose all there bravado. "Are you listening?" Roger asked again hoarsely, the man acknowledged by blinking his eyelids.

"Ok, I am going to release my hand over your mouth and you are going to tell me," and with that he took his hand off. As he did, the young man started to shout but was caught short literally by the blade slicing through his throat. Death came quickly as he drowned in his own blood and his eyes glazed over. Roger knelt by the man for a few minutes – he really did not want this to happen and so he whispered a silent prayer for the man and then brushed his hands over his eyes to close them. Raj felt sick that he had to push Roger's reflexes and motions but this had to be done – the boss had said this was written and their lives would not go to waste – it was their kismet.

At that point, his cell phone started to vibrate and he took it out of his pocket to answer it. It was Ken, "Roger you okay?"

"Yes Ken," he replied.

"The Boy he is safe dude, Oscar is looking after him with Dr Garcia. Oscar has assigned more guards at the clinic and has a swat team in waiting."

"Can he trust them Ken?"

"They're in his team Rog," replied Ken.

"Where are you now?" asked Roger, "you don't sound like you are in the clinic, more like in the car."

"One of Oscar's coppers dropped me off where the SVU was parked and I am heading towards Rosewood now. I should be there in ten minutes," he continued.

"Where are you now?" Roger he asked. Raj was annoyed but he could not stop Roger's friend from coming; "I am heading up Alder street at the moment and towards the Moonlight Club that Oscar mentioned on the phone."

"I am coming," Ken said and the cell phone cut off.

Roger put the cell phone away and then proceeded to drag the third man's dead body into the dark alleyway where he left him with the others. He then proceeded up Alder Street. Oscar had told him that the Homies' head office was the Moonlight Club. This is where all the deals went down. Gritting his teeth, he ventured on, moving using the plenty of dark hiding places up the street. One thing he had noticed about Alder street was that it was not looked after well by the local council, there was very little road lamps on, the streets were dirty and there was a stench in the air. As he travelled up more than another hundred yards, he could hear voices and loud music. He quickly darted behind a parked SUV to conceal himself and then peered above the bonnet of the car. Parked about fifteen yards down the street where two street rods and what looked like five to six men. They were having a laugh and drinking from what he could gather. There was also a couple of girls with them, dancing and cavorting with the men. The women were scantily dressed and the men were having a good time fondling the merchandise. They had no idea what had just went down further down the street until now.

Suddenly all the music stopped and the men turned around as he they heard cries coming up from the street. As Roger looked around, the young gang member he had left alive from the sleeper hold was running up the street, shouting for help. He had certainly caught their attention and two of them started to walk towards him. Roger had to make a decision here, was he going to sit it out or was he going to act. He took the second choice, he was going to act. Moving quickly down towards the boot of the SUV he quickly removed the only throwing star that he had and then launched it at the young man. He was about ten feet away and like the knives, the Shruiken struck home. The five-sided star buried itself neatly in the man's forehead and he fell backwards, blood spurted out from where the star had struck.

As all this happened, Roger pulled out the automatic piston out of his coat and squeezed out a couple of .45 rounds out towards the two men walking towards him. The men were caught by surprise and fell backwards as the bullets hit them in their chests. Roger fell forward and made it behind a car before a volley of semi-automatic fire came his way. He sat up and gasped to catch his breath because so many things were happening at the same time he had kept his head thinking straight and focused on his task. He waited for a moment and then he stuck his head out again and squeezed out a couple more rounds out at his assailants from his pistol. He couldn't be certain of whether he was successful or not in hitting them.

Suddenly from behind, he could hear the roar of an engine and headlights blaring at him. He recognised the lights of the car – it was the Escalade and Ken. He roared up the road and rammed hard and straight into the two hot rod streetcars killing two of the gang members instantly. The last member was caught by surprise and lost his footing and fell to the floor and dropped his weapon. As he fumbled to pick up his weapon, Roger pounced and threw his last knife as the man rose and hit it him in the neck. As he did this, Ken had reversed the big SUV out from the impact; it was badly damaged from the front but still driveable.

Ken got out of the car and greeted his friend, "you

alright?" They gave each other a hug and then both got in the SUV. The plan was to repeat the exercise a minute ago and ram the Escalade straight into the frontage of the club. At the minute of impact, they would both jump out.

Ken looked at Roger smiled and then floored the pedal to the metal and the Escalade responded with screeching tyres and a thunderous roar of the V12 engine. As they approached the club, a hail of gunfire met them. They both ducked and waited for the last minute to jump out of their respective doors. As they jumped out the escalade, it rammed into the front of the club. The men firing the guns stood no chance; the SUV hit everything in its path and took no prisoners.

The boys rolled out safely and saw the SUV crash into the club, Roger removed the kaftan from his coat, Raj felt like Christopher Lambert who played Highlander, and rushed forward. He caught his first assailants by surprise they were not expecting a man rushing them with a samurai sword. They did not stand a chance; the kaftan showed no mercy as it flashed with precision and accuracy.

The boys were in the club, there were bodies everywhere but they did not care – they were on a mission, their lives did not mean anything compared to what they had to achieve. They had blood on their hands but it was no time to feel remorseful now. Ken moved away from Roger and went down the right flank. He had an automatic rifle in his hand and was firing at his will. Roger moved more cautiously and his mind was set. He wanted to find Ramon and bring him down. He looked around and could not see Ken, he was worried but he had to keep moving, suddenly two assailants came out from nowhere. His lapse of concentration caused him to miss these guys. He had to react fast and he did, changing his position he caught the first man in the mid rib with the sword. The second man watched his partner fall, almost in half as the sword sliced through him, he froze in fright, and it looked like he was going to cry but it was too late – Roger was on him and he drove the sword through his chest.

Meanwhile, Ken pushed from the other side but he was caught off guard and he fell with a bullet in the shoulder. Before he could react, two gang members, who unarmed him and dragged him away into the darkness, rushed upon him.

Roger had seen none of this but he was thinking how his friend was doing – Raj pushed Roger along, he knew this was the end game. Roger made his way cautiously down to the dance floor, which was on the ground floor, surprisingly there was no resistance. Something was wrong; he had a horrible feeling in the pit of his stomach. Something was definitely not right, he hoped Ken was alright.

Raj was worried, "Please boss I hope Ken is okay," but there was no reply. Something indeed was wrong, so Raj pushed forward, he could not let Roger down. As he reached the bottom of the dance floor, he took a minute to look around. It was quite misty but then he froze.

The lights came on and on the far side of the dance floor stood Ken. He was bleeding from his right shoulder and his face showed signs of torture, with bruises and cuts to his eyes and bottom lip. Standing around Ken were four young man, holding semi-automatics in their hands?

"I would lower that sword if I was you, young man; you are in an impossible position. If you don't I will kill your friend in front of you, make a real mess on the floor with your friend's blood and then my men will cut you down with their guns."

The room was filled with laughter but Roger did not lower the kaftan, instead he relaxed his position with the sword pointing the blade downwards. He had no more throwing knives so what was he going to do? There was a 10ft gap between him and Ken and Ramon's men.

From behind Ken, the face of man appeared, it was Ramon. His sharp facial features reminded Raj of the *dark one* that he had met already. The eyes were a give-away for him, it was indeed him, and it was always him.

"Boss I need you now," he said.

"I am here Raj, just believe in yourself and I will deliver."

"I am not worried about myself, boss, I don't care about myself either."

"Ken. I know, don't lose heart now, my son, you have come so far."

Roger adjusted his stance again and inched his way forward, he decided to change his tactic and pulling the sword neatly into its sheath he straightened up his body. His eyes however never left Ramon and Ken.

"That's a wise move to lower your sword and sheath it," said Ramon. He then nodded towards his right and his men and they started to move forward. What happened next would live with Roger for the rest of his life and it almost reminded him of a scene out of a film he watched years ago. In his mind he had already seen this scene take place and as the men approached he drew the sword with lightening speed at the last moment and caught the first on coming assailant in the face as the kaftans' was drawn out of its sheath in a upward motion. He then followed the move by quickly moving steps to his left and drove the sword into his next opponent. As the man fell, he grabbed the man's gun and squeezed off a couple of rounds at the last two men on his left hand side who were caught by surprise as they looked on with bewilderment. They had not expected their opponent would do this.

Landing on one knee and holding the firearm in both hands, he fired his third shot at Ramon with pinpoint accuracy and hit him in the forehead. Ramon fell backwards and as he did, Ken crumbled forward. Roger dropped the gun and rushed to his friend side, "Ken!" he shouted.

He reached his friend as he hit floor and he scooped him up in his arms. "Ken wake up, it's me!" he cried, but Ken did not respond.

"Ken!" he screamed.

"He's gone Raj, I have taken him," and there was laughter. Raj looked up through Roger's eyes and there standing no more than three feet away was Satan himself. This time he looked different, his facial features looked distorted and grotesque. His body resembled the physique of man but the posture was of a demon. In his hand, he held a vicious looking trident, waiting to strike.

"Roger, this is mine," Raj whispered and he gently laid down Ken's limp body.

Slowly getting up, Raj walked over to where he had dropped the kaftan and picked it up. At that moment, he turned to face Satan.

"I see you have come looking like yourself, your ugliness," he gloated. "You are a fool, Raj, this dance you do with me... we have done this before many a time and you know this and we will keep on doing this in the next and next." "No," shouted Raj, "this is the last time I dance with you because now I know you are me and I am you." He paused for a minute to let his words sink in and he even managed to smile because he knew this would piss his opponent off.

"Is that what you wanted to hear? Is that what you

wanted from me? I would accept that I have evil inside me and that I....Yes, you are right, sir; you and I have danced many a time together, your ugliness, but not at the risk of other people losing their lives."

The dark one laughed, "Mock me all you like but I feel pity for you Raj, I feel sad for you; but I always told you that my brother would not have you. I have always been inside you and I have always made you do things."

"This is where you are wrong, Mr Horn," Raj said, "you are right; yes, I accept that you are inside all of us but we make our own decisions and we as human beings, we let you in because we are weak and we do not believe; but you know something," he said walking to his left, "I have accepted my demons but I have also accepted that I love, I laugh, I cry and that I have good inside of me and this overrules you. You hate this because you are the dark one, you spread your evil little hands everywhere but not today, I am sorry if this sounds clichéd when I describe you," he smiled, "but all you do is to manipulate our fear so we would crumble, but not today," he shouted; "today my sword will feel feed in your bosom and our dance will finish forever."

In an instant he withdrew the kaftan from his sheath and with both hands dug the blade into the dance floor to the hilt. Driving the sword through the dance floor felt so easy – the blade shone like when Hiruko used it the first time of pure white energy and it surged from every pour of his body. As he did this, he could swear he could hear all his re-incarnations shout with him.

The floor beneath him started to shake and started to rip up; he barely stayed in his feet and the ground opened up. "What have you done, little man?" shouted the Devil as the whole floor started to fall away, opening a huge black chasm.

"You are going home sir," replied Raj and from the void came light and it grew brighter and brighter,

"NO!" screamed the devil, "this cannot be... NO!" he screamed again as the light started to drag him into the void and as he was dragged. He screamed curses and a fire erupted around his body as invisible hands dragged him further down.

"What's the matter I thought you were going to have me? How does the light feel? It's warm, it's healing and it's full of love. Our dancing days are ove; no longer will I do the tango with you, sir, and you have no more hold over me; my Lord has delivered me from evil though I have walked in the valley of death I feared not from your shadows," he replied.

For Roger the light also felt it was healing and made him feel stronger. "Roger!" someone shouted and has he looked around it was Ken. He ran over to his friend, the light had healed him and brought him back, Roger was crying as he scooped Ken up from the floor and into an embrace.

For a split second Raj let Roger's conscience in and then he took control. Pulling Ken up, he whispered that this was not finished yet.

He ran over to where he had dug the sword in and pulled it out of the ground. The blade was in one piece and unbroken, he sheathed the sword and urged Ken to move. We have to get out of here he said before the cops arrive, Ken nodded he was exhausted but seemed to have recovered enough energy. They both ran up the stairs and to the first floor. When they reached there, they could hear sirens in the distance and so the need to get in the SUV was even stronger. Roger jumped into the driver's seat and once his friend was in he engaged the reverse gear and backed out of the club. Once out he took a deep breath and then floored the accelerator and the big V12 surged forward.

As the SUV roared off, the police arrived a few minutes later, no wiser to their presence. What they left behind was not just blood and destruction but also the end of the Homies of Compton. The gang after that was nothing and Oscar made sure that the remaining members were rounded up.

"You alright, Ken?" asked Roger who was breathing heavily in the driver's seat. His hands were sweating as they gripped the wheel hard.

"I am fine, for a minute I thought I was dead," he said, "I found myself in a really dark place and I couldn't breathe or get out."

"What happened back there Rog?" he asked and then as Roger drove he narrated the story back. "Technically mate you were dead, it was the light that brought you back and healed the wounds. Take a look he pointed towards his body and with that he did, there were no marks on him."

The boys drove a few miles down the road, until Roger decided that they had to dump the SUV, she had served her purpose, so he pulled into an alley man and parked up. There they removed as much of what they needed and left her there.

Once out on the street they broke into a parked truck and hotwired it. Next stop was the clinic and Jose.

The End Game

The ride to the clinic took fifteen minutes, they did not speak, and too much had happened over the last 24 hours. Now they felt remorse for the blood on their hands but they knew it had to happen. Roger turned to Ken, "You really okay? A lot of shit has gone down."

Ken smiled, "I am fine, I am with my friend, my family."

Ken picked up his cell home and called Oscar in advance to let them know they were coming, he spoke to Dr Garcia and informed him that Roger would need time with Jose. The doctor protested but Ken cut him and said, "Now is the time Doc."

They parked the car along the clinic driveway and were met by officers of Oscars Task force who lead them up to the ward that was isolated for the protection of the boy. They were met has they arrived by Oscar and the Dr Garcia, who were shocked at their appearance. It was Roger who ushered everyone away and told the Doctor that he had to meet Jose now. The Doctor was about to argue but he stopped, he saw the determination in Roger's eyes and knew he had to give in.

Dr Garcia took the short walk with Roger to Jose's room and told him to be gentle, as he was about to turn away, Roger stopped him.

"Hey Doc, Thank you very much for everything and Doc, look after your boys," and then he smiled and turned towards Jose's room. He pulled the handle, the catch clicked open and in he went. Jose was sitting on his bed, his eyes were staring into nowhere and he looked comatose.

As Roger entered, Jose turned his head towards him and as a reflex action he pulled away further into the corner of the bed.

Roger put his hands out in front him, "Jose I know everything that has happened has been traumatic and the scars will be with you for a long time but we are all here to help you."

Bending down on his knees, "Jose over twenty years ago I walked out of my family and it took me another life to realise how much I missed out. Son, I know you are hurt, I know you miss your father, but he is here and has always been here with you. I remember my son when he was your age – I would do everything for him and now he is married with his own family. Jose, the boss said to me, "Raj, I want you to look after a boy in LA but you, my son have helped me to find myself."

There were tears in Roger's eyes, Raj's emotions were coming out and Roger could feel all the hurt in him.

Roger's head dropped, Raj's emotions had poured out thinking about the kids, he looked back towards Jose, wiping away his tears; "Jose, there is one person here who wants to say hello to you and he's been here all this time."

Roger looked up and saw Jose's dad, he was standing in the corner of the room looking helplessly at his son. His eyes were swollen with tears and they were calling out for help. He has been watching Roger come in he saw Raj's form within and asked him to help his son, "that's why I am here sir," he replied without moving his mouth.

Roger turned his gaze to the boy; his eyes were full of compassion and assurance that everything would be okay. "Jose, listen to me," he said softly, "I know you are scared and hurting, I know you don't trust anyone but I am here to help you buddy."

He let his words sink in for a few minutes and then continued. "Jose there is someone in this room who you can see now and he is also here to talk to you. He has always been here for you, son; look up, buddy," he said.

Jose stopped muttering to himself and looked towards Roger and his eyes were transfixed.

For the first time in many weeks Jose spoke in a weak voice, "if my pa was here he would be disgusted at what I have turned up like. His dream when he came to America was that we would have a better life, but look at me, I deal in drugs, I mix with gangs and I am really messed up. When Pa was here, he was so proud of his Mexican heritage but he told us that we are in America now and we had to work hard. He worked hard, but no one gave him a proper job because he was a Mexican but he still did not complain and put food on the table."

"I miss you dad and I am sorry I could not do what you told me," and he started to cry.

Roger wanted to hold the young lad but he could not move something was stopping him.

Standing behind Roger was Jose's Father. "José mi hijo (Jose my son) soy you, Te quiero a mi hijo, (I love you), Papá me duele mucho, te extraño, es que realmente te? (Papa I hurt so much, I miss you, is that really you?). It's me, Jose. I have always been here, but hijo, you have always been too far away from me."

Jose's body language had softened and he had begun to relax slightly, "I am sorry Pa, I let you and Mama down but I had no one and I lost focus."

"No mi hijo, you did not let me down, it was just circumstance what happened and we have to learn and get stronger. That is what me and your Ma wants Jose, nothing else. I need to rest Jose but I cannot until my son is okay," he pleaded.

"Son, I am here now, let them help you, let this man help because I have to go soon." Jose raised his eyes through his tears, "Pa, please do not leave me again."

"I have to go Jose; your Mama is waiting for me. I told her that I would only leave until you were well and now I know you will be alright."

He then turned to Roger and asked if he could hold his son one more time. Roger simply nodded and Jose's father walked over to the bed. Both father and son wrapped their arms around each and hugged and wept. "Raj, your work is nearly done here," he sighed. The elation of seeing the reunion, and a feeling of happiness that everything had come together.

The guys in the observation room could not see who Jose was hugging but in their hearts they knew because they too had been there on this journey. They all had been touched by the events and they were touched because they were part of this story.

Jose's dad kissed his young son's forehead and whispered that he would always be here for him but also to be strong.

"Be proud of who you are, my son, that is why I came to America to make a better life for you."

"I know Pa," he whispered.

"I know and I love you," he cried softly.

"Tell mama I love her."

They held each other for a few minutes and then he was gone.

Jose was still crying as Roger scooped him up in his arms and the boy readily accepted him and held on. He then carried the boy to the bed and laid him down and whispered it is time to rest and sleep son and kissed his cheek. The boy was calmer now and his tired eyes began to close and so did Roger's.

"It's time, buddy," whispered Raj to Roger and with that because Raj hated saying goodbyes he stepped out of Roger's body. As he did so Roger's own true soul reclaimed its tired and worn out body.

Roger tried to look up but he was so tired and his

head fell back onto the bed next to Jose. Raj stood there for a minute, observing him and Jose and then he looked towards the observation privacy glass. Through he could see the other guys and mouthed them "goodbye", whether they could see him he did not know but he wished them the best and with that he left them.

The Wedding

After leaving the clinic, Raj did not know where he was going but he found himself sitting in a white empty room. It was completely sparse of anything including any furniture – it was simply empty. The room felt to Raj like one of those you would find in a mental hospital – but in this one, he felt safe and warm. He looked at his appearance, it was really tidy; there was no blood stained shirt and it was replaced with a white tank top and trousers. His feet were bare but it felt nice because there was warmth coming through the floor and it felt soothing.

Suddenly he noticed he was no longer alone and there was a man standing next to him. Raj smiled, he knew this guy, it was Danny De Vito.

"Hey, I am only joking, Boss," he said.

There was spontaneously laughter around, "I can be whoever you want Raj; you have known this, my son. I can be Lord Vishnu, I could be Lord Krishna or anyone – all these figureheads are me. No matter what colour or creed I am always here. You have done well my son he continued and you have understood as a human being you have to accept who you are and until that moment, you cannot live. That is why you went on this journey and I had to show you. You were quite right when you told my Brother that evil exists in everyone, because it is true and that is when you won the battle Raj. When I gave this gift to humankind, I was hoping they would use it well but over the eons man has become lustful, and he has lost is way. I am everywhere Raj, in different forms, in different lands and talking in different languages. You have always had the ability to reach me, my son and I am glad you went on this journey, I know you tried years ago to learn but the time was not right to unlock the past."

273

Raj smiled; "Where now boss?" there was laughter again.

"There is one last duty you must perform and this is the most important duty that a parent can perform, then we will see what jobs I have for you," he joked and with that, Raj's surroundings changed yet again.

"Boss," Raj called, "Thank you for believing in me when I was lost, Thank you for not giving up on me when I did." Tears again trickled down his cheeks. He wiped his face but this time he was happy, his mind was clear, his head was not clouded with thoughts of dismay or despair.

Raj found himself standing in the magnificent lobby of the very hotel that he had always wanted to stay in but never had the time; The Burj Al Arab in Dubai. This hotel was one of the world's most exclusive seven star hotels. Raj remembered years ago when they were at Jumeirah Beach complex they saw helicopters come in and land on the helipad on top of the hotel. This was very exclusive indeed and it cost a small fortune to stay here. What had caught his eyes though was the number of Asian people in very expensive clothes walking around the hotel, almost as if they were at a wedding. He then looked at his clothes, he was dressed in a very expensive looking silk suit and on top of his head, he was wearing a pink turban. He was confused but excited.

"Boss, where are we?"

"Don't you know my son?"

"Sonya…" he replied softly.

"Yes," came the reply. "Johnny's Grandfather after speaking to your daughter and family decided to bring everyone to this hotel. Your daughter told Johnny that her father would have loved to bring the kids here but could never afford it. Therefore, Johnny's grandfather decided that they would both marry here and not only that he also flew the majority of the families out and the hotel was exclusively for them. He's paid a fortune and not accepted any money from your children; he said he is paying a debt to someone who he thought he had met a few months ago."

"Can they see me boss?" he asked.

"Today Raj, yes your kids only will be able to see you and someone else who is standing over there waiting for you."

"Boss, thank you for believing in me."

"No Raj, I have always believed I just had to show you how to believe in yourself. Now go and enjoy yourself before I change my mind," he chuckled.

As Raj looked around, he saw an image that totally captivated him and sent a lovely warm feeling through him. It was Ash, she was standing a few yards in front of him and looked like a million dollars as she was dressed in a flowing baby pink embroidered saree. It was simple but looked so elegant on her. What he also noticed was that she had had her hair untied and grown long like the first time he had met her, before their marriage.

"Go to Ash and enjoy the day; you have earned it my son," and with that Raj walked over to Ash who sensed he was there. She looked up and gave him one of those lovely radiant smiles that always melted his heart.

"Raj," she whispered.

"Hi Ash," he grabbed her arms and hugged her tightly.

"Our daughter's getting married Raj," she said softly in his ears "and we are here, I cannot believe this."

As she pulled away, they shared a lingering kiss as they were two newlyweds on honeymoon. They giggled like little children and for a minute, he could not take his eyes on her. It was strange but he felt like he was waking up from a long coma and seeing her truly for the first time. She understood and then said, "Let's go or we will miss our daughter's marriage" and she giggled like a young girl.

Walking hand in hand, they mingled into the crowd walking towards the large Al Falkak Ballroom; over the years, they had increased the capacity of the Ball Room but the sight just blew both Ash and Raj away. The ballroom itself could only be described as one of the most beautiful venues in the world with its two tier circular design. The upper level of the ballroom had some magnificent views of the Jumeirah coastline, but the bottom tier just took their breath away.

As they walked in together hand in hand, it was like walking into a dream, in the middle of the ballroom dome was a magnificent chandelier but the overall design was awe-inspiring. The floor was made from the finest marble and magnificent pillars held the whole structure.

As they walked down some small marble stairs, they were greeted by two waiters, who were offering guests champagne in the finest crystal glasses. Strangely they offered both Ash and Raj a drink, how could this be – no one could see them – Raj could hear a chuckle in his head – before he could ask the question the boss answered that no one at the party would recognise them apart from the kids – "you guys have taken a mortal form – so enjoy."

They accepted the drinks and walked into the hall. The wedding mandap was setup in the middle of the hall and all guest tables were positioned all round. As they walked in and towards the mandap, they could see guest on the second floor as well have a birds eye few of the proceedings. At this stage, the couple could not see any of the kids or relations but Raj did see some familiar faces and he pointed them out to Ash. He saw Oscar and his family; he caught a glimpse of Ken and a very beautiful young lady with him. He then saw Roger; he was with Kate and another young man and that was Jose. Raj smiled and there was a tear in his eyes. Ash smiled at her husband as she intently watched him, he had not changed in some respect, always the soft guy and with that she gently wiped the tears from his eyes and gave him a kiss on his cheek.

They then walked closer to the mandap and then they recognised more familiar faces of their own families, it was fortunate that no one knew who they were.

"Hey let's sit down there," indicated Raj to Ash. She nodded and he led her to the nearest table opposite the front of the mandap.

As they sat down, the table was set for ten people. Surprisingly there were no names on the seating, which made it easier for them to steal the finest seats in the house. Ash squeezed his hand in anticipation on seeing the children, Raj could sense this and he smiled at her. A few minutes later, there came sound of a violin and as they looked around, a young man was walking out first. He was dressed in an embroided sherwani. A sherwani is a long coat like jacket fastened with buttons. It comes to just below the knees and the jacket has a Nehru collar. Johnny's sherwani was gold embroidery all the way down and looked lovely. To go along with the sherwani he was wearing plain white trousers (Pyjama) and draped along the side was a long scarf.

As tradition would have it a Turban was worn, with a sehera tied to the front. A sehera is a veil of flowers said to ward off the evil eye, much like the Christian custom of the bridal veil. The violinist led a small procession of Johnny and his immediate family to the mandap where he sat down on a large silk cushion on the floor. Next to Johnny on his left hand side sat his proud grandfather and grandmother. For the next ten minutes, the Hindu priest performed some rituals with the boy and then called for the girl.

As all the guests turned around, another violinist led out the girl's side. Sonya was accompanied by her sisters on either side and behind them were her relatives. For the first time Raj and Ash caught site of their children. Alongside his children were all their cousins who Raj had not seen for a very long time. Raj's parents would have been proud of this day if they were here. Their granddaughter marrying in style and hiding back his tears of joy were so hard at this precise moment.

Sonya looked so beautiful; she was not dressed in traditional red coloured lengha but a beautiful antique embroidered gold lengha. The procession came around to the right hand side of the mandap, very slowly; occasionally Sonya would look up and grab a cheeky look towards where Johnny was. The boy and his relatives at this stage all stood up as well and faced the girl's side. They then exchanged garlands around each other – first the boy to the girl and then the girl garlanded the boy. Tradition said that if the boy bent his head the girl would always lead the marriage – Johnny smiled and bowed his head and winked at her. She smiled and placed the garland over his head and everyone clapped. From there the wedding commenced and like all Indian ceremonies, the guests were asked to "please sit back and enjoy because it would take some time".

As Sonya sat down she glanced first around to Joy and her sister and then something drew her to look to her side and to a couple sitting near the stage. As she looked harder, she saw her mum and dad sitting at the table and watching the ceremony. She blinked her eyes because she was not sure this was real and how could it be real, but they were still there, smiling and looking so happy towards her. Tears welled in her eyes and she had to stop herself, so she looked at brother first because she knew her sister would react in a different way.

Joy stood up and went to her side, "what's up sis?" he whispered, "look in front you Joy and tell me who you see please?" He found this a strange request but he did, his sister had always been strange, he smiled thinking of that.

However, he too was caught at the sight of his parents and had to blink hard.

"It's Mum and Dad," she said whispered making sure no one else could hear.

"It is, Sis," and with that he left the mandap and walked towards the table where his parents were sitting. Johnny's grandfather looked concerned and asked if everything was okay, she said, "Everything is fine; they had just noticed some family that Joy had to meet." With that, the pundit carried on with the wedding.

Raj and Ash knew just what had happened and they knew the kids would recognise them and they saw Joy walking over. As their son approached, he stood by their table for a short time; he could not speak and then said, "Is this real?"

Raj nodded his head and whispered back, "only you and your sisters can see us truly – everyone else will not be able to, Joy."

Joy reached out with his hands and squeezed both of theirs and when he did, he knew that was true. "How?" he asked.

"Let's just say the big boss has allowed us to witness our daughter's wedding and to see you guys for the last time and say goodbye properly. Now you go

279

and enjoy the wedding and let us sit here."

Joy rubbed the tears from his eyes, nodded and went off to sit beside his family.

Both Ash and Raj nodded at Sonya and mouthed, "We love you."

At this moment, Joy told Ojal and she looked over. Ash squeezed Raj's hand; there were tears in her eyes – full of joy and happiness. Raj smiled, he had always wanted to see her like this, he loved her with all his heart and he understood today what it all meant and he had searched for this all his life. Love should be un-conditional, it's like wild magic sparks and light will fly in all direction. He looked up into the heavens, and thought, thank you for the lesson.

"No, my son it's not a lesson you needed, but direction on how to find what you most desired. I said to you: believe in me you will find everything; believe, trust with all your heart and it will be yours."

As the Marriage continued there was one last thing that Raj had to do, gently he turned to Ash, whispered in her ear and proceeded to get up from the table. He then started to thread his way through the other tables in the hall to the far side of the hall to a particular group of people seated at table 13.

As he approached the table, all the guests looked up and one in particular recognised Raj through his current disguise and smiled. Roger stood up and walked around, and reached out with his hand. Instead, Raj grasped the young man's hand and embraced him like a long lost friend. He whispered, "thank you for helping me and I wish you the best." Raj held Roger for a few minutes and then pulled away. Roger was left speechless, but he knew what had just happened. Raj then went around where young Jose sat and knelt on one knee in front of him. Looking into the young man's eyes, he no longer saw sadness but only hope and happiness. There were tears in Raj's eyes, and before he could wipe them away, it was Jose who gently wiped them for him with a tissue. Jose smiled and whispered, "Gracias por me ahorro con todo mi corazón y me rellenado con esperanza para el future."

Raj reached forward, kissed the boy's forehead and touched his face with his hand. He then slowly stood up, smiled at all the people that he had met and turned around, this time with tears of joy trickling down his cheeks and made his way back to Ash. This time he did not sit down, he whispered in her ear "its time to go, my darling, and leave our kids to their future." She looked up at him, smiled and acknowledged his words and with that both Raj and Ash looked up once again towards the kids smiled and mouthed a farewell, but see you again and then fade away as if they were never there…….

The old man smiled and chuckled to himself as he looked down, "no one is ever lost in my path and if they believe in what I offer they will succeed but for this you must transcend from all material desires and needs. Now he smiled again, his eyes shone brightly, his smile broadened across his face, the weathered cheeks of the old man were gone and his true infinite appearance took over. "Believe in me children and I will lead you where you may be. Race or creed makes no difference to me because we are all one colour, one person, this but a human trait.

"Think of me in your hearts and I will stand beside you and lead you and guide you in the path that has been written. Follow your duty and your heart and logic will see you through most things in life and remember that when you think you have lost, I will deliver thee. I will not measure you on your deeds but how good your heart is."

For Raj and Ash, they found themselves walking

hand in hand into a white hazy doorway into another life, everything felt safe, there were no barriers, no unturned stones to stumble over. They had left their past behind and the ritual of life begins all over again and their immortal souls moved on. They looked at each other with broad smiles, love and purity and then looked forward - they had shed their human bodily form and were one with their surroundings. In that, instant moment they faded away and took their place in the stars to be reborn again in a different time, different realm but their souls will also be linked together as in previous lives. They say love has no bounds and neither has time, but wounds do heal and the only thing that remains are memories.

This is not the end, but a continuation so you never really say Good Bye........., but 'hello, see u soon,' in another time and place.

Sir Isaac Newton quoted:

I do not know what I may appear to the world, but to myself I seem to have been only like a boy playing on the seashore, and diverting myself in now and then finding a smoother pebble or a prettier shell than ordinary, whilst the great ocean of truth lay all undiscovered before me.

To me, this is what life really means – a voyage of discovery and a vast chasm of mass that the soul can visit. Believe in yourself and your dreams will come true. Don't let our human traits of despair take over and then you have lost. When life knocks you down, you get up and push harder, but learn from your mistakes. My story portrayed the traditional fight between good and evil, but it was about deliverance, redemption and shedding the material things that we think are important.

To my Family – *I love you*, and to all the Rajs in the world – *you are not alone my friends.*

Lightning Source UK Ltd.
Milton Keynes UK
UKHW040820181122
412356UK00020B/750